Lover From
ANOTHER
WORLD

Lover From
ANOTHER
WORLD

RACHEL CARRINGTON,
ELIZABETH JEWELL, *and*
SHILOH WALKER

POCKET BOOKS

NEW YORK   LONDON   TORONTO   SYDNEY

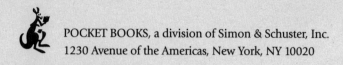

POCKET BOOKS, a division of Simon & Schuster, Inc.
1230 Avenue of the Americas, New York, NY 10020

Copyright © 2007 by Ellora's Cave Publishing, Inc.
Her Lover's World copyright © 2005 by Rachel Carrington
Lady of the Seals copyright © 2003 by Elizabeth Jewell
Voyeur copyright © 2003 by Shiloh Walker

Published by arrangement with Ellora's Cave Publishing, Inc.

ISBN-13: 978-1-4165-3612-3
ISBN-10:   1-4165-3612-4

This Pocket Books trade paperback edition March 2007

10 9 8 7 6 5 4 3 2 1

POCKET and colophon are registered trademarks of
Simon & Schuster, Inc.

Manufactured in the United States of America

For information regarding special discounts for bulk purchases,
please contact Simon & Schuster Special Sales at 1-800-456-6798
or business@simonandschuster.com

Contents

Her Lover's World

RACHEL CARRINGTON

1

HIS HAND BRUSHED *over her thigh, she sighed and moved her leg restlessly. The satin sheets burned her skin, scorching her from neck to ankle as she twisted over their silkiness. His hands were relentless, following each curve of her body, over the shadowy cleft between her breasts until his fingertips caressed her nipples, played with them, toyed with them. She bit down hard on her lower lip to keep from moaning aloud. And the assault on her senses continued. His long, daring fingers probed between her thighs, finding the hot wetness that invited him. "Open to me." His voice came as a deep, velvety-soft whisper. She couldn't picture the man as anything but hard, all strength and muscle.*

Helpless against the desires curling within the pit of her stomach, she opened her thighs and welcomed the hot, steely length of his cock. It touched the opening of her sheath, gliding over the glistening dampness, teasing her, taunting her, until she thrashed back and forth across the sheets.

The tip pressed against her clit, moving and grinding until Anna almost sat straight up in the bed. Her hair clung in damp strands to her face, and with gentle hands her lover brushed them away, soothing her, calming her.

"I need you," she whispered, desperation lining her voice.

"In due time, my love, in due time."

She bucked her hips, inviting yet demanding at the same time. And then, just when she couldn't take it any more, he . . .

The phone shrilled loud and long, dragging Anna out of the torrid, nightly fantasy and back into the cold, cruel harshness of reality. She came awake with a groan, slapping her hand to her forehead. Damn it! Why now? Pushing the thick mass of tangled curls away from her face, she silenced the painful sound by lifting the receiver from the cradle. "What?"

"Is that any way to greet your best friend?" Liz sounded damnably cheerful at so early an hour. Anna wished she could wake up like Liz did, but without her three cups of coffee, she functioned like a zombie, especially since she'd moved into this apartment and discovered a dream lover existed within its walls.

Or perhaps he didn't really exist. Maybe his touch was simply a product of an overworked imagination. She spent so much time surrounded by books, immersed in the fantasies within the pages that perhaps, out of sheer desperation, she'd created her own.

"Hello?" Liz's fingernail tapped against the receiver. "Are you still there?"

"What do you want?" Anna flopped back against the mattress, sliding one hand beneath the sheets to test the reality of her fantasy. The warm wetness attested to the strength of the dream.

"Did I wake you?"

"Yes." Anna felt strangely bereft, empty inside now that the dream had faded. Drawing her hand out from between her legs, she clutched the sheet up to her neck and wondered if her lover would return tonight.

"It's after eight."

"So? It's Saturday." And when she slept, her lover came.

"I thought you were meeting your mom for breakfast at eight-thirty," Liz gave the reminder in a perky voice which made Anna want to limit the woman's coffee intake.

Did he have dark hair and enticing silver eyes as she pictured in her dream? Were his hands large with long, sensual fingers? Shuddering a little, Anna forced a reply to her friend's question. "She canceled last night because her boyfriend made other plans for them." A long pause followed as if Liz awaited Anna's continuance of the conversation. She debated whether or not to talk about the dream, but then, Liz was her best friend. She told her everything. "I had another one of those dreams last night."

Liz sucked in a sharp breath. "You mean those wicked, wild dreams?"

"The same. I swear I haven't gotten a good night's sleep since I moved into this apartment." Anna jumped a little as the walls seemed to whisper to her, calling her name. Her eyes widening, she searched the room and saw nothing. She was still alone.

And still going crazy.

"Ooh, maybe it's haunted."

"I don't think a ghost could be doing the things this guy is doing to me."

Liz sighed, the sound of envy. "Honey, I'd give my right arm to be able to have even an inkling of what you have. I know it isn't real, but I'm here to tell you that reality can really suck. Sam's in bed by ten and out like a light by ten-fifteen. That gives us fifteen minutes for foreplay and sex. Sam's idea of the former is to turn off the bedroom light and the actual sex usually takes about five minutes and I'm being generous here. God, to have a secret lover."

Anna glared at the phone while her heart slammed against her breastbone. "I don't have a secret lover. I have fantasies. They're different."

"They're incredible," Liz gushed. "So get yourself together and meet me at the café for coffee and bagels. I'm buying and you're talking." She ended the phone conversation before Anna could respond.

Anna tossed back the sheets and climbed out of bed. Her legs shook and her knees wobbled. Since she'd moved in two weeks ago, she woke up the same way each morning, unfulfilled and frustrated. Each night, he reached out for her, teasing her, tantalizing her until she thought she would scream from sheer frustration. The same sexy, intoxicating voice, hard body and even harder cock, but none so far had culminated in what Anna desperately needed. Sweet release.

Her phantom lover enticed her, his ethereal hands gliding over her skin with slow, maddening strokes, but Anna wanted more. She wanted to feel his cock inside her, pushing deep, stretching her. Her body ached to feel the power of his cock and her pussy tingled with silent invitation. As crazy as it sounded, she wanted a man she'd never seen.

The hot spray of the shower stung her skin, the needle pricks wringing a sigh of pleasure from her. She bent her head beneath the steady stream, needing the heat to penetrate the taut muscles of her back and shoulders. Her hands fisted against the wall as the warmth spiraled down her spine, sliding between her thighs like a lover's fingers.

Anna spread her legs to allow the liquid to touch her intimately and closed her eyes. She pictured him again, not an actual image of the man, but more a feeling. He'd have a strong character and a gentle nature. He seemed to care about her even though he didn't know her. She wanted to see his face, to see what her mind already knew. His warmth and his touch, those she could imagine, but they weren't enough.

The hot water sluiced between her thighs and she moaned her pleasure, rocking her head back as the ribbons of heat caressed her clit. An orgasm was just what she needed to shake away the aftereffects of her dream lover.

Then she felt him, hard and strong, infinitely gentle hands probing the tender flesh between her thighs. Her eyes popped open and she tried to look over her shoulder, but he pushed her closer to the wall of the shower. Panic squeezed her heart as he caressed her skin. Doubts assailed her and for a brief moment, she thought about calling a halt to this, about demanding she see his face before she allowed him to continue.

"Easy, darlin'. I'm not going to hurt you."

His words proved to be her undoing, making the decision her body had already made. She gave in to his demands.

"Hold on, Anna. Brace your hands against the wall. I want to feel you, taste you."

Wild and wanton, she pushed back against the hardness of his thighs and the solid wall of his chest. His index finger spread the tender lips of her pussy and caressed her boldly.

"Ah, God," she moaned aloud.

"Yes, that's it." Cool lips nuzzled her neck. "Let me hear your sweet whispers. Your moans. I want to know when you come, Anna."

Her legs threatened to give way, but her phantom lover held her fast, keeping her upright with one solid arm wrapped around her stomach. *Am I losing my mind?* His finger continued to massage her, sending tiny spears of shock and delight shooting through her body. She leaned her head back and connected with a hard shoulder. Stunned, she tried to turn around, but he wouldn't allow it.

"I want to see you," she whispered.

"You will." He drove his fingers deep into her sheath and Anna cried out, the pleasure slicing through her, holding her riveted in place.

Dear God. Whatever he was, he was perfect. Much more than just a dream lover. He knew her every desire, her wildest fantasies. And fulfilled them, just by thought.

She heard his feet move against the shower floor, felt the glide of his hands down her thighs and then the press of a kiss against the globes of her ass. Her hands slapped against the wall overhead and her stance widened, parting in silent invitation.

"Arch your back," he commanded and the intensity of his tone caused a shiver to climb from the base of her spine up to her neck. And she obeyed without question.

Her reward came in the form of a simple stroke of his tongue over the center of her heat, and her pussy swelled even more. A trickle of juice dripped down her leg. He quickly captured it, sucking it from her skin.

Anna was sure any moment her legs would collapse. Even now her knees were jerking, her thighs constricting. She wanted to turn, to see the face of the man who drove her wild every night in her dreams, but he wouldn't allow it.

One hand fastened on her hips while two fingers of his other hand pushed deep inside of her, widening and flexing until Anna's back bowed further, threatening to snap from the pressure. Then his tongue began to push into her wetness, tickling her clit until her arms strained to hold her upright.

"Let go, my Anna. Let go."

Heat spiraled low in her abdomen and her legs began to shake. Her lover's tongue rotated against her clit in a maddening circle, moving the tiny nub of flesh until the pressure built inside of her, combustible and temperamental.

His mouth covered her pussy, his lips grinding against her flesh while his tongue danced and mated with her clit. Anna threw her head back and came on a long, loud scream.

His mouth covered the opening to her cleft, absorbing the spasms and drinking her juices. She quivered and moaned, thinking any minute now, her lover would fade away and she'd be left alone again, desperate to see him, to know his name, but even more desperate to fuck him.

"Come back to me, Anna," he whispered in her ear and she didn't know when he'd stood, but now she felt the press of his cock against her ass. She rubbed against the hardness as he moved it between her ass cheeks.

"Fuck me," she demanded.

"Not yet." He denied her the pleasure she craved.

Sheer frustration gave way to anger. "Then leave me! I don't want you here if I can't know you!"

He pressed a kiss between her shoulder blades. "My love, you must be patient."

"It's been two weeks."

Another kiss warmed her skin. "I know." He slipped one hand low again, gently massaging the dripping flesh between her legs. "Soon, my sweet, I will take you and you will know my name."

He thumbed her clit again and she jerked, reaching around behind him to grab hold of his ass. As she expected, his body was rock-hard, all lean muscle and sinew. God, how she wanted to turn in his arms, to feel the touch of his lips against hers, but she knew he would disappear.

Damn him anyway! What right did he have to invade her dreams, torment her like this and . . . Her thoughts scattered as the orgasm swamped her, dragging her under until she almost drowned in the sheer pleasure of the release. Almost sobbing, she rested her head against the tiled wall until the water ran cool over her spine and before she turned in the shower, she knew her dream lover wasn't behind her anymore. But he'd been there. Alive. With her. In the shower. *Hadn't he?*

He shouldn't have gone to her. He had no right. Each night, he invaded her dreams, easily slipping in to her mind by the allowances of his world. But it still didn't make it right. He had no place in her world and she had no place in his. Yet, from the moment he'd seen her, he knew she was the one he'd been searching for, the one woman who touched him not just in his soul but in his heart.

Fury swelled with him. He was a nomad, forced to wander the alternate universes searching for a new homeland for his people, a new Atlantis. As king, he had few choices in life other than to serve the people who believed in him.

Onyx tipped his face toward the weeping sky, quelling the urge to shake his fist at the unseen gods who ruled his life. "Damn you. Could I not just once have a love without having to consider the consequences of my people?"

He knew the answer before he voiced the question.

And he was trapped.

When Atlantis disappeared, so had Onyx's hope for a normal life. The gods had condemned him to a futile existence, a nebulous search for a new home. His people depended on him to lead them to a city they could call their own. Never mind that Onyx doubted they'd ever find it.

He had to try, and whatever he might have found with Anna couldn't last. Though his heart craved hers, eventually, he would have to leave her and pray she wouldn't hate him in the end.

2

"OH MY GOD!" Liz's eyes grew wide as hubcaps. "You mean you actually . . ." she lowered her voice and covered her coffee cup with one hand.

Anna still tingled from the aftereffects of her shower and as she'd relayed the events of that morning to her best friend, she relieved the moment again. "Yes, I actually."

"And you couldn't see his face?" Liz took a bite of bagel and chewed furiously. "My God, this is straight out of a movie." She blinked several times. "What did he sound like?"

Anna pushed her mug toward the edge of the table so she could lean in closer to Liz. "Foreign. I couldn't place the accent. He talked to me this time, more than he ever has before." She rubbed her hands together. "Liz, when he touched me, I felt something."

"I figured that much."

"No, I meant something more. I've never felt that way with a man before. It was like he owned my soul."

Liz rocked back and forth in her chair, her eyes wide. "Do you think he's real?"

Anna scrubbed her face with her hands and sat back in the chair. "I don't know what to think. But I have to find him. I need to see him face-to-face, find out why he's come to me."

With a sage nod, Liz grinned. "This is so wild! I can't

even imagine sleeping with someone I couldn't see. Well—" she tapped one finger against her chin, "—there has been that one fantasy, but that's another story." Her eyes still huge in her face, she leaned forward. "So was it any good?"

Anna smiled.

"From the look on your face, it was the best sex you've had since, well, ever." Liz's hands curled around her coffee mug and she brought it to her lips. "If I'm reading that smile correctly anyway."

"It was absolutely phenomenal." Anna released a sigh. "I mean, I can't even begin to describe it."

Liz grinned. "You don't have to. I'm jealous."

Anna waved a frantic hand. "Liz, I don't know how to fix this."

"And you want to fix it why? From where I'm sitting, you don't really have a reason to complain."

Anna glared at her and waved the approaching waitress away. The last thing she needed was another set of ears to catch wind of this. Next, it would be all over town that Anna had a phantom lover and she'd be looking for another job. "You're not helping."

Liz schooled her features into an appropriately helpful look. "Okay. Sorry. How about you go to one of those dream people? You know, the ones that analyze dreams?"

"How can he feel so real if he's a dream?" She shook her head almost violently. "He's not a dream. I could touch him, feel him and he could feel me. There's no way this was a dream, Liz."

"Ghostbusters then?" Liz continued her efforts to be helpful.

"I don't even want to think about that. A ghost just brought me to the best orgasm I've had in years. There's one for the books."

"Can I meet him?"

"*I* haven't even met him!" Realizing her voice had risen several octaves, Anna shared an apologetic glance with the café's patrons and lowered her voice. "But once I do, I'll be more than happy to introduce you to him."

Liz took a long, slow slurp of her coffee. "I'd go home if I were you. Try to flesh him out, get him to come back, no pun intended."

"He won't come if he knows I'm watching for him."

"How do you know? Some guys like that kind of stuff." Liz waggled her eyebrows suggestively.

"Will you be serious? I have a real problem here."

Liz leaned across the table and covered Anna's hand with her own. "Anna, honey, you're having sex. Does it really matter if your lover is corporeal or ethereal as long as he does the job?"

Anna tugged her hand free. "I still want to meet him, but I doubt he'll show up in the light of day. He never has before anyway."

"He's never joined you in the shower before, either."

Liz had a point there. Anna dabbed at her mouth with the napkin and got to her feet. "You're right. I have to find him. I need to know who he is."

"Well, he's obviously not there to hurt you and whoever he is, I'd hold onto him, in a manner of speaking."

Anna gave her friend a grimace and headed out into the bright North Carolina sun. Somehow, some way, she was going to meet her lover . . . today.

∽

He should leave her before things got out of hand, but even as the thought entered his conscience, Onyx knew he would not.

Though he was chosen by his people to lead them to the new promised land, he could not walk away from Anna, not when his soul had connected with hers. She'd felt it, too. And each time they were together, their hearts would knit a little more. He was sure of it. And yet, how could the fates be so cruel as to place his soul mate in a century he didn't belong?

Cruelty or not, he would take the few moments he could have with Anna. For now. And damn them both to a miserable existence once he left.

His people secured the lines on the ship, running back and forth to make sure she was seaworthy. She'd traveled many miles for them, gone through several time portals and had gotten them absolutely nowhere.

Onyx's lip curled in a measure of disdain. What good were the powers to travel through time's gate if it brought them to another dead end? The gods had assured him he would find a new home, a place for his people to rest their weary souls, raise their families and exist until their hearts ceased beating. And yet, centuries had passed with no such discovery.

His boots clicked loudly on the wooden deck as he tromped the stairs to the chambers below. He'd never wanted this responsibility, had even asked the gods to choose another leader, but as king of Atlantis, his duty was sealed. No matter how long it took, no matter how much time, he would continue to seek out this nebulous homeland.

"Damn you all to hell," he muttered the blasphemous words at the gods hidden from his view. "You hide behind your powers and condemn us to such a miserable existence. We have done everything you have commanded, followed your dictates to the letter in a futile attempt to find a new Atlantis and what have you given us in return? Longevity we neither want nor asked for." His hands clenched around the door handle to his quarters. "I should have been dead by now but for your interference. And now who must suffer the consequences? I have lived my life without love and am I now to lose this chance?"

Even now Onyx heard Anna's sweet voice and his muscles clenched. Were she not to be a part of his life, why did the gods allow them to meet? How was he able to reach out to her, to touch her? It had never happened before. The gods had never allowed him to converse with anyone outside of his people much less share such intimacies with her. They'd cursed him to an immortality that would sustain him until the new Atlantis materialized.

Flopping down atop the plush bedding, Onyx stacked his hands behind his head and glared at the ceiling.

"Well, if you're all so powerful, why can't you just create the damned city and be done with it?"

No answer. Just as he suspected. "Fuck all of you then," he grumbled and rolled to his side, knowing the gods would only consider his anger an amusing display of temper.

He closed his eyes and allowed the fantasy to carry him away. The images were so vivid, so real and Anna felt so right in his arms.

A blast of cold air met Anna the second she entered her apartment.

"Dammit. I know I didn't turn the air on." She headed down the hallway to the thermostat, surprised to find the needle stuck firmly on sixty degrees. She checked the air conditioner. With the temperature outside barely climbing to the low seventies, she couldn't imagine she would turn it on so early in the spring. "But I know I didn't turn it on." Her brain began to hum. "Now, I really think I'm going crazy."

Toeing off her shoes, she headed into the kitchen. Before her lover had joined her in the shower, she'd had plans for the day, but now, her only goal was to force his hand, to bring him out of hiding and meet him face-to-face. Whoever he was, he owed her that much.

She couldn't imagine why he'd chosen her anyway. Of all the apartments to enter, he picked hers. It didn't make sense, especially with Miss Henderson, Double D, living two doors down. Hell, even Eliza Marsetti on the third floor had more attributes than Anna did and she didn't need to look in the mirror to be reminded.

Though blessed with a trim figure and height most of her friends envied, Anna had always wished for bigger breasts, a little more in the ass department and even slightly wider hips. In her own opinion, she looked like an unadorned landscape, nothing spectacular to see.

Muttering to herself, Anna leaned down to see her reflection in the polished chrome toaster. Full lips. Wide, green eyes and thick auburn hair. Nothing special there, either, though she'd gotten plenty of compliments on her eyes.

A door creaked in the background and Anna straightened, her ears tuned toward the sound. Silence descended again, but uneasiness settled around her shoulders like a familiar sweater.

She wasn't alone.

Shivering, she headed down the hallway, her hands clenched into fists to still their shakes. Though she'd left the door to her bedroom opened, it was now only slightly ajar. She widened the gap by pressing against the wood and promptly froze.

The drawn shades blocked out the sunlight and everywhere she looked, she saw candles. Hundreds of them. Scented candles that filled the room with a heady fragrance.

Anna's heart began to beat faster. Soft music filtered from an unseen speaker, the sound dominating her senses. She swayed to the soft violin and felt her eyes drifting closed.

"Dance with me, Anna." The commanding voice welcomed her back to the pleasure of the dream. Thickly muscled arms wrapped around her waist from behind, drawing her close to his chest.

"Who are you?" Her voice came out a raspy whisper. She barely recognized it as her own. She tried to turn around. She wanted, no, she *needed* to see his face, but he embraced her tightly, preventing any movement other than the simple swaying of their bodies.

"You'll know soon enough. For now, just move with me."

Powerless to do anything else, Anna succumbed, allowing her fantasy to come to life. She shivered with anticipation. Something, she wasn't sure what, told her the fantasy would become a reality today. She'd finally feel him inside her, touching her mind, body and soul. Every nerve in her body tingled at the thought. And her heart reached out to his, needing to know if there was something more, something besides just sex that he wanted from her.

His warm breath caressed her cheek and Anna's head fell to one side as his lips moved over the softness of her skin. "Are you real?"

His hands cupped her breasts through her thin, cotton T-shirt. "Do I feel real?"

"This can't be happening."

"It's happening, Anna."

"I don't even know you." Yet, her heart told her she did know him. This man controlled her every waking moment and thoughts of him invaded her dreams at night. And now she didn't want to let him go. She couldn't explain the insanity.

"But you know you want me to make love to you. You want to feel me inside you."

"You're reading my mind."

"Move with me," he instructed. Anna didn't deny him his request. She danced with him toward the bed.

"Stop. Stand still." The heady accent swam around in her head. Who was this man? And how could he know her as well as he did? How could he touch her so intimately, know her so well? It all seemed impossible. She didn't know his name, where he came from or even where he would go when he left her. How could she allow him to take the liberties he took so freely now? Then, his hands massaged her flesh through the irritating barrier of her clothes and she wondered, how could she not?

Finally, he began to remove her clothing layer by layer, which took more time than Anna liked. His palm cupped her right cheek and she shivered.

"You are cold?"

"No." Her voice sounded thick to her own ears. "You make me shiver."

A warm chuckle was his only response and he continued to remove her clothes, stopping when she wore only the black lace thong. "What manner of clothing is this?" he whispered on a broken breath.

"It's called a thong." The blood rushed to her ears, sounding like pounding waves.

Gently, he hooked his finger in the thin strip of lace and tore through the material, allowing the backs of his knuckles to brush her ass. She shivered even more, but when he wedged that same finger into the crease, excitement licked at her spine like a long, wet tongue.

"Are you wet for me, Anna?"

She couldn't answer even if she wanted to. Her shoulders pressed back against his chest, her legs dipping to invite him to check for himself. Eyelids drooping, she moaned as he glided his finger further into her creaminess. He brushed it over her clit and she jumped.

"You are wet," he finally responded.

"Yes." She found her voice just as several of his fingers stretched open the gate of her pussy. "Ohhhhhhh." Her legs threatened to buckle.

"I want to fuck you now, Anna. I want to push so deep into your quim that you feel me everywhere." His hand tugged on the back of her hair. "Do you want me to fuck you, Anna?"

She couldn't find her voice.

He gave her hair another tug. "You're not answering my question."

"Yes, dammit!" She barked the response, needy and desperate. Her pussy throbbed and wept, her cream running in rivulets down her legs.

His fingers nipped into her hips. "Bend."

Anna tried to look over her shoulder, but again he stopped her. "Anna, bend, please." The strain in his voice soothed her somewhat. He needed to fuck her as much as she needed to be fucked, maybe even more.

Anna obeyed, bending over the bed, her hands clutching fistfuls of the wedding ring quilt her mother had given her for Christmas. The flame of the candles and the warmth of his hands on her flesh combined to make damp perspiration break out across Anna's body. She waited with anticipation for his next move.

One finger ran the length of her spine. Anna swallowed back a moan. She felt a hard thigh wedge in between her splayed legs and recognized the steely, solid length of his shaft.

He'd removed his clothing and now stood naked behind her. Anna reached around behind her thighs and touched him, almost groaning with the sheer perfection of his skin. Lightly sprinkled with hair, his taut flesh invited her touch. Her desire to look at him warred with her need to allow him to finish what he'd started.

His hand moved lower, testing the wetness of her pussy again. Her knees buckled, bumping against the mattress and the breath whooshed out of her lungs. His thumb flicked her clit and she jumped. Then he pinched it lightly, rolling it between his fingers until her eyes glazed.

She reached back to clutch at his arms, needing a solid crutch, anything to hold her aloft while his hand worked its magic inside the slick lips of her pussy. Time and again, he dipped into her creaminess, running the moisture up and down her pulsing valley only to return to her swollen clit.

"Oh, God, you're going to make me come," she told him, her voice tight with the approach of an orgasm.

"Perfect," he whispered in return. "I want to feel you pulsing all around my fingers, hear your soft moans and know that I brought you to this point. Come for me, Anna. Let me hear you moan for me." His finger pressed even harder into her clit and her knees threatened to buckle.

Warmth coated her from head to toe, encasing her in a cocoon of heat as one by one her muscles clenched and undulated. Her nails dug into his wrists, sinking deep enough to draw blood. Oxygen trapped in her lungs and she came hard and fast, her body going limp in his arms as she gave him the moan he'd asked for.

"That's it, my baby." He kissed her neck. "That's it." His cock bumped her ass. "Now, you're ready for me."

Anna closed her eyes as his hands settled against her hips,

his fingers biting into her skin. And then she felt him, pushing into her, stretching the limits of her body.

She knew she would explode with the pure joy of their joining once he surged into her. Her thighs pulsed, her hips convulsed and she urged him to go deeper, to plunge as far into her wetness as he could. She needed him to test the limits of her flesh, to stretch her, caress the walls of her pussy with the fiery length of his cock.

Big, hot, solid, he drove into her, pulling her back against the lower half of his body. Anna cried out and pushed back against him, her heels lifting off the floor. He claimed every inch of her sex from gate to womb.

He held still for a long moment, long enough to make Anna squirm. "Take me," she commanded. "I need this." She didn't think twice about pleading with him. She craved the thrusts, the powerful mating.

He eased back, almost drawing completely out of her body. Anna protested and reached behind her to curl her fingers around his wet cock. He gave a rumbling laugh which ended on a strangled note.

She tested his length, running her fingers over the taut skin until she heard his breath coming in short gasps behind her.

"By the gods, you're a vixen," the deep voice muttered before he pushed in further, ramming his cock deeper into her channel.

"Yes, that's it. Fuck me," she urged, splaying her legs to give him more room to move. The sweat poured over them, hot and steamy, combining with their heated breaths.

The gentleness broke away. Overtaken by wild, primitive need, her lover clamped his fingers deep into the flesh on her hips and pumped into her, his cock creating a perfect blend of friction and pressure. The force of his thrusts pushed Anna's arms into the mattress and her back arched. She braced her knees against the box spring and tossed her head back. With each slam of his balls against her ass, she moaned, wishing she could cry out his name.

One of his thick, large hands fisted in her hair, tugging her head back even further. With each stroke he took her further and further inside herself, climbing a wall, bridging the gap between passion and climax.

She felt him everywhere. He invaded her senses, obliterating all thought and sense of time. But she invited the eclipse, focusing on the stroke of his cock deep inside the walls of her pussy, the heat of his breath bathing the back of her neck and the feel of his fingers digging into her flesh.

And the scent. The smell of sex warred with the scented candles and Anna inhaled deeply.

She wanted to remember every moment of this, every sight, sound and feeling. How could she not? Even now, as her body accepted a man she barely knew, her mind lay claim to his memory. No, she couldn't forget him. Couldn't forget this exact moment when he whispered her name and rammed into her again and again, begging her to come.

"You're almost there, Anna," he warned her, but she knew. Her muscles tightened, spasming around his cock. And then she was there. The orgasm ripped through her, wringing a cry from the depths of her soul. As she tumbled over the edge, she collapsed against the mattress. He continued to pump for a few seconds longer and then he came on a long, guttural groan before resting his weight on top of her.

"My lovely Anna," he whispered before the weight disappeared.

Quickly, almost desperately, she rolled over, but he was gone. He'd left her alone once more. Anna couldn't stop the tears from leaking down her face.

How could he just leave?

She sat up in the bed and looked toward the window, imagining she could see the outline of his muscular frame, standing outside, watching her.

"Will you return?" Her hands bunched in the comforter. Why did she so desperately need him to return?

She couldn't be falling in love. Not yet. But it felt so right. So real. At that moment, she realized she wanted to love him.

3

"THE SON OF a bitch left you just like that? Well, I say, screw him." Liz examined her nails. "Oh, wait, you did that already." She paced back and forth in front of the stand-alone oval mirror in Anna's bedroom.

"Not funny, Liz. I called you for support." Anna drew her legs up beneath her and scooted to the top of her bed. "I don't even know if he really was here. Am I losing my mind?"

Liz hurried to the side of the bed closest to her friend. "I don't think you're losing your mind, sweetie, but I can see why you think that."

"You believe me, don't you? You don't think I'm imagining things." Anna tipped her face back to meet her friend's gaze.

Liz patted Anna's arm and scampered up to the top of the bed to join her. "Well, let's examine the evidence. Your clothes are on the floor where he left them. From the looks of this quilt, I can see where he had you and you look like a woman who's had incredible, mind-blowing sex. I'd say the evidence points to the reality of the situation."

"And he certainly felt real enough."

"You need to call someone."

"I did. I called you."

"No, I mean a specialist." Liz looked worried.

Anna wrinkled her nose. "You mean a shrink? What do you think a psychiatrist could actually do for me?"

"I was thinking more along the lines of an exorcist." Liz shivered. "What if he comes back?"

"He will." Anna didn't doubt her lover would return. He'd said in due time. Apparently, he had his own time schedule. She could wait, she had no other choice.

"You need to find out who he is . . . what he is."

"He's a man."

"Not an ordinary man. That much is apparent."

"True, but Liz, if you could feel him, hear him, you would probably feel the same way I do."

"And Sam would kill me." Liz rolled off the bed to get to her feet and turned to face Anna. "And speaking of Sam, I'd better get back to him before he calls looking for me to fix his lunch. Poor man doesn't know how to fix a sandwich." She walked around to the opposite side and enfolded Anna in a brief hug. "No matter what happens I'm on your side. Remember that."

How could she forget? Liz was the first person she called in life, be it for good news or bad. Anna smiled. "Thanks. That means a lot to me."

"Hey, what are friends for?" Liz strolled toward the door. "Call me if anything goes down. I mean besides him." She grinned and winked. "Pun intended. I'll be over in a flash."

Anna laughed and some of the pressure lifted from her shoulders. She might not understand who or what her lover was, but for now, she accepted that he existed. And Liz believed her. That would have to do for now.

"Good night, Liz."

Liz waggled her fingers over her shoulder before retreating, leaving Anna lying on the bed pondering her next encounter with a man she'd never really met.

☙

"You shouldn't have gone to her!" The explosion came out of nowhere and as the voice reached him, Onyx spun around.

"Don't you think I know that?" He gave his friend a look which bespoke of his own indecision before he resumed his pacing of the narrow hallway of the castle he'd chosen as yet another stop on their journey. His people grew weary of traveling by ship and needed a break from the monotony. Just as he needed a break from this life, this mundane existence. "I certainly do not need you to tell me what I should or shouldn't have done, Ezrel. I could not stop myself. It's as if there is an invisible string pulling me to her."

"She will not understand why you are . . . what you are." Ezrel, a short man with a bushy shock of white hair and equally bushy white eyebrows, clasped his hands together in front of him and rocked back on his heels. He'd spent his lifetime serving Onyx and such devotion had afforded him the ability to speak his mind. "She will not accept you as an immortal."

"Who said that I was going to ask her to accept me?" Onyx's hands clenched into fists, knowing the truth behind Ezrel's words. He could only imagine the fear in Anna's eyes were she to ever discover what he was.

Ezrel continued to rock. "She waits for you."

Onyx slammed one fist against the wall. The foundation shuddered. "I know that as well."

"And you will go to her again, knowing what it could do to her?"

"I will make sure that nothing will happen to her." He didn't know how, but he made the assurance to quell the censure he read in his friend's eyes.

"How? You are not even in control of your own destiny.

What can you promise her? We have no knowledge of how much longer will even be in this dimension. What will you tell her, Onyx? How can you explain to her that we have no home, that we travel from century to century, in and out of worlds, seeking that we cannot find? And what happens if she falls in love with you?"

"Enough! Leave me! I will decide what will be done." Onyx turned his back on his counselor, advisor and best friend, a man that had borne his sorrows and pain for the past century with the aplomb and grace any ordinary man would envy.

"Very well."

Onyx didn't need to turn around to know that his friend had obeyed his command. Fury swelled within him and he punched the solid stone wall. He had no choice.

He needed to walk away from Anna now . . . before his heart united with hers even more.

"My name is Onyx." The deep words woke Anna from a sound sleep, but she'd been praying for the dream, the touch of his hands once more and now, as her eyes blinked open and she saw him, the vision in her dreams, seated on the edge of her bed, she gasped. Broad-shouldered, with long, dark hair that hung down to her waist and eyes of glittering silver, he embodied every nuance of her fantasy. Pushing herself to a sitting position, she tugged the quilt up underneath her chin and stared into those eyes.

She reached out to touch him, wanting to feel the connection of her skin against his. He didn't back away from her. "Who—how—where did you come from?" Her palm rasped against his lower jaw, reassuring herself he was sitting in front of her.

"That is something for another time. You wanted to see me, to know my name. You wanted me to come to you. You were calling me in your sleep." He brushed a thick lock of hair away from her face and stared into her eyes. "You are beautiful."

"Who are you?" Anna could feel herself falling under the spell of his eyes.

"As I told you, my name is Onyx."

"I know, but that doesn't tell me who you are or how you get into my apartment or what you're doing here." Anna broke off to glare at him. "I was beginning to think you were a figment of my imagination . . . or a ghost."

Sensual lips twisted in a slight smile. "Perhaps I am both." His fingers caressed her cheek. "Or neither."

"You're speaking in riddles."

Onyx inclined his dark head in understanding. "Because I have no answers to your questions."

"You can't tell me how you get into my apartment?"

"I wish to be here and I am here."

Anna blinked at him. "You just visualize yourself here and suddenly you're here?" Her head swiveled as she began a sweeping search of the room. "Okay, this isn't funny anymore. Before, when you were in my dreams, I could convince myself you were just a fantasy, but now you're here. Real and—" she shook her head almost frantically, "—I'm not so sure I'm sane." Scrambling from the bed, Anna dragged the quilt with her and wrapped it around her body to cover the important parts from his view. It probably didn't matter considering if this man really was her dream guy, he'd already seen everything she considered important and then some. "Now, would you please leave my bedroom?" She gave a hysterical laugh. "I can't believe I'm asking a ghost to leave."

Onyx got to his feet and walked around the bed slowly, his

very movements intimidating. A large man, overwhelming in today's society, he carried his height with casual grace. Anna thought of Norse warriors when she looked at him and her mouth watered. She gave herself the luxury of a studied perusal beginning at the crown of his head and ending with his booted feet.

Her gaze lingered on each piece of clothing. Ancient at best, but well worn. Tight pants tucked into shiny, black boots and a leather vest that showed off his sculpted chest to perfection. Suddenly, her own chest grew tight, constricting with the need for oxygen.

"I will go if that is what you wish, but in your eyes, I see something different. I see your heart. You want me to stay."

"You made love to me." Anna couldn't keep the accusation out of her voice.

"Yes."

She closed her eyes and fisted her hands at her sides. "You're really not a ghost, are you?"

"I should be."

Her eyes popped open. "What does that mean?"

He held out both hands. "Look at me, Anna. Tell me what you see."

"Strange clothing and a very attractive man." Her brows lowered. "And your accent tells me you're not from around here. Are you from England?" His accent certainly sounded more British than American.

"I'm not from anywhere really, at least not any place you would know." He hedged and Anna's frustration intensified. He told her nothing. He approached her, reaching for her, but Anna backed off.

"Please don't touch me." Though she wanted him to. God how she wanted him to. But self-preservation warned her to protect her heart, that this man could be dangerous to her peace of mind.

His head tilted to one side. "Why do you tell me not to touch you when your body cries out for mine?" Onyx didn't stop coming until he pressed the massive length of his body against the thin material of her nightgown. "As my body yearns for yours. Do you think I could forget our first mating? It has never been more perfect for me, Anna." He lifted one of her hands and unfurled her fingers. "Touch me, my sweet." He held her hand captive against the wall of his chest. "Learn my body."

She hesitated. "Why are you here?"

"Because I cannot stay away from you."

Her voice lodged in her throat and she forced the words out. "But why?"

He rubbed her hand. "Perhaps we were lovers in a past life."

"I don't believe in reincarnation." Her breath caught at the look in his eyes. It seemed so familiar, like she'd know him for far longer than she actually had.

"Touch me, Anna. We can talk later, but for now, let's fall into each other's arms and seek what we both long for."

Anna swallowed hard. Voices in her head screamed, telling her to back away. She didn't know why she shut them out. Instincts told her she should run, put some distance between herself and this man who only existed when she fell asleep at night.

Should she stay, she'd fall further under his spell. While Onyx continued to watch her with those seductive eyes which reflected her own eyes, she knew he would overpower the voices. With a simple brush of his hand against her cheek, he made her defenses crumble, and she yielded, giving him what she craved just as much.

Her hands moved of their own volition, dropping lower to cup him through his pants, testing the weight of his cock in her palm. He felt so heavy, so full. Her fingers moved experimentally against the thickness and Onyx groaned.

"That's it, baby. Ahh, yes. That feels so good."

"I want to feel you fully, Onyx. I want to feel your cock in my hand."

He quickly tore open his pants and his cock sprang out, hard and hot with a drop of fluid clinging to the tip.

Anna's eyes widened with appreciation for the massive length and thickness. Her thumb rolled over the head and began to worry the most sensitive spot beneath his cock. The muscle jumped, the skin drawing tighter as she began to stroke him, eliciting pleading groans from deep within Onyx's throat.

"I want to come inside you," he muttered, catching hold of her chin in his palm. He tipped her face to his and lowered his head.

When he kissed her, Anna's world shifted and folded beneath her feet. She swirled in another dimension, a world where heat and light enveloped her, drowning out sounds and shapes. His hands caught her around the waist and lifted her easily, accommodating his height.

She recognized this man. This wild male with unrestrained feral strength, unleashed power, had tortured her beneath the spray of the shower and taken her on her own bed. His hands now tore at her panties, tossing the tiny scrap of material aside with little consequence.

Anna watched his cock, so close. His naked chest gleamed in the light and she didn't known how his vest had ended up across the room, but it didn't matter.

Onyx touched his cock to her clit and circled it. "By the gods, you feel so sweet."

"Onyx, I need to feel you inside me." Her pussy craved him, aching and weeping with desperation. She pushed upwards and felt just the tip of his cock, but it wasn't enough. "Onyx—" She didn't get any further words out before he slammed into her, holding her aloft, driving into her until the pressure built inside her like a maelstrom.

She cried out his name, her nails digging into his shoulders. Onyx spun around, allowing her to fall slightly back against the bed until only their lower halves touched. Anna's hands clawed at the satin sheets while he pumped into her.

His face wore a tortured look, almost one of a man condemned but his touch was one of a man who wanted her, needed her, would have her. His thumb dipped between their bodies and caught the tiny nub between the walls of her pussy. "Come for me, Anna. Let me feel your release." He flicked her clit back and forth, rotating the small nub until Anna jerked against him, shoving back against his hand.

Onyx worked his cock in and out of her opening until she ached with intense pleasure. He slammed into her hard and fast, pushing her, driving her while his fingers pinched and pressed her clit until her body began to jerk.

Anna pushed herself up, grinding her hips into his. "Onyx, please, please. Oh, God, oh, God." He was so hard and so deep she could feel him everywhere, his thickness stretching the walls of her pussy, his thighs rubbing against hers as he pumped.

"Yes, yes." He bent low and pressed a hot, spearing kiss against her neck. A harsh, almost guttural groan came from deep within the recesses of his stomach and his juices spilled into her. Anna caught and held her breath as the orgasm swept over her. She bucked off the bed and sank her teeth into his shoulder, shaking as he lifted her to hold her in his arms, tight against his chest.

∽

"Tell me why you're here. Tell me who you are," she pleaded. "You can't really believe we were lovers in a past life."

Onyx pressed a kiss against her forehead, her cheeks, before finally touching her lips. "I believe in a lot of things you would not understand. Perhaps it is because my life is so vastly different from yours."

"How did you know to come to me that first time?"

"I sensed you. Your heart felt so empty, so lonely and my heart recognized the same feelings. Now, I must go, my beautiful Anna." He pulled his body from hers and placed her gently on the bed. He allowed his eyes to drift over her from head to toe. His gaze lingered on the damp patch between her thighs. He wanted to take her again, but he knew he would never have enough of her.

"Stay with me, Onyx. I want you to stay with me tonight."

He fell to his knees beside the bed and cupped her face. "I wish I could, but there are no guarantees. There's nothing I can give you."

Anna cupped his face in return. "You can give me this. What we just shared together. I don't know what's going on here but I know that it's something special. Why else would you know that I needed you? How could you know that I went to bed early because I wanted you to come to me? There has to be some connection and maybe I don't understand and even if you told me, I probably still wouldn't understand it, but I don't want to lose you." She sat up and pressed her lips to his. "Please don't leave me."

Onyx closed his eyes and pulled in a shuddering breath. "Anna, I have no choice. I have to go." The desperate craving within his soul scared him, but walking away from this woman scared him even more. Would his heart return to the cold, empty shell it had been before Anna?

"Then take me with you."

He froze. He couldn't say that he hadn't considered the possibility and maybe, deep down inside, a part of him had been praying that she would ask that, but it was no solution to the problem. She would have no life, at least not the type of life that she had here. Here, she had her friends, her work, something to keep her going. With him, she would have nothing. Pained beyond measure, he got to his feet and placed her hands back down by her sides. "I cannot."

Tears poured down her cheeks. "Will you come again?"

He should tell her no, but instead he just brushed a finger over her lips. "Close your eyes."

"So that I can open them and be alone again?" Anna scrambled to her knees. "I'm not going to let you leave that easily again, Onyx." She brought her head waist-level to his body and with a slight movement of her face, her lips brushed his cock. His lungs constricted and he found it difficult to breathe.

Anna peeped up at him. "You don't like this?" She kissed him intimately again.

How could he tell her that in his time, women did not volunteer to take their man in such a way? Wives considered it a duty and husbands usually convinced them to take part in the act only through much coercion. "Anna, I do not ask you to . . . do this."

Anna's lips closed around his shaft. Onyx thought he would die right there, but then she twirled her tongue around the tip and his knees buckled. She laved him, worshiped him like she couldn't get enough of the taste of his cock. His hands fell to her shoulders, his hips beginning a slow, rocking rhythm as she feasted on his body. He couldn't stop touching her. He grabbed hold of her hair, wrapping the silken strands around his fists. Close to completion, his muscles strained as Anna's tight, wet mouth suckled him.

She moved her hands to his balls and began applying slow, steady pressure. He groaned and jerked, making inarticulate sounds. She transferred her lips to his sac and his self-control snapped. She captured his cock in her mouth seconds before an orgasm ripped through him. His legs shaky, he backed toward the bed and sat, pulling her onto his lap. Perhaps he didn't have to leave so soon. He still had time. He would make time. Time for Anna.

He pressed kisses against her coppery hair and smiled into her drowsy, green eyes. He didn't want to leave her, but soon, the option would be taken out of his hands. For now, he held her tightly, their bodies pressed intimately together. Whispering her name against her cheek, he felt her lips curve upwards in a smile. He needed her to know she would be in his memory forever. Would the words hurt her? Unsure of her feelings, he'd have to think of a way to remove himself from her life. Maybe, just maybe he could do it without hurting her.

His own pain would have to be dealt with alone. As always.

4

LIZ BARRELED THROUGH the front door of Anna's apartment, her eyes wide. "Thank God you called me. So, what happened? You sounded frantic on the phone."

Anna's arms were wrapped around her waist as she paced the living room in her tiny apartment. "His name is Onyx."

Liz's nose wrinkled. "Onyx? What in the hell kind of name is that?"

Anna sat down on the arm of the sofa she'd found at a local flea market and adjusted the folds of her robe. Underneath she was still naked and her skin burned from the touch of Onyx's hands and lips. "It's his name."

"And you know this how?"

"He told me when he came to me this time. And Liz, he's beautiful."

"Yeah, well, that's all well and good, but who is he really? Where does he come from?"

"I'm not sure. He wouldn't tell me that. He's different, Liz."

Liz came to stand in front of her friend, arms folded under her breasts. "Yeah, I figured that much already. So how different?"

Anna lowered her voice even though they were alone in her apartment. "I don't think he's from here."

Liz continued to watch her. "And you think he's alive then? Not a ghost like we thought?"

"No, he's not a ghost, but I'm not so sure he's supposed to be alive, either."

Liz's brows lowered. "You're not making much sense. He's not a ghost, but he's supposed to be one?" She shook her head and her ponytail bounced. "No, that doesn't make sense at all. You're going to have to help me out here."

Anna tucked her hair behind her ears and considered her next words. Probably, they would solidify her shaky mental status in Liz's mind. "I don't think he's from Earth, Liz."

Liz stared at her for a long, hard minute before taking a backward step. "What are you saying? You mean, like not from Earth as in an alien?" Her mouth worked. "I could handle the thought of a ghost, Anna, but a fucking alien?"

Anna nodded in complete understanding. She'd gone through the same intense feelings when she'd discovered Onyx's origins, or at least thought she discovered them. "This came as a shock to me, too, but he's here. Or at least he was here. He was gone when I woke up this morning."

"And you're sure he's not just a figment of your imagination?" Liz worked her hands together. "I think I could believe a powerful fantasy over some sort of outer space lover."

"Do you want to see my bed?"

Liz blanched. "I've seen it before, but wait—is this something different, something like that Monica Lewinsky deal where you kept something that the rest of us are going to find vulgar?"

Anna snatched her friend's wrist and frog-marched her down the hallway. "Come see for yourself." She stopped suddenly in the bedroom door, pointing to emphasize the dents in each pillow, one much larger than the other. The foam covering had left an imprint of Onyx's long form, he was taller than Anna by at least six inches. And as Anna watched Liz's color recede once more, she knew she wasn't the only one seeing something she shouldn't be seeing, something that couldn't possibly be happening. Only it was. It had.

Liz stood staring in the doorway, one hand gripping the frame. "This can't actually be happening." She shot a glance over her shoulder. "Can it? Surely, you're going to wake up tomorrow and all of this will have gone away." Her eyes returned to the rumpled bedcovers. "He can't be real."

Anna sighed. "I don't want to know if he isn't real, Liz."

Her friend wrapped an arm around her shoulder for support. "I know, but, honey, this is one time you have to know the truth."

"We will be leaving again soon," Ezrel pointed out the obvious as he adjusted the silk tie knotted at his throat.

"I am aware of that and why do you insist on dressing like that?"

"I blend in when I am dressed as they are."

"And you forget from where we come."

"Never, Onyx. I could never forget it." Ezrel spun around and faced his friend. "And it would appear that it is you who would forget. You should not have gotten involved with this woman. She is only going to get hurt and even now I can see your unwillingness to leave her behind when we leave here."

Onyx secured his long hair at the nape of his neck with a thong of leather and tugged his brown vest over his shoulders. "I would appreciate your letting me deal with this woman."

"How can I when it would seem that you are forgetting that you have nothing to offer her?"

Onyx's anger simmered below the surface, but the rage wasn't directed at his friend. Being with Anna had changed him and his inability to control his future haunted him now more than ever. He'd connected with Anna, but the ancient gods who still held the power over his life would not allow him to bring her with him. His destiny could not be hers. "This is the first time I've even wanted to bring a woman with me."

"But the journey is not hers."

"And what makes it ours, Ezrel? Whose choice was this journey anyway, because I do not remember being asked."

Ezrel blinked rapidly and twisted his hands in front of him. "Well, as you know, our choices were very limited. We were not able to simply pick and choose where we would go, what we would do and I can assure you that this was the best way for all of us."

Onyx clamped his hands on his hips and faced his friend. "Would everyone agree with you?" He watched a dull flush creep over the man's face and he let out a virulent curse. "Never mind. Forget it. We should not be talking about things we cannot change. This is what was handed to us and this is what we deal with." Walking past Ezrel, he clamped a hand down on the man's shoulder. "I know that I am taking a chance with Anna, but deep inside I do not feel that I have a choice."

Ezrel inclined his head shortly, obviously holding his tongue out of respect. "You are not thinking of telling this to Anna, are you?"

"Not yet."

"But you will tell her then?"

"When the time is right."

"And if she does not believe you?"

"Then I will go." But deep down inside, Onyx knew Anna would believe him. Their hearts had touched, their souls connected. He wished with all his heart he could take her with him, to another world, a place where they could exist as lovers and one life.

Ezrel studied Onyx with a discerning eye. "Why does my heart not believe you?"

Onyx sighed heavily. "She is like no other woman I have ever known. I never thought I would meet someone like Anna."

"You were never supposed to meet her."

"I do not believe that is true."

"You believe the fates would be so cruel as to allow the two of you to meet knowing that this brief encounter is all you will ever have with her?" Ezrel's voice was incredulous.

"Perhaps this brief encounter will be enough." But Onyx knew he spoke a lie, that there would never be enough time, enough days to spend with Anna. Each time he left her, he wanted more.

Anna couldn't explain why she felt so connected to Onyx and one look at Liz's face told her Liz didn't understand. "I know this is difficult for you. Hell, it's difficult for me, too." She turned and walked toward the kitchen. "Do you want some coffee? I feel like coffee."

Liz trailed after Anna into the kitchen and parked one hip against the counter. "No, I don't want coffee. What I want is to know you're going to be okay. I mean, we don't know much about this guy other than he's a great lover and can come and go as he pleases, no pun intended this time. He's not telling you much at all."

Anna ran her hands under the tap water. "Well, that's just it. He's not telling me anything. He hasn't told me anything but his name."

"And that reeks of a gold band on his left hand. Did you notice a white line there or were you even paying attention to his hands?"

Anna restrained herself from shivering. Oh, she'd been paying attention to his hands, all right, but probably not in the manner which Liz was referring. She thought she'd carry the feel of his hands with her to her grave. "Trust me. He wasn't married."

"How can you be so sure?"

"I just know."

"Could you possibly be a little blind when it comes to this man? I mean, I haven't even met him, but from the way you've described him, he's right up there with the Greek gods."

Anna chuckled a little and ran the coffee carafe under the water. "He's close." She dumped the water into the back of the coffeemaker and added grounds to the filter. "Very close actually."

Liz gave a snort of disbelief. "Think about what you're saying, Anna. You're a librarian, for Pete's sake. You read an almost inhuman amount of books each week and I'm sure those books work to feed your imagination. Is it possible that you're just building an everyday Joe up to meet your best fantasy?"

"He's not an everyday Joe, Liz. Just wait until you meet him."

"Do you really think that's going to happen? It doesn't appear to me that he wants anyone to know about him but you. Personally, I think . . ." Liz broke off.

Anna switched on the coffeemaker and tapped the side of the plastic to make sure the cranky old machine began to percolate. "You think what?" The ensuing long silence compelled Anna to turn around. "So you're just not going to talk to me now? What is it with you? Did you . . . ?" Out of the corner of her eye, she caught a flash of dark hair and her heart tripped over itself and then began a rapid beat beneath her breastbone. "Onyx. What are you doing here?"

He tipped his head to one side. "Apparently surprising your friend." He jerked his chin toward Liz's stunned form.

"This is my friend, Liz. Liz—" Anna waved her hand in front of Liz's ashen face, "—this is Onyx."

"Oh my God . . . Oh my God," Liz gushed. "You really are . . . Anna said you were . . . and you are. Tall, I mean. Tall and sexy and God, you're attractive."

Onyx's teeth flashed in a quicksilver grin. "Thank you. It is a pleasure to meet you, Liz."

Liz scrubbed her hand down the front leg of her jeans before sticking it out. "The pleasure is all mine." Ending the handshake, she tossed Anna a long look.

"We'll have to talk, but for now, I'll leave the two of you alone, although you can't imagine how much I'd love to stay." On her way toward the door, she stopped and looked Onyx over from head to toe. "I don't know where you come from, but they sure do make them attractive there."

Onyx didn't turn around to watch her leave, nor did he thank her again. Instead, he walked toward Anna, extending one hand. "Come. We should talk."

Anna swept one hand toward the coffeemaker. "I've made coffee. Would you like a cup? I like coffee. Even though I probably shouldn't be drinking all of this caffeine. It only stimulates my system. Maybe that's why I have insomnia so much. My doctor has told me before that I . . ."

"Anna," Onyx interrupted her with a soft whisper of her name.

She broke off and blinked at him. Her tongue darted out to lick her dry lips. "I'm sorry. I guess I'm a little nervous. I tend to talk a lot when I get nervous. Just like I'm doing now." She pulled in a deep breath. "Okay, I'll shut up and let you do the talking now."

Onyx took her hand and guided her out of the kitchen. "Your bedroom?"

"We don't really talk much in there."

His lips twitched. "This other room in here, then?"

Anna eyed him strangely. "It's the living room and yes, that would probably be the best place."

Onyx waited until she was seated on the sofa before he knelt in front of her, taking both of her hands in his. "Anna, I cannot come back to see you after today."

Her eyes widened, her mouth gaped open slightly. "What are you talking about?"

"My time here is up and I must move on."

"You're talking like you don't have a choice."

His lips twisted into a grimace. "Unfortunately, I don't."

"That's crazy." Anna leaped to her feet, dislodging his hands. "We always have a choice, Onyx. That's what makes us human." But was he human? The thought shook her.

She spun around and realized that Onyx was staring at her strangely as if he hadn't understood a word she'd said and perhaps he hadn't. Anna pulled in a steadying breath and began backing up, moving toward the hall. "Okay, fine. If you want to leave, you go right ahead and leave. I won't try to stop you." She held her head high and marched out of the living room, walking down the hallway with a regal stride befitting a queen.

"Anna." Onyx came after her, his long strides making it easy for him to catch her before she could barricade herself inside her bedroom. "Please. You do not understand how difficult this is for me. I should never have come to you and I knew I was taking a risk by doing so, but once I saw you, I could not stop."

He cupped her face. "I'll never forget that day." His thumb stroked her lower lip. "You were walking down the street, the wind blowing your hair and lifting the edge of your dress. It had just started to rain and the wetness coated your face. I knew from the moment I saw you that I would have to meet you."

Anna's hands curled into fists against his chest. "So what has changed? You've met me and that's enough? You come to me in my dreams and make love to me and then you speak in riddles. I just want to know whatever it is that you aren't telling me." She dropped her head. "I need to know."

Onyx stroked her back gently and kissed the top of her head. "You would not understand."

"I'll never understand if you don't give me that choice. Tell me. The least you can do is tell me and then I can try to understand."

"I was never supposed to come to you." Onyx's voice rang thick with regret. "Had I stayed where I belonged, this never would have happened. I could have left you behind without regret."

"It's too late for that now," Anna whispered against the leather of his vest. "I want to know the truth."

"I didn't see you as a normal man would see you, Anna. I looked at you from another world." Onyx pulled away and searched her face, his eyes guarded. "That's right. My life isn't here. It never has been. It exists beyond these borders."

Anna watched his face, uncertainty warring with her. What he was saying wasn't possible. She'd read enough fantasy to know that it wasn't possible. Time travel simply hadn't been achieved. "How? How could you exist beyond this world?"

Onyx took her hand and led her into the bedroom. He stopped just over the threshold and turned to face her. "Ancient gods have controlled my life for centuries. Though I say it simply, it's anything but simple. I don't belong here, Anna, but then, I don't really belong anywhere."

Anna sat down on the edge of the bed, tugging the rumpled quilt out from under her. She patted the mattress beside her, urging him to join her, but Onyx began to pace the room instead. "Where are you from?"

Onyx stopped and pivoted while Anna held her breath, wondering if he would really tell her. There was something in his eyes, something painful that told her he wanted to tell her, had to tell someone, that he'd been holding it in far too long. So she waited.

"I'm from the city of Atlantis." The words fell on dead silence.

Anna's eyes widened as she watched him, debating whether to believe him or debate him. Atlantis was a fictional city in ancient times, oft debated by scholars as a mythical place much like the gods Onyx spoke of. So far, no proof had been shown as to its true existence and yet, here stood a man, with clothes from centuries ago, a demeanor which bespoke of another era, and eyes that were portals to another dimension. And Anna believed him. Didn't understand everything about his existence, but she believed him. "I thought Atlantis was a myth."

Onyx did sit down then and he captured her hand with his. "I have heard that many times before. I can assure you my city was not a myth. It existed."

"Your city?"

His lips curled. "I was—I am—the ruler of Atlantis, the king."

Anna rested her head on his shoulder. "What happened?"

"The city was destroyed and the remainder of my people were trapped in another dimension, traveling through time."

"Like *Quantum Leap?*" Anna raised her head to look at him.

Onyx blinked at her. "I do not know this *Quantum Leap.*"

She waved a hand in dismissal. "It's a television show." At his blank look, she shook her head. "Never mind. Long story. So why do you have to leave now and where will you go?"

Onyx sighed and squeezed her hand. "My people are in search of a home, a place to start fresh, but they want to go back, to use the knowledge they have learned in these centuries to repair the errors of the past. They believe they can save Atlantis."

"They want to finish out their lives on Atlantis?"

"Yes."

"Is that what you want?"

"It isn't about what I want and the gods would never allow it anyway. They have determined we will build a new Atlantis and as they have decreed that shall I do."

"But that didn't answer my question. Is that really what you want to do?"

Onyx met her gaze boldly and lifted one hand to stroke her face. "Before I met you, I was convinced this was my destiny."

Anna's hand covered his. "Then don't go. Let your people go on and try to find their way back to Atlantis." She lowered her gaze, biting her lower lip. Sparks tiptoed down her spine and though she might regret her next words, she voiced them anyway. "You can stay here with me."

The look he gave her was filled with sadness. "And what would my people do without me, Anna? They need a leader. They need their king."

"But you don't want to go anymore!"

"A true king is not controlled by his desires. He is controlled by his destiny, the love for his people." He sighed heavily. "Besides that, the gods would never allow my desertion. My existence is at their whim."

Anna decided at that moment that she hated those mythological gods that could control a man's destiny and rip him so cruelly out of her reach. Tears built in her eyes and she squeezed her lids shut, desperately trying not to cry. "So that's it, then. You will walk away and never look back."

Onyx pulled her to him in a crushing embrace. "I never said I would never look back, Anna. I will always look back and I will always remember you."

Anna began to cry against his chest, though it didn't make sense. They barely knew one another and yet, she felt like she'd known him forever. "When will you go?"

"Tomorrow at dawn."

"Will you stay with me tonight?"

Onyx pressed her back against the mattress. "I would not be anywhere but here tonight."

With a soft sigh of invitation, Anna opened her arms. "Let's take it slow this time. I want the night to last as long as it can."

Onyx caught the tears in her eyes with his knuckles. "No tears. Not tonight, Anna. Tonight, it will be just you—" he pressed a soft kiss against her lips, "—and me. We will not worry about dawn or what the future will hold. We will—" he kissed her again, "—think about us." He parted the folds of her robe, laying her bare body open to his gaze.

Anna's hands framed his face. "How could I have fallen in love with you in such a short time? I don't even know you, but then I feel like I've known you forever. I feel like you're a part of me."

"I am here." Onyx touched the place over her breastbone. "And I always will be. Just as I will carry you with me in my heart." His words soothed her and his hand slipped down to nestle between her thighs. "Tonight I will love you with more than just my body. I will love you with my heart, my soul and everything that I am." His fingers began to move, parting the folds of her body to massage her intimately.

Anna began to relax beneath the touch of his fingers and she whimpered slightly. Onyx's thumb kept a steady, even pace as he slipped two fingers inside her, drawing out her wetness. Then, bringing his fingers to his lips, he suckled them, keeping his eyes locked on Anna's.

Anna's body responded instantly to the erotic gesture and she reached for him, drawing him close to her once more. Hard and solid against her abdomen, the thickness of his erection pressed hotly against her flesh. "Make love to me." But he resisted. "Not yet." His hands were almost harsh as they moved over her hips, pressing her back against the mattress. Keeping his eyes trained on her face, he lowered himself, pushing the sheets out of the way with his feet. His skin contrasted sharply with the pink satin sheets as he slipped between her thighs.

Anna watched his dark head dip between her legs and held her breath, waiting for that magical moment when his lips would touch her intimately. She felt the warmth of his breath as he hovered over her and her heart thumped against the wall of her chest. Seconds passed and still he didn't move. Anna's hands fisted in the sheets and her legs moved restlessly against the sheets. "Onyx, please."

"Shhh," he whispered, trailing one finger along the inner side of her thigh. "I want to remember every minute of this, Anna. I want to remember how the sunlight bathed your skin. I want to recall the feel of you, your scent, and—" he brushed his lips over the tight nest of curls, "—your taste."

Anna's breath exploded out of her lungs and her back

arched off the bed, but she didn't try to move away. As she connected with satin once more, Onyx's tongue dipped between the velvety folds and fondled her, tasting the wetness, the heat and he groaned low and long.

"I knew you would taste sweet, like the petals on a rose in the early morning dew." Onyx drew back long enough to see her face. His eyes locked with Anna's glazed ones. "My heart is yours, Anna."

Her breath caught in her throat. Knowing he felt the connection just as strongly only made her pain that much worse. Somehow, for some inexplicable reason, her soul knew his and that was all that mattered.

Onyx's hands slid beneath her buttocks and lifted her easily. He pressed slow, languorous kisses against her pussy, sliding his tongue along the damp valley to her pussy. Anna moaned and thrashed beneath his attention and still the charge continued. He suckled her, nibbled her and enjoyed her much as a connoisseur would a fine wine. He supped at her liquid and caressed the ultimate pinnacle until Anna's back bowed off the bed, her hands fisted in his hair and she cried out his name in reckless abandonment.

Anna grasped the headboard, her hands curling around sturdy wood, needing a solid force to hold onto before she toppled over the precipice, hurtling into that shadowy realm where fantasy became the victor over reality.

She basked in the aftereffect of her orgasm while Onyx stroked her thighs, her stomach. Her pussy still quivered with the aftershocks. As he finally slid up her body, she commanded on a purr, "Now fuck me."

Onyx needed no further invitation . . . or demand. Standing, he ripped his clothes from his body, freeing his pounding cock. He'd never been this hard, this solid and as his gaze met Anna's he wondered that a woman could entice him like this, hold him in the palm of her hand. Enthrall him.

Caught in her web, he succumbed to his own need. Her legs went around his hips, completing the invitation.

Anna's fingers dug into his shoulders, her nails scoring his skin. "Fuck me. Fuck me now."

"Oh, yeah, baby." He swept his cock up and down her channel, swirling the head over her clit. She gasped and squirmed, growing wild in his arms.

Arching her back and grinding her pussy against his cock, she panted the demand, "Onyx, now."

Onyx hooked his hands underneath her thighs and plunged into her heat, going deep. She was wet. Tight. Perfect. Her pussy clenched around his cock with a firm grasp and he moved. The friction made him catch his breath.

"Faster." Anna pumped in time with his thrusts.

The gods take him. He knew he'd never feel this way again, this sweet heat and such powerful emotions. And then Anna's teeth sank into his shoulder and he came with such force that even the muscles in his chest clenched. Head tossed back, he let loose a loud, long roar before finally collapsing on top of her.

And still the night continued as time and time again, they turned to one another, loving and sharing until spent, they finally closed their eyes in sleep.

Anna woke at three a.m. She gave into her first instinct and reached out to touch him, to make sure Onyx still rested beside her. She comforted herself with the feel of his warm skin. His body was still relaxed in sleep, but Anna knew that before dawn, he would awaken. She couldn't hold him now. Slowly, carefully, she pushed back the sheets and climbed out of the bed, snagging her robe from the floor where Onyx had finally left it the night before.

Her steps were quiet as she made her way out of the bedroom and down the hallway. Belting the robe around her, she captured the cordless phone from the kitchen counter and tiptoed into the living room. She didn't think twice about dialing Liz's number.

"Hullo?" Sam answered in a gruff, sleepy voice.

"Sam, it's Anna. I'm sorry to wake you but I need to talk to Liz."

"Is something wrong?" Sam yawned into the receiver.

"No. Yes. I just need to talk to Liz."

"'Kay." There was a rustle of sheets as Sam turned to hand the phone to Liz.

"Hello?"

"Liz, it's me. Onyx is here."

"And you called me to tell me that at three a.m.? Anna, this isn't news."

"He's leaving at dawn. . .for good."

"Okay, this is news. Hold on. I'm going to take the phone into the living room so Sam can sleep. He has to get up at six and he gets grumpy if he doesn't get his usual eight hours."

Anna waited impatiently while Liz had a short conversation with her husband before finally making it out of the bedroom.

"Sorry, he wanted to know what was wrong. I told him you were having man troubles. He kind of tuned me out after that. So." Liz opened the door for an explanation. "Tell me what's going on. Why is Onyx leaving?"

"He says he has to." Anna tossed a look over her shoulder to make sure they were still alone. "He told me everything last night, well, probably not everything, but possibly all that he could tell me without the top of my head coming off."

"Yeah? Like what? Hold on, let me grab a cigarette."

"I thought you stopped smoking."

"I did, but this just seems like it deserves a cigarette." A lighter clicked and Anna heard Liz draw the nicotine in before she bade her to continue the conversation.

"He's not from here and I mean nowhere near here. He's from, are you ready for this? Atlantis."

"Atlantis? You're kidding."

"No, I'm not. Onyx was the king of Atlantis."

Liz yawned loudly. "And you bought this story?"

"If you're asking if I believed him, then the answer is yes. I did."

"Is this some kind of a joke? Anna, honey, a man just told you that he is centuries old and you believed him. What happened to that skeptical mind of yours?"

"It probably went the same place my sanity did after I started getting late-night visits from a man I could never touch. Liz, will you listen to me? This is real. Everything he says makes sense. And he's leaving at dawn."

"Why dawn? Is the mother ship coming to take him back?"

Anna held the receiver away from her ear to glare at it, as if she could transport her disapproval across the line. "Will you get serious?"

"Okay, sorry. I'm trying to think here, but my brain's a little fuzzy." Liz lowered her voice to a whisper. "Did he tell you he's leaving?"

"Yes, and—" Anna carried the phone back into the kitchen. "I know you're probably going to think I'm crazy, but I plan to go with him when he leaves."

"What?!?" Liz's voice screeched into the phone. "Are you out of your mind? Sorry, honey, just go back to sleep. I woke

Sam back up. You're not thinking clearly, Anna. You're plan-ning to run away, to leave behind the only life you've ever known to head off for parts unknown with a man you don't know well."

Anna felt a cold chill race down her spine. "Liz, wait." Dropping the phone, she raced down the hallway and stood transfixed in the doorway. Her bed was empty, Onyx was gone. Pain so strong it pierced her heart brought her to her knees and clutching her hands against her chest, she sobbed.

Liz banged on the front door until Anna's ears reverberated. "Come on, Anna. Open up. I know you're in there. Open the damn door or I'm going to call your landlord and have her open it. I'll tell her you're suicidal or something. So open the door. Now."

Anna didn't doubt that Liz would search out her landlord and the last thing she wanted right now was for other people to find out what was going on in her life. Reluctantly, she shuffled to the door, clutching a box of tissues in one hand and the television remote in the other. Switching the box to her arm, she clicked open the locks on the door and swung it open. "It's four-thirty in the morning."

"You were talking to me one minute, telling me to hold on and then there was this long silence. You never came back to the phone and I knew something was up. I kept trying to dial your number but the line was busy." Anna followed Liz's gaze to the discarded receiver on the floor halfway outside the kitchen door. "That could possibly be the reason why." Liz marched across plush carpeting to retrieve the phone and switch it off. "Now, do you want to tell me what's going on?"

"Onyx left while I was talking to you."

"Talk about taking the easy way out."

"He'd already told me that he had to go." Anna's voice was defensive.

"Yeah, after giving you this cock-and-bull story about having to go back to his home place. Anna, honey." Liz wrapped one arm around Anna's shoulders and guided her toward the sofa. "Why don't you sit down and I'll fix us some tea? Where do you keep your brandy? You look like you could use a dash of some liquid fortitude in yours."

"Left-hand cabinet beside the refrigerator." Anna curled her legs up beneath her on the sofa. "I can't believe he's gone. I won't see him again. Ever."

"You don't know that. After all, you didn't know that he would even come to you to begin with. This guy has been an enigma from the beginning. Maybe he won't stay gone."

Anna shook her head. "No. I know he's gone."

"Okay, the way I see it, you don't really have many options here. I know this hurts a little, but you didn't have a lot invested in this guy." Liz's hands paused, the tea kettle hovering over the stove. "I'm sorry. That didn't come out right. I doubt I'd feel any better about it if I were in your shoes."

"He's not coming back and there's not a damned thing I can do about it. That's what hurts the most." Anna clenched her hands into fists. "Oh, Liz, how do I get myself into these things?"

"Well, you had help this time, honey. So don't beat yourself up about it."

"I wish I could have gotten to known him better, learned more about him. And I should have asked him why I couldn't go with him."

Liz switched on the stove to heat the water. "Would you really have gone, left your life here to traipse off to parts unknown? Tea bags?"

"Canister at the back of the counter and absolutely. He was unlike any man I've ever known."

Liz busied herself with retrieving china cups and saucers. "I could tell that from your first encounter with him. He kinda stays with you, doesn't he?"

Anna felt the tears building again and she quickly dabbed at the moisture at the corners of her eyes. "It didn't take long, Liz. There was something there."

Liz turned slightly to better enable her to see her friend's face. "You felt a connection."

Relief coursed through Anna's veins. Liz did understand. Maybe not all of it, but at least the most important part. "Yes, a connection and while we were talking, you and I, I knew when he'd left. It was like the warmth had gone out of me. How can you explain that?"

Liz whistled low. "I can't and I know that doesn't really help you much, but you're going to have to face facts. Whoever he was, he's gone now and you're going to have to get back to life as usual."

Anna gave her friend a bleak look. "How, Liz? How do I do that? I know it might not have been a long time but there was something there, a tie, a bond and now that it's broken, I know that I will never meet another man like Onyx."

"That could be for the best, you know. Could you imagine having to introduce him to your friends? First, with a name like Onyx, he had to have been kicked around in school. Second, most of our friends would pay more attention to him than you and with those eyes of his, well, let's just say you'd spend most of your time worrying about whether or not he would be faithful to you because he could charm his way into any woman's bed. Look how long it took him to get into yours."

"Onyx isn't like that, Liz."

Even from the distance separating them, Anna saw Liz roll her eyes. "Okay, I'm going to dismiss that because right now you're swept up in this fairy tale, but when sunlight gets here, if you're not thinking more rationally, I'm going to call a doctor, one who can prescribe medication to make you sleep this off." As the tea kettle began to whistle, Liz switched off the stove and began preparing the tray. "You know, honestly, I'm kind of glad this is over. I know that might sound cold to you, but you haven't been yourself since all this started. In fact, you've been acting kind of spooky. It'll be a relief to have things get back to normal. We'll hook you up with a nice, ordinary guy, one who doesn't slip out of your bed at three in the morning. How does that sound? Anna?" Liz turned around. "Anna?" She forgot all about the tea tray and headed down the hallway to find Anna curled on her side on the bed, clinging tightly to the pillow Onyx had used. "Oh for the love of Pete, you're going to have to . . ."

"He told me goodbye," Anna whispered.

Liz's mouth rounded to an "o." "What do you mean he told you goodbye? I thought you said he left without telling you."

"While you were talking. He whispered in my ear. Told me he loved me and that he would miss me."

"This is so bizarre. What can't this guy do?" Liz peered into Anna's face. "You know, you really don't look okay. I'm calling the doctor now."

"Liz, wait. I'm okay." Anna sat up, pushed the hair out of her eyes. "Really." She even managed a small smile. "I'm going to be okay. As long as I know that he's going to be okay."

"You know, you're certifiable."

"Probably. So where's that tea?"

Liz gave her a wary look. "In the kitchen, but I'm warning you. One more weird outburst or strange comment about voices in your ear and I will call the doctor. I mean, honestly, what did the two of you really share beyond great sex?" She paused. "I'm assuming it was great sex because I haven't really gotten all of the details since the two of you actually started, well, you know. You told me about the shower and all and casually mentioned when you first had sex with him, but since then, you've been strangely mum. So did the good sex continue?"

Anna stuffed her feet into her bedroom slippers and rolled off the bed. "Liz, I'll never find another man like him." She walked out of the room.

"Wow," Liz mumbled.

5

"I DON'T EVEN know why I'm here." Anna glowered at her best friend and shifted her position away from the woman hacking beside her. She hated doctors' offices. Ordinarily, she only went for her annual checkups, but this time, she'd been forced to make an appointment at Liz's insistence. Okay, so maybe she had been a little pale lately and her stomach hadn't felt quite right, but Onyx had only been gone two weeks. To her, she was still in mourning.

She wasn't sleeping well and it was going to take her some time to adjust to never seeing him again. Ever. It wasn't like she could hop on a plane and go visit him. He was gone for good and she had to come to terms with that, no matter how much it hurt.

"Because you've been sick."

"I haven't been sleeping well." Anna gave the same excuse she'd been giving for the past week.

"Then you should be ready to collapse by now. If you could see yourself, you would know why I brought you here. Your doctor needs to be the one to tell you that you're going to kill yourself."

"My doctor barely knows me. I see him once a year whether I like it or not. That's it."

"But you'll listen to his advice, I'm sure."

"I doubt it."

"Ms. Barker?" A portly nurse in brightly flowered scrubs beckoned Anna from a swinging door. "If you'll come with me, we'll get you set up."

"If I have to take my clothes off for this, I'm not going to be happy with you," Anna snarled over her shoulder.

Liz waved a hand and picked up a magazine dated two years ago.

"This can't be happening." Anna kept repeating the mantra when Liz's minivan slowed to a stop in the parking lot of her apartment complex. "Do you have any idea what this means?"

Liz nodded in complete understanding and killed the engine. "Come on. We're going to go inside and I'm going to fix you some hot soup and some ginger ale. Now that we know what's causing the nausea, we can certainly treat it." She unfastened her seat belt and opened the car door, but Anna's hand clenched around her wrist, stopping her progress.

"I don't think you really understand this, Liz. I am thirty-three years old and I'm about to become a mother for the very first time."

"Honey, plenty of women have done it. You won't be the first and you certainly won't be the last. And if anyone is capable of raising a child alone, you are. Besides that, you know you're not in this alone. I'll be there every step of the way." She flashed a bright smile. "I'll even help you decorate the nursery. Now, unbuckle and let's go inside." Liz hopped out and headed toward the main entrance of the complex.

Slow, wooden steps carried Anna toward the front door. She walked in a fog behind Liz. Pregnant. She was going to have a baby. Alone. She would be a single parent. Just like her mother had been. Her mother had always told her that it was no picnic raising a child alone with little or no support. Well, how could she expect support from Onyx when she didn't know where he was or how to find him? Hell, she didn't even know his last name.

Her hand shook as she stuck the key inside the lock. "Liz, I'm pregnant," she parroted for the fifth time.

Liz placed her hand against Anna's back and steered her down the hallway. "Yes, dear, I know. Now, go change into your jammies and I'll whir open a can of soup. My mother's cure-all to all the ills of the world. Now, go, go." She shooed her down the hallway before she headed into the kitchen.

Onyx stared out across the open ocean, his arms folded across his chest. His eyes were narrowed against the glare of the sun bouncing off the crystal-blue waters of the Aegean Sea.

He finally knew the way to his new home. It had come to him in a dream and at first, he'd dismissed the visions. But this morning, he'd awaken with a sense of purpose and belief that his dream had guided him.

Now, his people would be home soon and they could put down roots, start afresh. There was an air of excitement on the ship, whispers of joy shared between friends and family.

But Onyx felt no joy, only a deep, abiding sadness. He didn't hear Ezrel join him at the bow, but he sensed him. The man moved with an ageless grace, quietly. "Before you say anything, I know."

Ezrel's brows puckered. "This was not supposed to happen, Onyx."

Onyx's arms dropped to his sides but he didn't turn around, didn't look at his friend. "That I already know."

"There is no solution."

"She cries to me in her dreams."

Ezrel harrumphed. "But do you know why she cries?"

"That is not important. I only know that she hurts."

"You did not expect any less when you left her." Ezrel remained the voice of reason.

"I never wanted to hurt her." Onyx knew the choice he had made. It had been painful for him as well. But he did not like the feel of Anna's pain deep within his heart. Every night, he heard her cries, but lately the cries had been more insistent, the pleas almost deafening, drowning out his own thoughts. It seemed that her pain was giving him no other choice but to return to her.

As if Ezrel could read Onyx's mind, his voice became firm. "This cannot be."

Onyx ignored the words. "I must go back."

"The people will not want to turn back."

Onyx whirled, fire in his eyes. "Then tell the people to go on without me."

Ezrel blinked rapidly. "You know that will not happen. The people need you. You are our leader."

"Perhaps it is time they found a new leader. We are almost home. We all know that and once the ship has arrived, they will no longer need my guidance."

"That is not for you to decide," Ezrel snapped.

"Perhaps it is. Perhaps it is time for me to start making my own personal decisions."

More rapid-fire blinking accompanied this statement. "You are not thinking clearly, my king." Very rarely did Ezrel resort to formality, usually under the most extreme circumstances. "We are close to our new Atlantis. You cannot desert us now, and this woman, what can you offer her? For that matter, what can she offer you? And were you to disobey the gods, they would not look favorably on you." He shuddered as he said the words. "You do not want to anger the gods, Onyx."

"I have broken her heart. Her spirit is not the same as when I went to her." Onyx's hands twisted around the railing, barely acknowledging his friend's words.

"Did you expect it to be any different? I tried to warn you that no good could come of this union, but you would not listen. You travel two very different paths."

"Then why do I feel connected to her?" Onyx looked at Ezrel, his own eyes filled with a bitter pain. "Why does my heart ache in time with hers?"

Ezrel licked his lips and turned his attention toward the swelling tides. "What will you do?"

"I will go back to her."

"And if the fates will not allow it?"

"Then I will find a way."

Ezrel sighed and nodded his head shortly. "Then we shall come with you." He held up one hand to silence Onyx's interruption. "It is no use, Onyx. We will not go on without you and you will not go on without this woman. Perhaps, this is meant to be. We shall return with you to this woman's time and find out what the fates would have your path be. Should we learn that it is different than ours, then, and only then, will we go on without you." He placed a hand on the taller man's shoulder. "Until then, we stay with our king."

Onyx nodded. "Thank you."

Ezrel didn't speak another word, he simply turned and walked away, leaving his king to consider the consequences of his next move.

∽

Anna moved slowly around the nursery, putting the finishing touches on the crib, adjusting the drapes. She walked with difficulty as the baby within her was close to his or her birth day. She backed toward the door to get a better view. One protective hand rested on her abdomen.

"I wish you could see what I see, little one." Anna spoke in a soothing tone of voice. "But since you can't, I'll describe it to you. I didn't know if you were going to be a boy or a girl. I asked the doctor not to tell me because I just wanted to love you for you. The nursery is painted yellow. You'll understand all about neutral colors when you're older. I hope you like teddy bears and stuffed animals. I think most babies do. Anyway, the nursery is full of them. It's a beautiful room, sweetheart. I just wish your daddy could be here to see it, too." She turned and switched off the light, lingering for a moment in the darkness to drink in the smell of the new border, the fresh scent of clean linen. Soon this room would be put to use. Soon, she would have a baby in her arms to remember Onyx by.

She couldn't believe he'd been gone for almost nine months. She still thought about him every day. Still heard his voice whispering in her ear. And once, she even thought she'd heard him say he was coming back to her. Or maybe that had been her mind playing tricks on her. Either way, she held out hope that one day, he really would return to her. She wanted him to know his child and to see what their love had given them.

∽

Home. The word had a foreign sound to it, but as the boat dropped anchor in the crisp blue waters off the small island with stark white sands and rippling waters, Onyx knew they were indeed, home. They'd traveled through time, from century to century and finally, a new world had emerged. He felt it in his soul.

Onyx walked down the boat's plank, hearing the excited whispers behind him. As king, he would be the first to inspect the city, to determine if his people would be safe here. But he already had his answer. Everywhere he look, he saw fresh green grass, ice-tipped mountains and a sky so blue his eyes hurt. And in the distance, a castle, constructed of polished stone . . . and onyx. His namesake.

There could be no question. The city of Atlantis would be resurrected on this small island. And life would start anew for his people and their families. They'd find happiness here.

Everyone except him.

∽

The rain slashed against the window of the castle, obliterating the view of the street below. Darkness had taken the city and even with the lighted torches, very little could be seen.

Onyx pulled his cloak closer around his frame and turned from the inky blackness. He squared his shoulders as he made his way across the floor, back to the long, wooden table that centered the dining area.

"I am sorry, Your Majesty. I have known for a long time that the fates could be cruel, but I never imagined that they would take away your opportunity to see your Anna again."

Onyx flung his long, dark hair back over his shoulders and looked away. "It is of no importance now. Too much time has passed." Though it had crawled by for him, he knew many months had gone by in Anna's world. She had to have moved on . . . hadn't she? "I'm sure Anna has gone on with her life and it is better this way. This—" his hand swept out to encompass the castle, "—is our life now. We are centuries away from the life that Anna knows. She lives in a world that we could never understand just as she could never understand ours. I could not ask her to give up the comforts of her life to join me here."

"I do not believe that any of us expected to find the new Atlantis. To us, it has been a dream a long time in the making. To you, it comes at a time when you least wanted it."

"I wanted it for my people," Onyx corrected. "Selfishly, I wanted more time with Anna, but I must go on. Anna would not want me to be unhappy any more than I would want her to drown in misery."

Ezrel cleared his throat. "The people are talking. That is—" he coughed, "—they have mentioned that perhaps it is time for you to—" another cough, "—you see, the people want you to be happy and they believe that for a man to be happy, he needs a wife, someone to care for him, nurture him. The people have asked when you shall take a queen."

The mere thought made Onyx cringe inwardly. He wanted no other woman to lie in his bed. He could not imagine making love to any other woman but Anna. His heart was hers and he cursed the cruelty of the fates for keeping them separate. But he knew that he must do right by his people. The people made him king and he must honor their requests no matter how much those requests hurt him inside.

"Tell them I will look into the matter but it will take some time to choose my bride." He turned and gave Ezrel a long, hard look, willing him to interpret the words in the right manner. He needed time and Ezrel could give him that time.

Ezrel bobbed his head in completed understanding. "Certainly, Your Majesty. I will inform the people that you will take your time in choosing a bride as these matters cannot be rushed into without the proper thought and care." He began to back toward the doorway. "Perhaps even a winter or two."

Onyx felt some of the weight slip off his shoulders. "Thank you. You serve your king well."

"You are my friend," Ezrel pointed out quietly before he slipped into the darkened corridor.

∞

Anna woke up in a cold sweat, perspiration clinging damply to her skin. She tossed back the sheets and got to her feet, dragging her hands through her hair, trying to make sense of the fear taking root inside her heart. Quietly, she walked to the nursery, her steps muffled against the carpeting. One peek inside the narrow opening reassured her that Alex still slept soundly. At just over a month old, he was growing by leaps and bounds and Anna regretted what Onyx was missing. He hadn't seen Alex's first smile or felt his baby's soft body in his arms just after his birth. Now, Anna's hope had diminished. She didn't believe she would ever see him again.

She retreated back to her bedroom, pushing aside the frilly, white curtain to stare out into the night. Stars winked in the sky and moonlight slashed across the tiny backyard of the house she'd bought months before Alex's birth. She'd thought that every baby needed to grow up in a home, to have a yard to play in, a place to put a swing set. Afterward, she'd been dismayed to think that maybe Onyx had come back to her in the apartment and she'd been gone.

A sick sensation curled in the pit of her stomach and she pressed one hand against the cold windowpane. Winter had settled over the city, wrapping its residents in a cocoon of ice and snow. Ordinarily, Anna loved this time of the year. With Christmas just a few short weeks away, the festive lights glowed along the streets and she'd always looked forward to drinking hot chocolate and listening to the carolers outside her windows. But not this year. This year was different.

"Anna." She whirled around, hearing his voice as clearly as if he was standing over her shoulder. "Onyx?" With frantic steps, she searched the house. He called to her from somewhere. She couldn't find him, but she could feel him, reaching out to her. Her heart connected with his and she closed her eyes, standing in the middle of the hallway of her two-bedroom house. "Onyx, where are you?"

The cold chill of the night enveloped her and she wrapped her arms around her waist. Why had he called to her? Was he ill? Did he need her like she needed him? "Dammit, Onyx, let me know you're okay."

6

ONYX CAME AWAKE with a start, his heart thundering in his chest. He'd heard her. She'd called out to him. He propped his hands on the mattress and breathed in deeply. He could almost smell her, recall her scent with vivid clarity.

Her eyes flashed into his line of vision and Onyx pushed aside the heavy quilts covering him. "Damnation! How could you be so cruel?" He railed to the fates as he climbed out of the bed. "If I cannot be with her, why must I see her, feel her, hear her every waking hour of every day? I cannot look at another woman without seeing Anna, much less think about taking a queen." He paced the spacious area of his living quarters, his bare feet slapping against the cold floor. "I cannot live like this!"

"We should not interfere any further, Sisters. Their destinies have been chosen, woven into the fabric of time." Clotho, the youngest of the fates, made the announcement in her most solemn of voices.

Lachesis folded her arms across her bosom and looked down into the time bubble. "How can we not interfere? Can we really leave Anna as she is, unhappy and miserable in an existence without the man she has fallen in love with?"

Atropos, the sister who wielded the most control—the ability to cut the cords of life, surveyed her sisters with something akin to distaste. "Did we not interfere when we allowed Onyx to breach time? Did we not interfere when we turned our backs on his love affair with Anna?"

Clotho shook her head, her long hair swinging freely about her waist. "Onyx allowed his heart to rule him and we don't come between a man and his heart. But it was necessary that he find the new Atlantis." She sank down atop a velvet settee, nibbling on her lower lip. "We could not allow those souls to be lost."

Lachesis held up one hand. "We are the fates. We are not gatekeepers for souls, and we allowed ourselves to get involved in matters of the heart." She placed her hand on her youngest sister's shoulder. "Therefore, it behooves us to help resolve the situation and set things to right."

"Then we are all agreed." Atropos swept a hand toward the clear bubble below which enabled the three fates to see into Anna's life. "The lovers will be reunited and at least given the ability to say their final goodbyes."

Anna's eyes popped open and suddenly, her heart eased. She knew what needed to be done. Calmly, she retraced her steps to her bedroom and quickly dressed in jeans and a pullover sweater. Sliding her feet into boots, she straightened and ran her fingers through her tousled hair. If Onyx could not come to her, she would go to him. She wasn't quite sure how she was going to go about doing that just yet, but she would find a way. There had to be a way, perhaps some spell, a time portal or something.

Halfway to Alex's room, she stopped, her eyes widening. A time portal? What in the hell was she thinking? There was no such thing as a time portal. And even though she knew Onyx had not been a figment of her imagination—she had Alex to disprove that theory—she believed that there was a logical reason for his appearance and disappearance. She had to believe that or she would drive herself crazy thinking that he was in another time dimension and couldn't get back to her.

"I'm going to find you, Onyx. I'm tired of waiting around here for you to reappear. My heart is with yours. I can feel it and I'm going to come to you."

Determination in every step, she hurried into her son's room and after making sure he was properly bundled, she pressed him to her shoulder. "Hang on, honey. It's going to be okay. You're about to meet your daddy."

∞

"No!" Onyx's hands fisted at his sides as he whirled around. "She cannot come here! She does not belong here! She would never be happy."

Ezrel folded his hands in front of him and bobbed his head in understanding. "I can only tell you what the seer has told me, Your Majesty, and you know she is in tune with the fates."

"So we are back to formalities again, I see." Onyx's lips twisted into a bitter parody of a smile. Where once he had a friend, now he had another subject, another man to bow and scrape and answer his every command. "Anna does not belong here."

"And yet, the seer said she would come."

"How? I can't imagine the fates would take part in this. Their job is only to watch our lives, not rework them." Though Onyx knew deep in his heart that Anna would never fit in with this lifestyle, that he would have to send her back, he couldn't deny the thrill racing through him at the thought of seeing her again, holding her again.

"The seer could not say, but you know she communes with the fates on a daily basis," Ezrel hedged, looking away from the probing eyes of his king.

"You know more than what you are telling me."

"Perhaps, but surely how she arrives is not as important as the fact that she will be coming, Your Majesty. And soon."

"How soon?" Onyx's hands unclenched and he walked toward his friend.

Ezrel shrugged. "I do not know that."

Onyx's eyes flicked back toward the window. "I can feel her."

Ezrel cleared his throat. "Perhaps you would like to be alone."

"How am I going to tell her she cannot stay, Ezrel?"

Decidedly uncomfortable now, the smaller man cleared his throat, coughed and backed toward the door of the royal chambers. "I am sure that it will come to you, Onyx. You have never been a man short on words."

"But I have never told my heart to leave before." Onyx heard the door click shut and knew he was alone again.

Anna didn't know where she was or how she'd gotten there but when she opened her eyes, her bedroom had disappeared. The safety net she knew fell away and she found herself in a dark, damp and uninviting corridor reminiscent of an Alfred Hitchcock movie. Alex stirred against her shoulder and she soothed him by gentle pats on his back as she moved cautiously down the hallway. Where in the hell were the lights? She slid one hand along the wall, searching for a light switch, but cold stone scratched her palm. Stone? Who in the hell lived in a stone house? Okay, she was going crazy, losing her mind. That was the only explanation she could think of to explain her presence in this dank, lightless corridor.

And she couldn't sense Onyx. She wished for him, certain by mere desire alone she could find the portal to him, but now, she wasn't so sure. Holding Alex tight against her chest, she blinked into the darkness. What had she done?

"The king has summoned you," came a deep voice from out of the dark.

Anna shrank back against the wall and clutched Alex even tighter. She held her breath as the military-type voice barked out another order. She prayed the order wasn't directed at her, but then footsteps receded and she was alone again. With plenty of time to mull over the man's words. The king has summoned you? The king? Now, she was starting to get worried, but hadn't Onyx mentioned he led the people of Atlantis? Excitement speared through her, but didn't totally erase the fear.

Creeping forward, Anna felt her way toward the end of the hallway, rounding a corner to find a narrow pathway of stone steps. "It's a castle. I'm in a friggin' castle," she exclaimed aloud. "Boy, Anna, when you dream, you dream big. Okay, just stay calm. You'll find a way out of this. After all, you got here, so that means there has to be a way to go back." But she wasn't so sure. She didn't even know how she'd gotten here . . . unless her wishes alone had done it.

Firelight flickered at her feet and Anna shrieked in terror, startling Alex from a sound sleep. He protested with loud wails and while Anna tried to shush him, the light grew closer. "Get away from me." She kept her voice stern, praying that the force of it alone would intimidate her would-be attacker.

"You have no reason to fear me, Anna." The deep voice reassured her and as the torch lifted, the light played across a face lined with age and wisdom.

Anna bounced Alex to quiet him. "How do you know my name? No, never mind that question. Where in the hell am I and how do I get home?"

The man leaned forward with his free hand and patted Alex's back. The baby's cries grew silent and Anna took a step back, but with the wall against her spine, there was nowhere for her to run. "As I said, do not fear me. I know of you because our king speaks of you often."

"Your king?" Anna's voice squeaked out. She was trapped inside a bad *Twilight Zone* episode.

"Come with me. I shall take you to him."

Anna didn't move. "I'm not so sure I want to go to your king."

The man raised the torch higher. "But the king will want to see you." He made the words sound like a command from on high.

"Yeah, well, I have more important things on my mind right now. My child is going to be hungry in a few minutes and I didn't take the time to pack a bag for him. I wasn't sure it would have traveled with me anyway." Hysterical laughter bubbled up in her throat. "What am I saying? I didn't really know I was going anywhere. I mean, I hoped, but plenty of people hope and nothing happens. So I couldn't be sure. Do you understand what I'm saying?"

He gave her a blank look. "We shall provide a wet nurse for your son."

Anna held tighter to Alex. "I don't think so. I just want to go home."

"And you shall. As soon as you speak with the king."

"Okay, fine. I'll meet with your damned king, but he'd better have a really good reason for wanting to see me." Anna began to move, heading up the steps illuminated by the torch the king's lackey held aloft. She stopped on the third step and looked over her shoulder. "Could you at least tell me where I am?"

The man's lips twitched. "You are in the new Atlantis."

Onyx turned as the door opened, releasing a breath he'd been holding since he'd known that Anna had arrived in the castle. He didn't know how she'd gotten here or how long she could stay, but for now, it was enough that she was here. Two steps and he stood in front of her. "Anna."

Her mouth slightly agape, Anna stared up into the face of the man she thought she'd never see again. "Onyx? Is it really you? I hoped—the man outside said that this is the new Atlantis and before that could register, he was pushing me toward this door and here you are and I thought I'd never see you again. No matter how much I prayed for this. And—" she tossed a look over her shoulder, "—then he disappeared before I could even reach the door."

Giving in to his need to touch her, Onyx brushed his hand over her hair, allowing his palm to rest against her cheek. "You are here." He couldn't believe his eyes or his good fortune. She actually was standing in front of him and he realized he'd missed her so much that his heart ached.

Alex stirred once more, letting out a soft whine that Anna recognized as the beginning sign of hunger. She cradled him in her arms, feeling Onyx's silver eyes burning a path across her child's slight form.

"Who is this?" Onyx's voice thickened as his fingers parted the heavy quilt Anna had wrapped Alex in before her departure.

Anna's head lifted and she felt her eyes fill with tears as she responded. "His name is Alex. And he's your son."

His breath leaving his body, Onyx staggered back, his hand extended. "My son? No. That cannot be possible. Something must be wrong." He took a backward step, then another before the backs of his knees connected with the feather mattress. He sat down abruptly on the edge.

Anna advanced into the room as Alex began to whimper in earnest. "I was hoping for a better reaction than this, but I can assure you that he is your son, Onyx. He is one month old. You only have to look at him to see that he is your son. He has your eyes."

Onyx heard the tears in her voice and he quickly raised his eyes to her face. "Anna, please do not cry. I believe you." He managed to push himself to his feet. "May I hold him?"

Anna extended their son, carefully passing him into Onyx's outstretched arms.

His eyes welling with tears, Onyx looked down into Alex's wide eyes. His heart seized in his chest, overflowing with love and the need to protect. "My son. He is beautiful." He ran a finger down the boy's soft cheek and Alex gurgled his approval. The gods had indeed blessed him. Seeing the slight touch of silver in the boy's small eyes, he smiled. "He does have my eyes."

"And your nose," Anna replied, her voice choked.

Onyx jostled the baby onto his shoulder and Alex gave a chortle. Surprise colored Onyx's face. "He likes this."

"He's not used to being that high up." She swiped tears off her own cheeks.

"This changes everything," Onyx whispered.

"Changes what? What are you talking about?"

"You were not supposed to come, Anna. The fates are not allowed to tamper with the future. By allowing you to come, they have changed things. By the birth of our son, we have changed the future." Onyx's eyes were bright with unshed tears when he looked at her.

"We have changed our future, that is all," Anna responded with a sharp bite to her voice. "And if you stand there and tell me that our son is a mistake or wasn't meant to be, I'm going to hit you."

One eyebrow lifted as Onyx continued to watch her. "You would strike a king?"

"I would strike anyone who considered my son a mistake."

"He is not a mistake, Anna, but I do not understand how this can be."

"Perhaps you aren't supposed to understand it. Don't you ever just accept things for how they are? Maybe this wasn't supposed to happen, but it did happen. You and I met and now we have a child. Tell me that you regret any of this, Onyx." Anna took a step forward and grasped his wrist. "Tell me."

Onyx swallowed the lump in his throat and cradled Alex against his broad chest. "He needs food. I shall call Ezrel and . . ."

"No, you won't call Ezrel, whoever in the hell Ezrel is. You'll give me my son," Anna snapped as she lifted her sweater up over her stomach until her breast was bared.

The lump climbed back into his throat, bigger than ever. Onyx passed Alex into the arms of his mother without another word, but the sight of Alex feeding at Anna's breast rendered him speechless, unmovable. He searched for an answer, a reason behind Anna's arrival but nothing came to mind. "You cannot stay." The harsh words were a surprise to himself and Anna.

Anna sat down on the edge of the bed and continued to nurse their son. "I'm not going back."

Onyx stared at her. "You have no choice. This is not your life."

"It is now."

"You would not like it here, Anna. I have seen how you live, the comforts that exist in your world. They do not exist here."

Anna lifted her head, fixing her lover with a studious look. "Oh, I don't know. Being with you offered some comfort that my world doesn't offer without you."

"We speak of different types of comfort."

"Do you still love me?"

His eyes narrowed to slits. "In my world, a woman does not ask that of a man."

"Yeah, well, I come from modern America. So answer the question."

"It makes no difference. Love does not change . . ."

"Onyx, just answer the damn question!" Anna's voice sharpened.

"You are much different in this world than you are in your own time," Onyx observed with a wry twist of his lips.

"I didn't even know I was in another world until you just told me!" Anna shifted Alex to burp him and continued to glare upwards. "So are you going to answer the question?"

"No, I think I am not." He watched her shoulders sag. "Only because my love for you changes nothing. You cannot stay in this world. The fates will not allow it."

"They've brought me here."

"I am not so sure that it was the fates."

"Who else could it be?"

Onyx sighed and sat down beside her on the edge of the bed. "In my world, there are gods and goddesses who do not always do what is right for their people. They can be cruel and when they are bored, they will use their people as pawns in a game to amuse themselves."

"Okay, wait." Anna scooted back on the bed so she could see his face. "Let me get this straight. First, you appear in my bedroom out of nowhere. We have incredible sex. I get pregnant and you leave because you're searching for your new Atlantis. All this happened supposedly because of the fates, a tale I'm supposed to believe. But now, you're telling me that this might be the acts of some vengeful god or goddess who just wants to have a little fun on a rainy day." She got to her feet and began walking toward the door.

"Anna, where are you going?"

"Home. I'm going home because none of this is making sense, Onyx. You don't exist. This place doesn't exist. All of this—" her free hand swept out to encompass Onyx's quarters, "—is in my imagination and I'm going to wake up tomorrow and hopefully, none of this will exist."

"That would mean that Alex will not exist," Onyx's quiet voice stopped her progress toward the door.

Anna turned slowly, holding Alex a little too tightly. "What are you saying?"

Onyx walked toward her, one hand held out to reach for hers. "If this is your imagination, then our son is a figment of that same imagination."

Anna dropped her cheek to Alex's downy soft head. Onyx watched her inhale the fragrant baby scent of his shampoo. "He exists, Onyx."

"Then so does this. This is not a dream."

Anna closed her eyes but a tear leaked out to scramble down her cheek before she could prevent its escape. "I don't know what to do."

"I do." Onyx carefully removed Alex from her arms and carried him across the floor to a long, sturdy rope with a sash. With one sharp tug, he rang the bell, calling Ezrel back to his king's chambers. "I will have Sarah put Alex down. He is tired and needs his sleep. He will be safe." His voice reassured Anna in ways the stout man who appeared at the door moments later could not. "Take my son. Make sure he is safely down for the night."

Ezrel accepted the baby in his arms and bowed low. "As you wish."

Onyx could feel Anna's eyes on his back before he turned around. "What do you desire to say, Anna? I can see something in your eyes and I must admit that I am not aware of your thoughts at present."

Anna pulled her lower lip in with her teeth and observed him quietly for a moment longer before she responded. "I have never met a true king before. Oh, I've met plenty of men who thought they were king, but never one that really deserved the title. Do people really bow like that all the time?"

Onyx smiled a little. "Yes and I have to admit that it does grow a little tiresome, but enough talk about my title. Come, we will go to bed and let the night take away our worries. Perhaps in the morning, things will be different."

Anna backed away a little from his approach. "Do you know something that you aren't telling me?"

Onyx lifted an eyebrow. "And what would that be?"

"Obviously I don't know or I wouldn't be asking you."

He only smiled and took her hand to lead her to the bed. "I only know that I want to make love to you again, to feel your body give beneath mine." He stopped beside the bed and turned her in his arms. "You have only to tell me if you do not want the same thing tonight."

Anna shifted slightly against him and tipped her head back, surrendering with a slow, welcoming smile.

Desire slammed through his body, rocking him back on his heels and later, when he had only his memories to keep him company, Onyx knew he would remember everything about this night. Anna's eyes when she pushed against his chest, asking silently for space, the way she stood in the center of the room, undressing so methodically he thought he would explode.

At night, when he was alone once again, he would recall the way her fingers trailed over her thighs before they crept up to the waistband of her panties. She pulled them down with such care that Onyx's mouth watered. And once she'd removed her boots and socks, he saw pink toenails curling against the bearskin rug. Yeah, he'd remember that, too. He would hear the sounds of her breath, in and out, her chest expanding with every inhalation, each one deeper than the last.

He heard his own heartbeat, his own footsteps as he approached Anna once more, slowly, his eyes meeting hers. Less than an inch away, the solid wall of his chest brushing her sensitized skin, he tipped her face back with a finger under her chin and he kissed her, gently. His lips against hers were reassuring, comforting, but Anna didn't want comfort, she wanted the passion she knew would explode between them at any moment.

Drawing away from him, she stood on tiptoe and grazed her teeth along his jawline, his breath shot from his lungs in a loud burst of air. Nimble fingers slid against his chest, caressing the taut flesh that fell prey to her lips and teeth. Hard, male nipples were caught inside the dampness of her mouth and Onyx's hands framed her face, fingers tangling in the silky length of her auburn tresses.

Anna pressed her body against his, enjoying the feel of textured hair against her breasts, the masculine bulge against her thigh. Her hands on a journey propelled by her imagination, they traveled down the broad expanse of his chest, across his lean hips, forward to cup him through the material of his pants.

In an instant, Onyx's control snapped and desire clouded his vision. Instincts took over, guiding his hands over her bare skin as he fell to his knees in front of her. His fingers bit into her hips as he remained bowed before her, almost worshiping.

Anna rested her hands on his head, tilting her face back, waiting for his touch. It came . . . lightly at first, over her toes, her foot, before ghosting up her leg. He still knelt before her, one hand holding the back of her thigh as if to keep himself steady. She thought she was prepared for him to touch her more, ready for his hand against the silk and lace covering her pussy. She was wrong. His fingers streaked across the sensitive flesh and she gasped, biting back a louder cry.

Onyx hooked his fingers in the elastic and rocked back on his heels to drink in the full sight of supple body. Golden skin, perfect curves melded into a woman he knew he would love forever even if she was not with him for that long. The gauzy panties came off easily and Onyx lifted her feet one by one to rid her of the material. Then, tossing them to one side, Onyx leaned forward, inhaling the scent of her. His breath brushed her, teasing her. Anna heard her own voice. She whispered his name and maybe a plea, she wasn't sure. The muscles in the backs of her thighs quivered and her knees weakened, but still Onyx waited, dragging out the moment until Anna was sure she would collapse with wanting him.

And then he tipped forward, drawing even closer to the compelling warmth at the apex of her thighs. Drawing a damp path along her bikini line with his tongue, he murmured his approval while her hands flexed on his shoulders. Then he kissed her, his lips against her most intimate place and this time, Anna was sure the cry on her lips was a plea. He parted the soft petals of her pussy and her breath exhaled on a sob. His tongue caressed her and she bit down on her lower lip.

Soft, suckling sounds echoed in the silence of the king's chambers. His teeth caught the small bud hidden between the folds of her body and he grazed her. Sharp pinpoints of pleasure shot through her, electrifying her spine and Anna dug her nails into his skin, more to hold on than anything else. Stroke after stroke, he brought her to the edge of reality, coaxing her to let go, to fall over the edge. Convinced he would catch her, she fell, his name on her lips, a damp sheen spreading across her body. Before her muscles could betray her, Onyx caught her against him.

His steps guided them toward the bed and Anna felt the mattress against the backs of her knees. She opened her eyes and saw his face, inches away from hers. She couldn't speak, she didn't know what to say, but he smiled at her and it was enough. Without a sound, she sat down on the edge of the bed, her hands going to the waistband of his pants. He stood in front of her, his hands at his sides, allowing her free rein.

The buttons opened with simple flicks of her fingers and Anna pushed the fabric aside, over taut hips, her knuckles brushing against his abdomen, just grazing the sides of his cock. She felt him tighten, read the strain in his posture and leaning forward, she pressed her lips against the cotton material covering his erection. An expletive exploded out of his throat and he tried to pull her to her feet or push her away, but Anna hooked her fingers in the waistband of his pants and shoved them down his legs.

Onyx managed to catch her hands this time. "You'd better let me do the rest."

Anna leaned back on her elbows and smiled.

He quickly divested himself of the remainder of his clothing, his boots hitting the wall with a thump. His eyes swept
over her prone body, his breath clogging in his throat. One
knee depressed the mattress as he joined her on the bed.
He wanted to tell her how beautiful she was, but the words
wouldn't come. Hoping his hands told her what he couldn't
say, he touched her, caressed her, traveling across the warm skin
with gentle strokes. Her eyelids concealed green eyes frosted
with desire and he had his answer. He shifted on the bed, taking her with him. Lying side-to-side, he slid one hand over
her face, her breasts, before allowing it to stop against her hip.
Then, he kissed her again, deeper, more possessively than the
last time. There was no comfort, only passion and an intensity
that startled them both. Rolling, he tucked her beneath him.

Anna moved against the coverlet, adjusting her body to
welcome the weight of his. His skin warmed to her touch.
Perspiration coated his body and her palms grew damp with
each caress. Her hands drifted down his spine, massaging every
ridge before gripping the firm skin of his buttocks. Her fingers
contracted against the muscles and Onyx's breath hissed out
against her ear.

His lips found the hollow of her neck, leaving wet kisses
that cooled her skin. One hand pushed against a breast, drawing the nipple into his line of vision. His head dipped and he
tasted her. She wiggled beneath him, her nails digging into
his sensitive flesh. Then, turning the tables, she slid one hand
between their bodies, her fingers curling around his cock.

Onyx groaned low in his throat and shifted, loving and hat-
ing the play of her fingers around him. Her hand moved faster,
harder, sliding up and down his shaft. His breath hitched in
his throat and he caught her wrist, wanting to stop her, but

needing her to continue. He closed his eyes, nearing the end, but wanting more.

Still holding him, Anna slid down the bed, her lips warm against his abdomen, the muscles knotted. Framing her hands at the base of his shaft, she propped herself up on her elbows and ran her wet, hot tongue down the length. A small gurgle of sound caught in his throat as she took him in her mouth.

Her tongue laved circles around the tip of his cock as her teeth grazed the taut skin. Her mind registered the harsh sounds of his breath, the way his hands tightened on her shoulders and she increased the pace, pulling back until just her lips touched him. His stomach quivered beneath the light graze of her fingertips. Then, she took him in again, her fingers rolling forward to cup his balls. Massaging him, she took him deeper into her mouth, leaning forward on her elbows. With teeth, lips and tongue, she teased him, coaxed him until with a harsh, guttural groan, he came, his muscles jerking with the release. Only then did Anna relinquish her hold on him.

Hands framing her face, Onyx looked down into her eyes, saw her womanly smile, the way her lips glistened and his breath shuddered out of his lungs. He was lost. Her hands glided over his sweat-slicked body and he found his way again.

With a sudden movement, he rolled her flat against the mattress, hitched his body up on his elbows and pressed his manhood against the entrance to her body. He became hard again, desire curling hot and fiery in his stomach. Blood raced downward, filling his erection, making him ache with wanting her. Her legs parted in open invitation and he guided himself home. Silken velvet closed around steely muscle and breaths clashed in the air.

His hands found hers, fingers entwining, drawing her arms above her head. His lips fused to hers and the rhythm of his body lifted hers, arching her back. Thrusting deep within her warmth, Onyx deepened the kiss, his tongue dueling with hers. The mattress gave with each pump of his hips, the headboard bumping the wall. He felt the muscles of her sheath contract around him, heard her soft whimper of release and he let go, driving himself into her one last time before following her.

Heartbeat to heartbeat, they rested against one another. His kisses were gentle against her temple, her hands soft against his chest. And Onyx knew as he lay there that he would never forget this woman, never forget the feel of her in his arms or the sound of his name on her lips. He would love her but he would not be able to keep her.

"I don't want to leave you," Anna whispered in the darkness.

"Shhh." Onyx brushed a kiss against her brow, knowing she would have no choice in the matter. "We have tonight."

Anna turned in his arms, pressing her body against his. "And will tonight be enough? Because I know that it won't be for me. My life has changed because of you, Onyx." Her hands framed his face, sifted through his long, beautiful hair. "I love you. I will always love you."

Onyx didn't doubt that. He felt the same. His love for her burned within him, but he knew that it was a hopeless cause. The fates would not change history to allow them to be together, at least, he didn't think so. But perhaps he was wrong. It didn't matter, though. Whoever had allowed Anna to be with him tonight had given them a gift and they would take this night that wasn't meant to be and make it last for eternity as would their love. He pressed a hard kiss against her lips. "And I love you, my beautiful, sweet Anna." He rested his forehead against hers. "Promise me that you will take care of our son and that you will make sure that he knows that I love him, will always love him. As I will you."

Anna's breath hitched in her throat and she could feel the tears burning the back of her throat. "This sounds like goodbye."

"Not yet. Not now. For now, we still have tonight." Onyx slipped a hand down between their bodies and found her warm, wet center. "And for tonight, I am going to love you until I am branded on your soul, Anna. You will never forget me."

Anna's back arched as thick fingers slipped inside her pussy. "I could never forget you."

Onyx's thumb caressed that sensitive spot between her thighs. "I like the way you whimper when I am touching you like this and the way your eyes change colors when you give yourself to me. Your wetness flows over my hand and yet, there is always more. You always have more to give, Anna." He increased the tempo and Anna gave a little cry as her vision clouded with the release. "Promise me you will never forget me."

"I promise." Anna sobbed against his shoulder. "But I'm not leaving you. I don't care who brought me here. I am not leaving you. They can't make me leave."

Onyx soothed her with gentle kisses and soft touches, but deep down in his heart he knew that she would leave. Because they could make her.

Anna opened her eyes and lay there in the early morning light, moving only slightly against the mattress as she tried to acclimate herself to her surroundings. Where was she? But more importantly, where was Onyx? By the light of dawn she could make out the room where she lay and her heart sank as she recognized her mother's old armoire, the wicker rocking chair she'd owned since college. Tears scalded her cheeks as she closed her eyes once more. She was home. And she was alone.

Then, her eyes popping open, she scrambled out of the bed, fear licking at her insides as she tore down the hallway. She skidded to a stop in front of the only other bedroom in her house and with a shaking hand, she turned the doorknob. Relief poured through her as the crib came into her line of vision. The crib with Alex nestled safely inside, breathing evenly and deeply, and having no memory of the night's happenings. Or of his father.

Okay, so, she'd been returned to her home. No worse off than when she'd been determined to find Onyx. And she had found him. And he'd told her that he loved her. It had to be enough to carry her through, to help her raise their son.

She walked back down the hallway on wobbly legs and sank down on the edge of her bed.

"Sweetheart, are you all right?" A deep, masculine voice queried over her shoulder.

Anna jumped, shrieked and spun around, one hand clutching her heart. Her eyes squinted in the dim lighting. "Wh-what? Onyx?" She blinked rapidly. He looked like Onyx, only his hair was shorter and he was wearing boxer shorts. She'd never seen Onyx in a pair of boxer shorts.

The double image of Onyx frowned. "Who or what in the hell is Onyx?"

Anna didn't know how she'd managed to extricate herself from the potential confrontation with the man in her bedroom who looked like Onyx, sounded like Onyx, but clearly wasn't Onyx. As she stood beneath the spray of the shower, she now wondered who exactly he was supposed to be.

A tapping on the bathroom door had her drawing the shower curtain close around her soapy body. "Yes?"

The man stuck his head inside the steam. "Are you okay?"

"I'm fine. Perfectly fine." She beamed, trying to throw him off-guard. What in the hell was she supposed to call him?

"Well, you were acting a bit strange out there." He advanced into the bathroom and as he hooked his fingers into the waistband of his boxer shorts, Anna's eyes widened.

"What are you doing?" she squeaked.

He gave her a wary look. "Joining you."

Her hands fisted in the shower curtain. "I don't think that's a good idea. I don't feel well."

He stepped into the shower from the other end. "What's wrong?" He walked up close behind her and Anna couldn't think of one symptom to create. Well, she could possibly tell him her blood pressure rose several notches and her heart now beat erratically.

"Nothing. Nothing," she finally managed to say. "I'm just a bit, well, I'm just not feeling well, that's all."

He chuckled and pressed his lips to the side of her neck. Instant heat stabbed her midsection. He certainly felt like Onyx. "You never have gotten used to the idea that I'm a doctor, have you?"

Her head tilted back. "A doctor? You?"

His hands dropped to his sides. "Okay. Now, I know there's something wrong."

Her eyes dropped to the impressive erection. "No, nothing's wrong. I guess I'm just thinking about Alex."

The man continued to watch her quizzically. "Are you sure that's all it is?"

She pasted a bright smile on her face. "Of course. Now, stop worrying."

He rocked forward on his heels, his eyes narrowed. "Well, okay. If you're sure."

Her smile faded and her eyes dropped. She really wished she could finagle his name out of him considering she could only call him honey for so long. He reached out for her and she went willingly into his arms. Somewhere, somehow, Onyx existed inside this body. Standing on tiptoe, Anna kissed his neck.

"Now that's more like it," he growled. When his hand slid down to her side, Anna inspected it quickly. The gold wedding band gave her all the information she needed to begin the inquisition.

"Honey, how long have we been married?"

He lifted his head. "You're testing me now?"

She affected a pout. "I'm just curious if you . . ."

He pressed one finger against her lips. "I know, I know. We got married a little after Alex was born. Did you really think I could forget?"

She turned in his arms. Had it been her imagination or had an accent coated his voice? "I'm sorry. I just get a little insecure sometimes."

He cupped her bottom and brought her hard against his cock. "My Anna, you have no reason to feel insecure about my love for you. We are two halves of the same whole. Our souls are connected."

At his words, her face lifted and she met his gaze, searching for some sign of recognition, but all she saw was love, pure, unfiltered love. Perhaps this would be enough. Those meddling gods had taken away her Onyx, but given him a replacement. Even as the thought reached her, she knew it wouldn't be enough. She didn't want a carbon copy. She wanted Onyx.

"Anna?" His voice broke into her reverie, calling her back to the present.

She managed to give him a wan smile. "I just need a few minutes by myself."

He watched her for a moment longer before stepping back out of the shower. "If that's what you want. I'll be out here when you decide you want to talk."

The second the bathroom door closed, Anna tipped her face to the tiled ceiling above her. "Okay, whoever you are, whatever you are. This isn't funny. I don't want a clone. I want Onyx. It's not the same." Her tears mixed with the spray of the shower. "It will never be the same." She bumped her head against the wall. "I would give up everything in this life to be with him. Can't you understand that or are all of you so cynical?"

Switching off the faucets, she straightened and yanked back the curtain. "You might control Onyx's life, but I won't allow you to control mine. Take this man out there away. If I can't have Onyx, I don't want him. I will never settle." As she said the words, the truth broke her heart. She couldn't settle for anyone. Only Onyx would fill the void in her soul.

Stepping out of the shower, she snagged the towel off the rack and wrapped it around her body. "Please, if you have any decency within you, take away the imitation." After the final prayer, she yanked open the door.

The bedroom was empty and save for the ticking of the bedside clock, silence settled over the house.

She tiptoed to the nursery to check on Alex, relieved to see he slept soundly in his crib. Patting his back, she watched him sleep, his tiny fist curled next to his face. "I'm sorry, Alex, but I will never let any man take the place of your Daddy."

∽

A long silence ensconced the temple as the three sisters exchanged glances. One by one, they shifted in their seats, turning toward the time window which enabled them to see Anna and hear her pain.

"I believe we're all thinking the same thing," Atropos said with a sigh. "Shall I rework a few threads?"

Both sisters nodded and Atropos got to her feet. "So be it."

"Hello, Anna."

The deep voice brought her whirling around. Her mouth open, hands shaking, she stared up into Onyx's face. "Onyx?"

He nodded slowly and her heart began to beat faster. "The fates sent me back. I think it might have had something to do with those fervent prayers of yours."

Her lips wobbled. "And to think I've never really believed in prayer."

His eyes feasted on her and warmed her. She held herself back a second longer before running toward him. He caught her in his arms and swung her around, laughing with joy.

Her hands framed his face. "I can't believe you're here. Do you remember leaving Atlantis? What happened? Were you asleep when the fates sent you?"

He bumped his forehead against hers and settled his hands on her hips. "I remember everything, Anna. The last night I spent with you in Atlantis, the feel of the sheets against my skin and the taste of your woman spot."

Anna gave him a mock-glare. "That's not what I'm talking about. I believe I specifically asked if you remembered leaving Atlantis?"

His eyes clouded. "No, I do not." A pained expression on his face, he took hold of her hands and backed toward the bed.

"I have to contact Ezrel. He will know what's going on."

Anna felt his uncertainty, his fear even. This was a different world for him, a new one, and here he was no longer in control. "Onyx, why are you here, though? If the fates sent you here, they must have a reason. Did they tell you how long you're here?" She stopped, her breath catching in her throat. "Can you stay?"

He stopped by the bed and dipped down to rest his hands on the mattress. "I don't know, but I would imagine I'm here for you."

The pain in his voice tore at her heart. She rubbed one hand up and down his spine. "I'm sorry. You probably didn't want to come back. I didn't know they would do this to you. I'm so sorry." She leaned her head against his shoulder. "I never wanted them to hurt you. We'll ask them to send you back. Atlantis needs you. Or they can send all of us back." She managed to turn him around. "Alex and I will go with you."

Onyx cupped her face. "Anna, do you think I hurt because I am here with you?"

She nodded slowly.

He kissed her briefly. "That is not so. I do not hurt." He took her hand and placed it over his heart. "I am alive in here." He curled her fingers between his. "The gods have given me a chance at another life, a life to spend with you. Where once I thought them cruel, they have now proven they believe in love." He kissed her again and Anna stood on tiptoe to meet him halfway.

"But why the sadness I saw in your eyes, then?"

"I will miss my people. That is true, but they have a new king now."

She leaned back to blink up at him. "They do? And you know so soon?"

He ran a finger down the tip of her nose. "They do and I

do." He held up his left hand to survey the gold band on his third finger. "What is this circle of gold here?"

She laughingly took hold of his hand. "It's called a wedding band. It means the gods have sent you back as my husband."

"And men willingly wear this type of jewelry on their fingers?"

She held up her own hand. "Just as I wear it on mine."

"I can see I have a lot to learn in this century."

She cupped his face. "I will help you. I will teach you everything you need to know, Onyx. And I promise you'll be happy here."

He pressed a finger against her lips. "Anna, that was not a complaint. I will never complain about this opportunity." His arms closed around her waist. "You are my love, my life and I will always . . ."

A loud, shrill wail interrupted the speech and Anna instantly pulled out of his embrace. She backed toward the door, one finger held aloft. "Hold that thought. Your son is hungry."

Onyx's face took on a wondrous expression. "My son." He took two steps toward her. "I will watch you feed him just as I did last night . . . in Atlantis."

She held out one hand. "It will be my pleasure, Your Majesty."

He shook his head. "I am not a king any more, Anna."

She hooked onto his wrist. "That's where you're wrong. You'll always be my king."

Lady of the Seals

ELIZABETH JEWELL

1

SEVEN DAYS. SEVEN days alone at sea in a lifeboat and still no sign of land.

He was nearly out of water. The food had been gone for two days. He had been hungry so long he couldn't feel it anymore. Only the tarp from the bottom of the boat had kept him sheltered from the relentless sun. Still, his back was tight and painful from sunburn, his lips cracked and dry.

He hunched in the bottom of the boat, aching with hunger, with thirst, with the sun. The drinking water was almost gone.

He had a knife. He could slit his throat, bleed himself out into the water. It would be better than this. Or he could cut himself and go overboard. The sharks would come. Painful, perhaps, but it would be quick.

Picking up the knife, he turned it in his hand, watching the glint of the sun off the blade. Then he looked up, into the sky, the sea.

A dark streak on the horizon.

Land. Finally, land.

He picked up an oar and began to paddle.

Just past noon, the clouds came. The dark hump of land was no closer.

As the clouds lowered, panic set in. This was no light rain shower coming in. He could tell by the smell and the way the wind felt on his face. And the dark ridge of land was still far away. Too far away. The hope it had brought him faded.

Rage flared hot in his chest, and he flung the oar, watching it sail through the air, into the rising waves. He flung himself to the bottom of the boat and wept.

The rain came. The wind came. The waves lifted the tiny boat, flung it with a sickening crack down against the ocean's surface. His mouth filled with water. He was too tired now even to weep.

Another wave took the boat, higher this time, and there was nothing he could do as it cracked open under him and delivered him to the ocean. Nothing he could do as the waves broke over his wearied body.

And as the ocean took him, he could think only, *Thank God there is no pain.*

She loved storms. The smell, the wind, the movement of the ocean. She had watched this one as it came, and had slipped off into the water to ride the glorious tumult.

She didn't dare go too far from the shore. In calm water, she could swim for hours, but in the storm she had to stay within sight of land or risk drowning. But the sheer beauty of the gale lured her. A little farther. A little more . . .

Something brushed against her lower body. Startled, she dove under, fast. Surely not a shark. It was dark under the surface, but she could see enough to tell it wasn't a shark. It was a man.

She slid up under him, catching his weight on her shoulders. He was not a small man, and his weight unbalanced her for a moment. But the buoyancy of the water helped, and soon she was making headway, swimming him out of the storm. But he was so still she feared it might be too late.

The waves took them the last few yards. Landing on the beach, she took a moment to catch her breath. Then she rolled toward the man's still, silent form.

He wasn't breathing. His lips were gray. If he were to live, she would have to save him.

She changed quickly; she couldn't help him at all if she wasn't in human form. She laid her head against his chest. His heartbeat made little more than a murmur. Putting her mouth to his, she breathed for him until he suddenly convulsed, spewing water. She rolled him to his side as he vomited up the ocean.

Still, he was cold and seemed not to have the strength even to move. He just lay there on the sand, breathing, eyes closed.

"Shh," she whispered. "'Tis all right. You're well now, lad, you're all well."

His lips moved but no sound came from them. She bent close, until his breath touched her ear, but still could not make out the words.

"I'll be back," she whispered into his ear. "You'll no' last the night like this. I have to be keeping you warm."

It was a dream, he thought. It had to be a dream. Or maybe it was heaven, because how else could this have come to pass? He had been halfway to death—more than halfway—and now he lay on the beach in the arms of a beautiful woman with large, brown eyes.

Barely conscious, he registered her presence as if she were a dream. But her skin against him warmed him, gave back some of the life the cold ocean had tried to take.

She was naked, he realized slowly, and so was he. They were rolled up together in a mass of heavy wool blankets, skin to skin, her breasts against his chest, her long legs scissored between his. He remembered, vaguely, the touch of her mouth on his as she put her own life's breath into him. Now she shared her heat.

He looked at her in the darkness as she lay there against him. Her eyes were closed, and he was almost certain she slept. Gently, he drew his hands down her back and set his lips against hers. She tasted of life, and the salty ocean. He opened her mouth with his, tasting more deeply, and she stirred against him and opened her eyes with a smile.

His hands slid down her body, cupping the soft, warm roundness of her buttocks. Her thighs pressed against his and then opened loosely, inviting him in. Wrapped as they were in the blankets, it was difficult for him to align his body the right way, but he eased his thigh between hers as he kissed her. The wetness of her sex made hot dew on the skin of his leg.

She moved closer to him, all of her body a warm welcome to his. He hefted her breasts, bent to take one, then the other, into his mouth. Warmth and more warmth, silky and soft and beautiful.

"I'll no' hurt you," he whispered, though she seemed to have no fear of him. Her hand slid between his thighs, pressing his scrotum against his body. The heat flashed through him, bringing him to life where the ocean had tried so hard to send him to death. She shifted her legs against his and the blankets eased around them. Her fingers, rising up the heavy length of his erection, eased him inside her.

He stilled there, enraptured by her heat. Everything the

sea had taken from him—his breath, his warmth, his very life—she had given back. The heat radiated from his sex up through the core of his body, through his limbs, to his skin. Through his heart.

Her legs went around his waist, her calves pressing his buttocks, driving him a little deeper as she clenched the channel of her sex hard down on the full length of his. He moaned at the sweet, hot tightness, then she shifted her hips, drawing away from him. He moved with her, the tight sheath of her vagina sliding back down the length of his cock then pressing him back in. The movement was like the movement of the ocean, a steady, consuming rhythm. Soon he was lost in it, lost in her heat, the rapid sound of her breathing as her desire rose.

Then she arched under him as she cried out her release and her body pulsed around his. He pressed harder into her as she came, impossibly far, feeling the hot pounding of her climax, letting it carry him into his own, until the heat flooded his body and poured out of him, thick and hot, into her.

And suddenly he was so consumingly tired. He pulled her closer, cradling her against him, and let the dragging tide of weariness pull him down.

2

SHE WOKE AT the touch of the sun on her face. He still slept, his arms around her, his head cradled against her breasts. He had slept soundly through the night. He must have dreamed, though, for she had awakened once to hear him moaning, his hands clutching at her back.

Gently, she slid out of the clasp of the woolen blankets. He seemed warm enough now for her to safely leave him. She crept across the beach to where she'd left her clothes and his. She'd stripped him before crawling into the blankets naked herself, knowing this to be the best way to restore his warmth. At first, pressed into his cold chest, she'd thought it might prove the best way to freeze them both to death, but gradually his body had returned to a normal temperature, and the heat had suffused them both, filling the cocoon of the woolen blankets.

She dressed quickly then came back to him, carrying his clothes. He still slept. She laid his torn, still-wet clothing down next to him, spreading them out so the early heat of the morning might dry them, if only a little.

He made a small noise behind her and she turned to look at him. Dreams again, she thought, for he hadn't opened his eyes.

She hadn't been able to see much of him last night, either

in the ocean or in the darkness. Now, with the pale morning touching his face, she could. The light was still dim—dawn had not quite passed—but she could see more than she had before.

His face and wide shoulders were reddened with sunburn. He must have floated for a time before the storm had dragged him into the sea. His dark hair fell a bit past his shoulders and hung lankly now, still wet. He had a square face, rough now with stubble, a high forehead, dark, straight, low-slung brows. His eyes would be dark, she was certain. His straight mouth tipped up slightly at the corners, but even now, in repose, it had a harshness to it. She couldn't judge him by that, though, by the dark, straight, severe slashes of his brows and his mouth. Not until he woke, and she could see how they moved.

Gently, unable to help herself, she reached out and touched his lips. They were hot and dry, damaged by the sun. He needed tending to. He would need food, water, medicine for his skin. Leaving him to sleep, she went to prepare for his waking.

◌⃝◌

He had fallen into icy cold—now he woke to the warmth of sun and heavy woolen blankets. He opened his eyes, squinting against the light. There had been a woman. Hadn't there? Or was he delusional from journeying too close to death?

Slowly, he sat up. He was naked under the blankets. Looking around, he found his clothes lying next to him. He picked up the trousers, stood and put them on. They were still damp and clung to him uncomfortably. He left his shirt and his shoes where he'd found them.

He appeared to be alone. If so, where had the blankets come from? And who had stripped him and wrapped him up? Someone had saved his life, that much was certain. He suspected whoever that had been was still here.

The woman. She hadn't been a dream. He was certain of that. Feeling the dead weariness in his body, he rather doubted the sex had been real, but he was certain the girl had been. He trudged up the hill, away from the shore. He was hungry. And thirsty. So thirsty, his mouth so dry it was hard to swallow. Surely there was fresh water here somewhere.

A rustling sound caught his ear and he glanced toward it. She was there, coming toward him, carrying a bucket. A heavy bucket, by the look of it. She stopped when she saw him.

This, then, was the girl he remembered. The one who had saved him with the warmth of her body. She was tall, with a strength about her that reminded him of the girls in his village back home, who spent their days hauling water, spinning, digging peat. Long black hair tumbled down around her shoulders, and she regarded him through big, round, dark eyes. She wasn't so much beautiful as arresting. Intriguing.

"I've water for ye, lad," she said gently, her voice carrying easily even over the sound of the surf.

He closed the distance between them and knelt next to the bucket, drinking greedily from it with his hands. She dropped quickly to her knees next to him, her long-fingered hand clasping his bare shoulder.

"Easy. Slower. Too fast and you'll be bringing it back up."

She was right. He forced himself to slow down. What he'd drunk had already balled into a knot in his stomach. But he was so thirsty, his lips and tongue so parched and dry. He filled his mouth again and just held the water there, letting the cold moisture bathe the starved tissues. After a few seconds, he swallowed.

"I'm beholden to ye," he said. His lips were still dry enough to make it hard to speak.

"Aye," she answered. "You were dead when I brought you up on the beach." She smiled a little. "And now you're not."

He smiled back. "Then I'm more beholden than I realized. Are you having a name?"

"Aye. Gilly, they call me. And yourself?"

"David. David Fraser."

She nodded. "Drink again. Slowly."

He drank. After a time, she touched him again, on the back of his head this time, her fingers light on his still-wet hair. "Come with me. I've a house nearby, and it's there I can get you something for the sunburn. And food."

"Food." He straightened. Thirst still nagged, but he would be a long time ending that. "Food would be a good thing, I'm thinking."

She lifted the half-empty bucket. "Then come."

He had expected to hear voices as she led him to a village or town somewhere nearby, but her small house sat alone, just where the scattered trees along the shoreline began to cluster into the edge of a forest. It was a cottage, old but carefully kept. Flowers grew in neat rows in front of it.

"Where's your family?" he asked her.

"I've no family," she answered, a misty sadness in her voice. "Not for a long time."

"'Tis sad," he said. "You're living all alone here, then?"

"Nay." She smiled. "There are the seals."

He nodded, intrigued. His dream shimmered through his mind and he wondered if it had been more than a dream. A portent, perhaps. What would she do if he were to kiss her?

She led the way into the small house. "I've bread and cheese and little else right now," she said. "There'll be fish later, when I've caught it. And milk when I've seen to the rest of my morning chores."

He sat on a wooden rocking chair next to the fire, which burned low and filled the small room with the rich odor of peat smoke.

"Anything you have," he said, "and with thanks."

She brought him a plate with bread and cheese, an apple and a tankard filled with a weak but somehow satisfying beer. He ate a bit, remembering this time to be careful, and sipped from the tankard. She sat next to him on the floor, her legs curled under her.

"So, David Fraser," she said after a time, "I'm given to think you're a sailor?"

"Aye. I was first mate on the *Silver Swan*. We were on our way back from France when she went down in a gale."

"But you survived."

"Only to find death in another gale." He took another bite, chewed fastidiously. "But I also found you, and glad I am for it."

Her smile came warm and bright, and he was glad he'd lived to see it. She was a strong girl and somewhat plain, but when she smiled it was like the sun coming up in mid-winter when the nights in northern Scotland lasted forever.

He found himself smiling back, though it hurt his still-dry lips. "Where are we?"

"'Tis an island."

"Is there anyone else living here?"

She nodded. Strangely, her eyes had widened. She seemed to be afraid. "Aye. A village on the east side, closest to the mainland."

Why was she afraid? Her dark eyes held his, pleading. She

didn't want him to ask any more questions. He wasn't sure why, nor was he sure how he knew that.

"You stay here by yourself, then?"

"Aye." Her wide eyes blinked, the fear still there.

He nodded. He would find the village later. He knew something about the small islands on the west coast of Scotland, and he was certain this was one of the smaller ones. It would be a simple matter to slip off and find the island's other inhabitants. For now, though, he would honor the wishes of the woman who had saved his life.

"'Tis a nice place you've made for yourself here," he said.

She nodded, the panic fading from her face. "You'll be staying?"

"If you'll have me."

"Stay as long as you like. I'll make certain you've food and water."

"'Tis greatly appreciated." He took another bite of cheese and felt his lower lip split. Wincing, he touched the wound, came back with blood on his finger.

"Let me get something for that." She stood quickly, going to the back part of the cottage where he could see her small bed, little more than a mat and blankets on the floor. From a low table by the bed she took a seashell and brought it back to him. Salve of some kind glistened within the curve of the gray shell.

Kneeling next to his chair, she daubed a bit of the salve onto her finger then reached to his face. Gently, she applied the soft, oily stuff to his lips. The pressure of her finger against his mouth aroused him more than it should have, especially since it was a healer's touch, not a lover's. He'd been too long without a woman, that was certain, but even long abstinence didn't explain the way his body responded to her. He held very still, letting her minister to him, trying to rein in the heat that had so thoroughly and unexpectedly filled him.

She felt it too and was equally startled. This wasn't right—she was tending to his wounds, not trying to seduce or arouse him. But she could tell by the way he had stilled under her touch that he had been affected by it. And her own heart had begun a rapid pattering she could feel in her chest and her throat.

His lip still bled where the skin had broken. She scooped out a little more salve and touched it to the wound, gently rubbing it in.

The shape of his mouth fascinated her. It was so blatantly a man's mouth, straight and wide, with a wide dip in the center of the upper lip. She thought about the shape of her own, fuller lips, then found herself wondering exactly how his mouth might fit against hers. Finished with the salve, she brushed her thumb over his lips then experimentally tipped her head toward him.

He seemed to know what she was doing, what she wanted. The line of his mouth softened a little as she cautiously moved toward him and finally, gently, touched her lips to his.

He made a soft sound, and for a moment she thought she might have hurt him, pressed too hard on his broken lip, but he cupped her cheek in his hand and held her there, gently.

She had never desired a man before. Had never wanted anything but the surf or the sun or the deep, dark rhythms of the ocean. But something as primal as the tide woke in her at this man's touch, gentle as it was. The sensation thrilled and frightened her. She wasn't sure what to do with it.

His mouth shifted on hers as he kissed her top lip, then her bottom lip, with careful attention. His hand on her face held her still against him; his other hand slid up her back, clasping her closer against his still-bare chest. Reflexively, she reached out to him, clasped his shoulders. He flinched.

She pulled back, the moment broken, or at least strained. The skin of his shoulders was dry and hot under her hands, and she remembered the red rage of sunburn she'd seen there.

"Your back," she whispered. "Let me see to it too."

He looked down into her face, his dark eyes even darker with arousal, the low brows drawn together. Finally he traced his fingers along the line of her cheekbone and drew his hand away.

She rose from her stool and stood behind him, gathering more of the salve onto her fingers. It was a special concoction she made of herbs and carefully strained fats, effective for sunburn and chapping and any number of ailments.

His shoulders were red and peeling, but the sunburn wasn't as bad as it could have been. He closed his eyes and took a long breath as she kneaded the oil into his skin.

She rubbed gently, feeling the thick cords of muscle beneath, the solid structure of bone. He had good, strong shoulders. There was a stretch of pitted scarring there, she noticed, and also along his jawline. She had seen this on men before but didn't know enough of the human world to know what caused it. It intrigued her—everything about him did.

He touched her hand suddenly, stopping the movement of her fingers over the top of his shoulder. The herbal smell of the salve filled her nostrils—wild mint and lavender.

"It's hurting me," he said softly.

"I'm sorry." She had felt the knots in his shoulders and hadn't given enough consideration to his sunburn, trying to knead them away.

"Nay. 'Tis all right. You've a healer's hands. I'm just no' quite ready yet to be healed, I suppose."

She smiled as he turned back toward her. "You'll be well soon. Eat. You're needing your strength."

"Aye. And when I'm done, is there a place to rinse off the salt?"

"Aye. I'll take you there."

3

WHEN HE WAS finished eating, she led him up the hill,
to the lake where she gathered her water. A stream tumbled
down a craggy cliff into a waterfall to feed the lake with
cold, fresh water. She bathed here herself from time to time,
though she didn't mind the salt from the ocean. Sometimes
her human skin protested it. But when it did, she preferred
to transform rather than wash. Her other skin loved the ocean
water.

"'Tis a beautiful place," he said, smiling at her.

"The water's cold," she warned.

"Come with me. Keep me warm."

Startled, she took a step back. His grin was bright and welcoming but offered something she wasn't sure she wanted.

The grin faded as she stood there, speechless.

"I'm sorry," he finally said. "I just thought . . . well, there's
nothing here ye havenae seen, aye?"

She couldn't help it; her gaze fell to his trousers. "I saw . . .
nothing. It was dark. I was careful not to be looking or . . .
touching . . . where I shouldnae." She had felt him, though,
his solid body against hers, his arms around her. She hadn't
tried to feel him, had kept her hands folded against his chest,
but his legs had wound between hers and though she hadn't
looked she had felt the hardness and the softness and the heat

of his sex rising and falling against her thighs. "I didnae . . . I didnae want to take advantage."

He laughed. "Well, I thank you for it, then. But if you come now, it'll no' be taking advantage, will it?"

She stepped forward, putting herself back where she'd started. "I can't . . . I've never . . ."

His smile gentled. "Oh. Well. Then it's I who'll no' take advantage."

"Aye." She moved back again, away from him. His smile now seemed to hold regret. He turned his back to her and began to unlace his trousers.

She should go. If she went to him now, it would only mean hurting him later, when she had to leave him. Because she would, eventually. She would have to.

Turning away, she took a few steps back down the hill then stopped. Her mother had told stories of sailors, men whose lives she'd saved, who'd come to her in gratitude. Gilly herself had been the result of such a union, as had her siblings, all sisters.

Perhaps it was time for her to carry on the tradition. It was what her people did, after all. Saved sailors, loved them, let them go. This David Fraser wasn't the first man she'd saved, but he was the first she'd wanted.

Remembering the way his body had felt against hers, the way his arms had held her through the night, the way his lips had moved on hers, she made her decision.

She turned around. He was naked now, his back to her, and in the sunlight she could see all the sleek textures of his body that had been covered before by darkness. His wide shoulders tapered to a slim waist, then taut, rounded buttocks, long, lean legs.

For a moment she just stood there, looking at him. He

stepped forward into the water, stopped then looked over his shoulder. His dark eyes under the low, straight brows met hers, and he smiled. This was a different smile than the open grin he'd given her before—a devilish tilt of his mouth that made her quiver. He watched her, inviting her with that wicked smile, then lifted an eyebrow in question.

In answer, she walked the few steps back to the pool. He turned to face her and the sunlight showed her everything the night had hidden.

She hesitated just a moment, and mostly so she could look at him. She didn't think she had ever seen anything so beautiful as his tapered male body in the sunlight, the curves of his chest and the flat plane of his belly. He seemed blithely unaware of—or at least not embarrassed by—the rise of his erection as he stood there, waiting for her to decide what to do.

Decisively, she drew down the shoulders of her shift and let it slide to the ground. Then she took the last few steps to join him in the pool.

The water wasn't as cold as she'd expected. She walked up to him and pressed her body against his, her breasts mounding against his chest, his hard cock prodding into her abdomen.

With a soft smile, he put his arms around her, sliding his hands down her back. She closed her eyes, the better to feel the slide of his palms over her skin, the press of his hard chest against her softness.

Until now she hadn't given much thought to the differences between men and women, besides the obvious. But this man made her want to explore all of them, from the squareness of his jaw to the breadth and strength of his shoulders to . . . well, to the obvious.

He shifted his hands, sliding his fingertips down the groove of her spine until they reached the concavity at the small of her back. His touch slipped sideways then, feathering the tops of her buttocks. She shivered against him, and not from the cold. Tentative, she set her lips against his shoulder, touched her tongue to his skin. He tasted of the ocean.

He laughed a little at the touch and she withdrew, thinking she might have offended him. But when she looked up, searching for clues in his face, he dipped his head and kissed her.

She liked this. She thought perhaps she could spend hours exploring just this—all the ways his mouth could fit against hers. The other body parts could wait. They didn't seem to want to, hot and prodding as they were against her, but she wanted them to.

Her sailor seemed willing to cooperate, kissing her thoroughly with a heady mixture of carefulness and enthusiasm. She pressed closer to him, into the heat of his body. One hand slipped down his stomach, her fingers finding the curls of coarse hair low on his abdomen, down into the fold of his groin.

Suddenly he broke away, laughing, catching her errant hands in his.

"I came here to wash," he said, "and I'll no' be doing it if you're distracting me."

She wasn't sure what to say. Had she angered him? Why was he laughing?

Before she could answer any of her doubts, he bent and splashed water at her, then ran into the deeper part of the pool and fell in, splashing hard. He went under for a moment then came back up, still laughing.

"'Tis aye cold, as you said!" he called. "Come in and join me!"

It was his laugh that did it. It was lilting and infectious and, hearing it, she could not help but smile. She flung herself after him into the chilly water, her feet sliding on the stones, until she tripped into the deeper part of the pool and found herself falling into his arms. He caught her, steadied her then found her mouth again with his. The kiss brought his laughter into her mouth and she clung to him, amazed at the joyousness of it.

He clasped her buttocks in his big hands, lifting her off her feet. Reflexively, she wrapped her legs around his waist. The bulge of his sex pressed, beguiling, against the heat of hers, but there was no hardness there anymore. Perhaps because of the cold water, she thought. It had cooled her own ardor fairly thoroughly.

The kiss was heated, though. He wasn't laughing now. His tongue outlined the seam of her lips and she opened to him. The inside of his mouth still held heat and she sought after it, echoing the movement of his tongue as he licked into her mouth. The sensation dizzied her. He explored her thoroughly, building a soft rhythm, then eased back. She held tight to his wide shoulders as he moved, but his arms around her, his big hands splayed against her back, held her steady.

"Are you wanting to wash your hair?" he said.

She didn't quite know what to say. But apparently he didn't really need an answer because he shifted, easing her backward, holding her as he dipped her back toward the water.

His strength surprised her. She didn't know why—he was a sailor, after all, spending months at sea hauling ropes and fishing lines, pulling oars from time to time. She could feel that strength in his arms, his chest, his back, as he eased her down until her hair went into the water.

Smiling, luxuriating in the masculine power that supported her, she ran her hands through her hair, making sure the water touched it all, right down to the scalp. It was cold, but it was clean, and she would feel better for it once she'd warmed up and dried off.

He drew her back up to him and kissed her again before he let her go and dunked his own head, wetting down his dark hair. When he came up, he scraped his hair back from his face and shuddered.

"Aye, 'tis all I can take for now."

He headed back toward the grass and she followed.

"We can go back home. I'll make a fire."

He nodded. "It sounds grand."

Much to his dismay, she pulled her shift back on when she came out of the water. He'd been surprised she'd joined him so boldly in the first place, particularly if she really was a virgin. He had a feeling he'd be finding out soon enough. She certainly seemed willing.

He pulled his trousers on as best he could with his skin still wet and followed her back down the hill to her cottage. She was already inside, laying sticks on the fire. He came to stand next to her, not touching her, just holding his hands out to the glowing fire.

"There," she said. "You'll be warm soon enough."

He nodded, slanted her a look. She was staring resolutely into the fire.

"You're a bonnie wee lassie," he ventured softly.

She looked sidelong at him. "I'm no' wee."

Laughing, he conceded, "Aye, I suppose not. And a good thing that is for me, or else you'd no' have been able to bring me in."

She studied him for the space of a few breaths, far too seriously, he thought. Then she lifted a hand to his face, brushing her fingers down his jawline. He had some growth there, though only a little. He was certainly old enough for a beard but had never had much luck coaxing one to grow. Her fingers explored the sparse, soft hair then slid forward to touch his lips.

He hardly dared to move, afraid he might spook her, like a wild animal. She lifted her other hand to his face, tracing his features as a blind person might, drawing her thumbs along the ridges of his brows, a finger down the bridge of his nose.

"Have ye no' seen a man before?" he said finally.

"Oh, aye." She let her fingers trail down his neck, over the tops of his shoulders. "But never one so young and pretty as you." Her hands slid flat down his chest. "D'ye want me, lad?"

"Aye." He could barely force the word out. He had gone hard again under her touch, and it was all he could do to hold still while her hands explored him.

"You can have me then," she said. "But you must remember—ye cannae keep me. No man can."

"Oh, aye." He barely heard what she said, as his face dipped closer to hers.

"You must understand that. D'ye understand?"

"Aye," he said, because he would have agreed to almost anything just to feel her lips against his, and he had lowered his head, and they were little more than a breath away . . .

He wasn't paying attention—she could tell by the mindless, lusty look that had come into his eyes. She grabbed him hard by the chin, forcing him to look her in the eye.

"David Fraser, you'll be listening to me."

Some of the lust cleared out of his expression; it appeared she'd finally gotten his attention.

"Ye cannae keep me. No man can claim me as his. I belong to the ocean, and when the time comes for me to go back there, you'll no' be able to stop me. D'ye understand me?"

"Aye." It puzzled him, she could tell, but he seemed willing to accept it.

"Then touch me, bonnie lad, and show me exactly what it is a man can do."

He did more than touch her—he bent and picked her up and carried her to the rumpled pile of blankets and sheepskins where she slept, and he laid her down there and lowered himself next to her.

"I think it's you who should touch me," he said gently. "If you've no' had a man before, then perhaps that would be easier for you."

His consideration touched her, and the thought of exploring him aroused her. The heat and wetness rising between her legs was not unfamiliar—she had learned much of her own body in the time she'd spent alone in this place—but it was somehow different, more pervasive. She slid back out of her shift, pleased to find his hands assisting her in the effort. She wanted her skin to find his, wanted to explore him with more than just her fingers.

He tossed her shift aside and lay back again, just looking at her. His brown gaze explored her inch by inch, touching her breasts, drifting down her belly, settling on the triangle of dark curls between her legs. But his hands lay still, fingers folded together atop his flat abdomen. He had pretty hands, she noticed, wide palms, long fingers. They would be marred with calluses, she knew, from the work of a sailor, but the shape was perfect.

She reached for his hands, tracing the blue veins that rose from the backs, the strong tendons running from fingers to wrists. His eyes rose back to hers and stayed there. His mouth was set in a straight, neutral line, waiting.

So she touched him there. Traced his lips, the firm, straight line, the wide "v" at the top of his upper lip. He responded then, his lips parting, his tongue touching the tip of her finger, drawing it into his mouth. He swirled his tongue around her fingertip and she closed her eyes, amazed at the sensation.

After a few seconds, he let her go. *Aye, and he's a clever one,* she thought, but didn't dare say it aloud. She needed the silence now, just for a time.

Her fingers traced his straight nose, up to the low brows and high forehead, down to his temples, over the soft, half-hearted growth on his face, to his neck, over his collarbones. The wideness of his shoulders entranced her, the poetic arrangement of bone and muscle that created them. The arrangement of muscles in his upper arms, as her fingers explored there, sliding down to his elbows, finally across and over to brush again over his hands, which hadn't moved.

Other parts of his body had, though. His eyes betrayed no emotion as of yet, but his erection made a long, hard line under the clinging fabric of his trousers. She pulled the laces loose and eased the damp material off him. That was better. Naked, she'd decided, was always better.

And this was an intriguing piece of him, the long, firm cock that arched as it came to rise over his belly. A pretty thing, she thought, in its own way. She wondered what it tasted like. Maybe she would find out.

Right now, she slid her hands back up his body, up his belly to his chest, across to explore his nipples, which rose under her fingers into small, hard nubs. She bent her face to him and licked them—one, then the other, rewarded when he made a small sound in his throat, squirming just a little under her ministrations.

She lowered her body to his then, brushing her breasts

against his chest. Her eyes locked to his and she stared into their dark, smoldering depths, reading the promise there but not entirely certain what it meant.

"There's more to see," he said softly. "There's no stopping now."

She didn't want to stop. But she wanted more than just her hands on him. She wanted his hands on her. He was right, though—there was more of him to explore, and it might be better for her to have seen and touched and possibly tasted all of it before they moved on to other mysteries.

First, though, she wanted to kiss him again. She licked the line of his closed lips, and they opened to her. For a long moment she explored his mouth, experimenting with the slide of his lips against hers. There were so many different ways she could kiss him, even just here, mouth to mouth. His lips remained soft and undemanding, letting her take what she wanted and demanding no more.

She leaned back finally, studying his face again. He smiled a little, just the corners of his mouth tipping up, encouraging her.

Encouragement, at this point, was welcome but not necessary. If she had felt any embarrassment or shyness before, it was gone by now, and she kissed her way softly down his neck, onto his chest, down to the firm, rippled muscles of his abdomen. His navel tempted her so she dipped the tip of her tongue into it. He shifted his hips and the head of his cock bumped her in the chin. Smiling, she turned her head and took it into her mouth.

She wasn't sure it was the right thing to do, but his hips rose under her and he drew in a sharp breath. She drew back.

"Am I hurting you?"

"Ah, God, no."

Still, his reaction had disconcerted her. She had a feeling this was a good thing but she wasn't quite certain how to respond. So she continued with more caution.

Gently, she sucked the head of his cock again then let it go and licked down the length of it. Glancing to the side, she saw his fists clench. This must be good, then, if it eroded even the edges of his composure. Perhaps it was too much, though, for the moment. Instead of trying it again, she smoothed her cheek against the nest of dark, wiry hair there between his thighs then kissed the soft bulge of his scrotum. And he squirmed again.

"Laddie," she ventured. "David. Are ye well?"

"Aye, quite well." His voice was taut, strained. "You'll no' be stopping, aye?"

She slid her hands down the length of his hard thighs. "I'm thinking perhaps it's your turn."

He rose abruptly under her, clasping her arms and rolling her over on the pile of blankets until he was atop her, his broad body pinning her to the floor. It startled her, almost frightened her for a moment, then he kissed her, his mouth seeking and plundering. She wasn't sure whether to pull him closer or push him away. But he wasn't hurting her.

The urgency of his kiss faded after a time, and he drew back, resting his forehead against her shoulder. He was breathing hard, and she noticed then that his hips pulsed against her, his hard cock prodding against her thigh.

"You're wanting inside," she whispered.

"Aye," he said. "But not yet. I'll no' hurt you more than I have to. I want it to be easy for you."

She slid her fingers into his hair, combing through the dark length of it. "It'll be what it is, laddie." Her other hand slipped down his back. "Love me."

He took a moment to gather himself then his face shifted

against her shoulder, his lips touching her throat. He kissed her there, then his mouth went soft down across her collar-bones, down to her breasts. Her breath caught in her throat as he closed his mouth over her small breast, drawing it deep. His tongue twirled around her nipple, sending fire through her body. She knew her own body, knew what it could do and what awoke when she touched herself, her breasts and between her legs, but it had been nothing like this. Her skin was alight, fiery against his, and the sensation arrowing from her breast to her sex was almost more than her body could contain.

Gently then, he drew his mouth away from her, his teeth sliding against the delicate skin of her breast then nipping her pebbled nipple. Not quite hard enough to hurt, just a bit too hard to be comfortable. She gasped at the sensation. Heat had begun to pool between her legs, a relentless, demanding desire. Her body wanted him inside as much as his did.

But it wasn't time. He had done this before and she hadn't, so she made herself wait for him. After all, he seemed to have a plan.

The plan seemed to involve hot, wet kissing, to which she found no reason to object. He left the mark of his mouth across her body on the way to her other breast, where he suckled and nipped until she clutched at his wide shoulders, whimpering with need. Then he let her go and gave her that wicked smile, looking up at her through the frame of her breasts.

"Is it well, lassie?" he said.

"Aye." Her legs lifted instinctively against him, her knees pressing against his ribs. His body eased downward through this embrace as he slid his hands, then his lips, down her stomach. There was a certain reverence to his touch, as if he had never felt such skin as hers, or as if it were an honor that she allowed him to touch her at all. She knew the truth of that—it surprised her that he might understand it.

His fingers slipped down her belly to the tops of her thighs then feathered sideways, tracing the curves of her hips and slipping light and ticklish down the backs of her thighs to the bends of her knees. Then a slow glide down the backs of her calves until finally he cupped her heels in his hands. He sat there a moment looking down at her, sitting between her cocked legs, a foot in each hand, her toes against his shoulders. Even the look in his eyes was soft, reverent. Then he let his smile return and it tilted wickedly across his mouth.

"Do you trust me?" he asked.

She lifted an eyebrow. "Wi' ye looking at me like that, as if I'm a bit of cake you're about to gobble up? I'm thinking not." But she smiled when she said it because the mischief in his eyes made her warm, the wicked tilt of his smile made her want him that much more.

He grinned then, flashing his teeth, and bent to bite her big toe. She laughed. "Yes, I trust you."

Nodding, he licked the sole of her foot, heel to toe. She shivered and smiled, then laughed again. His answering smile turned into a kiss against her ankle, then the trail of his hot mouth continued up the inside of her calf, over her thigh, up to her navel. Her hips tilted up toward him as he moved, but his kisses went around the mound of her sex. How long was he going to make her wait?

Then, with his tongue dipping into her navel, his fingers surprised her, settling against the dark curls between her thighs. He stroked her softly and she gasped, feeling the spiraling rise of heat beneath his touch.

His fingers caressed her damp curls and slipped past them,

opening her labia. He touched the round, hardening pearl of her clit with the tip of his finger, making her squirm. She looked down at him and he tilted his head to look into her eyes as he squeezed her gently between his first two fingers. She forced herself to hold still, to hold his eyes with hers, as his fingers slid down her inner lips, slipping over the slick wetness of her arousal. A sound came from her throat—begging, anticipating, she wasn't sure which. But he only circled the mouth of her vagina with one finger, awakening her there but not penetrating. Then he lowered his eyes, and his head dipped between her legs.

She moaned when his tongue touched her. It rolled against the ache of her clit then licked into her labia, into her vagina. She had never felt anything like it. Wonderfully soft, intimately invasive, but welcome as his mouth pressed into her, as his tongue thrust into and against her. The taut spiral of fiery need built and swirled beneath that joining of moist flesh, rose and flashed under her skin. He suckled at her, pulling at her clit, at the soft inner tissues of her labia, until she keened with the intensity of the fire he stoked, until her body tautened, and her hips arched into him. His big hands clutched her buttocks, holding her steady against his working mouth. She flung her arms back, giving herself up to it. Her body had taken over and she was helpless in the grip of her pounding, pulsing release.

He held her there until she was finished, until she had to push his head away because she could no longer stand the intensity. Then he lifted himself back over her and looked again into her eyes. His face was sober now. Waiting.

There was no need for him to speak. She knew what he was waiting for. She reached down, curled her hand around the long, hard jut of his cock and pulled him toward her.

She thought he might kiss her, but he held her eyes with his and eased forward. The head of his cock pressed into her, into the hot wetness of her sex. It slid over the fading pebble of her clit, which rose again under the contact. And slid down to touch the edges of her vagina.

Reaching down, he took hold of his cock and stroked her with it a few times then slid the head slickly down the open folds of her sex, until the fire had risen again inside her. She clutched at his shoulders, gasping with need.

"Now?" he asked her finally.

"Now. God, please, now."

He pushed hard inside her. The sharp, tearing sensation surprised a cry out of her, brought tears to her eyes. She'd known it would happen but had hoped perhaps it would not be so bad.

He stopped, trembling a little as he braced himself above her, his hands on either side of her.

"Gilly," he said softly. "Is it all right?"

She blinked back the tears. The pain had faded, but she was afraid it would come back if he moved.

"Let it go," he said. He shifted his weight, lifted a hand to stroke her face. "Let it all go, lassie. Soft and gentle."

His soft hand on her face, the easiness of his voice, settled her. She let herself go lax, made her muscles unclench, loosening around his shaft. Bending down, he kissed her, deep but careful, then slowly slid the rest of the way into her.

He filled her, the sensation intense but no longer painful. It was easier now to relax, now that the pain had passed. He nibbled at her mouth, holding her lower lip between his teeth for a moment, then let go and smiled against her mouth.

"'Tis all right now?" he murmured.

"Aye."

He started a rhythm then, drawing partially out of her then pressing, sliding back in. The friction made her gasp, but the pain was past and forgotten now. He seemed to know the sounds she made were born of pleasure, perhaps by the tone, or perhaps because now he kept his eyes locked to hers, watching her as he pulsed in, slipped back, pulsed in again. Easing himself down to his elbows, he reached for her hands and wove his fingers through hers, holding her, his thumbs caressing hers. His smile had tilted up again, then it faded as his rhythm quickened. The line of his mouth went harsh and straight again, then his lips parted and his breath deepened, rasping out of him.

The rise and fall of his body above her, inside her, quickened her own response again. There was still some pain, but the rending sensation was gone. Now the vague, rasping discomfort simply heightened her need, fed the fire. Instinctively, she matched his rhythm, let her body tighten on him, her inner muscles trying to hold him inside her even as he pulled out then pressed back in again.

His hands tightened on hers, squeezing hard as he rose over her, as deep inside her as he could be. A low, guttural gasp tore from his throat and she clenched on him as hard as she could, feeling the taut pulsation of his cock as he emptied himself into her. He was vulnerable here, she realized. Strong as he was, big as he was, in this place he was vulnerable and she had a kind of power over him.

And he let her see it, opening his eyes suddenly, just as the last shudders of completion passed through his body. He was as open to her, there in his eyes, as she was to him, letting her inside him as profoundly as she had let him inside her.

It lasted only a moment, then his eyes drifted shut again, and he smiled and leaned down to kiss her softly on the mouth.

His hands still held hers against the blankets. She lifted her legs and embraced him that way, pressing her knees against his hips.

He let go of her hand then, and to her surprise, he reached down between her legs again. His fingers soft but demanding, he circled her clit, slowly, then faster, until she fell to pieces once again, shuddering in ecstasy against his clever fingers.

Finally, when she thought she might die of the pleasure, it ended, fading softly. His hand slid over her stomach and he rolled away from her, to lie next to her. She turned toward him, resting her head against his chest.

"Are you all right?" he asked her.

"Aye. 'Twas like joy and sadness and beauty all together."

"I'm sorry if I hurt you."

"It cannae be helped, aye?"

"Sometimes it can. I did the best I could."

"I'm thinking ye did well."

He stroked her hair, and something in his smile touched her. "I may be gone in the morning," he said, "but I'll be back."

She frowned up at him. "Where will you be going?"

"Just down to the town. I'm needing some things."

"For instance?"

"Clothes, to start."

"Aye. Then I'll be here when you come back."

4

HE LEFT IN the early hours, while morning crept along the horizon. In the summertime the days began early here, so he would have plenty of time to reach the town, wherever on the east side of the island it might lie.

He found it hard to leave Gilly though. She lay soft in the bed, one hand curled under her cheek, a smile curving her sleeping lips. Bending, he kissed her smile gently, not enough to wake her. He straightened the blanket over her shoulders and went on his way.

First he went back down to the beach, where he found his shirt—or what was left of it—and pulled it on. Tattered as it was, it still offered some protection from the sun. His shoulders still ached and itched from sunburn. Even the shirt scraped uncomfortably. Perhaps he should have waited for Gilly to awaken so she could treat him again with the soft, soothing salve. He could go back, but now that he'd started he wanted only to finish his errand so he could come back to her.

As he had suspected, the island was small, and it took him only a few hours to walk from Gilly's side of the shore to the town on the other side. It wasn't much of a town—perhaps twelve houses, all facing toward the mainland, which he could see looming beyond the swells of a few miles of ocean.

A dock jutted out into the dark blue waves, several boats gathered around it like chicks around a hen.

On the rise of a hill, a shepherd caught sight of him and waved. David changed his course, picking his way over the rocky slope to join the other man.

"'Tisnae often we see a stranger here," said the shepherd. "Where have you come from?"

"The other side of the island," David replied. "I was washed up there."

"Ah, a sailor. It's lucky you are, then, that you've lived to tell the tale."

"Aye." Normally he might have discussed the particulars of his rescue, but for some reason he had no desire to. As long as he didn't speak of her, Gilly was his alone.

The shepherd began to head down the slope of the hill, toward the town. "What's your name being then, lad?"

"David Fraser. First mate on the *Silver Swan,* may its captain and crew rest in peace."

"There are no other survivors then?"

"Not that I'm knowing."

The shepherd shook his head. "'Tis a cruel mistress, is the sea." He gave David an appraising look. "You'll be wanting a boat to the mainland then?"

David looked at the loom of Scotland's shore, beyond the swell of ocean and a drift of mist. "Aye," he said, reluctant. "And supplies. A shirt would be welcome."

The shepherd laughed. "You are looking a bit ragged, at that." He put out his hand and David took it. "I'm Hamish MacIver. I've work for you, if you want it, and I'm thinking I could spare a shirt."

"That'd be grand."

So David acquired a new shirt and spent the day mending fences for Hamish. Hamish's wife Mary, a short, blunt woman with bright blue eyes and red hair, fawned over him as she fed him cheese and fresh bread at noon.

"And how long were you lost, lad?" she asked, sitting down across the table from him. Hamish watched the exchange with amusement.

"Three days at sea in a lifeboat," David replied. "'Twas the brutal sun and little water, less food. And then a gale tossed me out of the boat, and the waves brought me here."

Hamish cocked an eyebrow. "'Tis a wonder ye werenae drowned, lad."

"Aye, that it is." He bent his head to his bread and cheese, uncomfortable for the moment with meeting their eyes. He wasn't sure why he felt such a need to keep Gilly a secret, but somehow it just didn't feel right to speak of her.

"You'll be needing a place to stay then," said Mary. She reached across the table and touched David's hand. "We've a bit of room to spare."

David looked at Hamish, who only smiled, apparently amused at his wife's obvious flirting. "Nay," David said. "I'll be heading back to where I've been."

Mary frowned. "There's nowt on that side of the island but seals, lad."

David shifted in his chair. "There's a bit of a cave. I'm well there for now."

Hamish's look had become suddenly narrow, evaluating. "Aye, you'll be well there for now." He stuffed a chunk of bread into his mouth. "You'll be wanting a boat. Come back tomorrow and I'll have someone ready to take you."

David nodded. "Aye."

He spent the afternoon finishing the fence then mending a hole in the roof of Hamish's barn. Mary sent him off with a basket of bread and cheese as well as a skin of ale.

"We'll be seeing you tomorrow then," she said, blinking her eyes at him just a little. She was nearly fifteen years his senior, he thought, old enough to be his mother. He indulged her as she rose on tiptoe to kiss his cheek.

"Thank you for all you've done," he said, making no commitment for tomorrow.

Hamish walked with him for a while, just to the top of the hill. There he whistled up his dog and sent the animal off to bring in the sheep.

"David Fraser," he said as David began his way down the hill.

"Aye?"

"You be careful of those seals."

Puzzled, David only frowned and nodded.

There was no sign of Gilly as he wound his way back down the hill toward her cottage. Smoke curled from the chimney, blue and thin. She was surely inside the house, he thought. The evening was wearing on, though the sun had yet to go down. The nights were short these days.

He came into the cottage, carrying his basket of bread and cheese, but she wasn't there.

"Gilly?" he called, as if there might be some hidden room somewhere in the tiny house where she might be secreted away. There was no answer.

She'd lived here on her own for quite some time, he'd gathered, but he couldn't help but worry. He set the basket down on the table, checked the fire then headed out, walking down the slope toward the ocean.

He heard her singing before he saw her, though at first he thought it might be his imagination, as entwined as the sound was with the sound of the waves. But as he grew closer, her voice rose above that of the ocean, and he stopped a moment, just listening, before he went on.

Finally he came to a place where he could see her. He stopped there, not certain why he was so reluctant to go on. But from here he could hear her, and watch, without her knowing he was there. He leaned against an outcropping of rock and stood silent.

She wasn't far away, sitting on a rock that jutted out into the pounding ocean. Her knees were drawn up to her chest, her arms around them, the breeze blowing her long, dark hair back and playing with its errant strands. And she sang. Her voice high and clear, pure, forming words in Gaelic that spoke of the width and loneliness of the sea. The crystalline sound brought tears to his eyes.

His attention had been so captivated by her voice that at first he didn't see the seals. They registered slowly, imprinting their dark forms on the periphery of his vision, until finally he dragged his eyes away from Gilly to look at them. There were perhaps twenty-five, black and sleek, clustered around the rock where she sat. Watching her. They seemed as enthralled by her music as David was. Strange, he thought, but he'd heard of stranger things regarding music and animals. She seemed unaware of them, directing her song toward the sea. But they sat silent and regarded her with their large, wet, black eyes, and only when she finally fell silent did they slip away from her, sliding back down into the water.

The spell seemed also to release David—he too pushed

away from the outcropping to make his way down to the place where she sat. By the time he got there, she had slid off the rock and was walking back toward the cottage. Toward him.

She caught sight of him after a few steps and smiled. "You're back," she said, quickening her pace to meet him halfway.

"Aye." He bent to kiss her, taking a moment to caress her mouth with his, to remind himself of her taste and her softness.

"I see you've a new shirt," she said when he finally drew back. She ran her hand down his chest, feeling the fabric but arousing the flesh beneath. He smiled at her, wanting her.

"Aye. I've worked the day away to earn it, that and a bit of food."

She smiled and took his hand, weaving her fingers between his as they walked back up the shore. "So you've met the folk of the village."

"Just a shepherd and his wife."

"Aye. Hamish and Mary, was it?"

"Aye. You're knowing them?"

"No, not really. I've seen them, though, him and his dog and his sheep, and she sometimes outside their cottage, sitting spinning in the sun." Her soft, contented smile faded. "You'll be meeting a boat tomorrow then? To take you on to Scotland?"

"I'm thinking no."

And the smile came back, lighting her face like sunshine. He smiled in return and wondered how in the world he would ever be able to leave her.

5

IT WAS PERHAPS a week before David found a reason to think about anything but Gilly. There was food, of course, to worry about, but she went down nearly every morning to the sea's edge and came back with fish, and she made bread in the late morning. Her routine went smoothly from hour to hour, day to day, as she went about her life as she apparently had for years, living alone on this island.

There was little for him to do, then, but think about her, look at her, touch her, make love to her. She seemed always eager for his touch, and he was always eager for hers.

He grew restless though after a time. It was nice to be without the backbreaking labor he knew from shipboard, but being so dependent on Gilly made him uncomfortable. So finally, one early morning when he lay with her in his arms, the taste of her still pungent on his tongue, he said, "I've a mind to go to the mainland today."

She stilled in his arms, frozen as if in fear. "To the mainland?"

"Aye."

"And you'll no' be coming back?"

He closed his arms around her, pulling her close against his chest. "Aye, I'll be coming back. I only want to find a bit of work, bring back some food and perhaps a wee gift or two for my bonnie lassie."

She relaxed a little, but he still felt tension in her back, under his hands. "We have food enough here."

"And you're working every day for it. Let me go and earn my way, at least for a day or two."

She was silent for a moment then nodded her understanding. "Come back to me, laddie. I'll no' be the same without ye."

He kissed the top of her head. "I'll be back in a few days."

There was some work to be had in the village, so he took advantage of that to earn the silver he needed to pay for passage to the mainland. Hamish and Mary had more work—a farm such as theirs never lacked for chores. They must have spoken to others in the village, for when he came back from the field, Mary had messages for him from several others asking if he could do work for them as well.

"I thank you for this," he said to Hamish as the farmer passed a few coins into David's hand.

"You're a good worker," Hamish said. "A good worker is always welcome."

David smiled. "You're too kind, all of you."

"Perhaps you could stay," said Mary, catching his arm as he started out the door. "You'd have plenty of work here, food. 'Tis better, certainly, than living alone on the other side of the island. There's room here with us, if you've a mind. You could stay as long as you like."

"I'm fine there. 'Tis a pleasant place to be."

"He's no' alone," said Hamish wisely. "There are the seals."

Mary's brow creased in concern. "'Tisnae a wise thing to linger with the seals."

David shrugged. "The seals cannae harm me."

"Just be careful of yourself on those shores." Mary let go of his arm but touched his back protectively, in a motherly gesture.

Puzzled, he nodded. "Aye. I will be. I am."

So he slept that night, and the next, in Hamish and Mary's barn. After two days working for the villagers, he missed Gilly so intensely he could hardly bear it. But he had enough money now to pay for the ship to the mainland, so he booked passage, and by his third day on the mainland he had arranged to trade work for room and board in an inn by the docks.

"'Tis hard to find a strong back to tend to these things," the innkeeper told him. He was somewhat elderly, his hands gnarled and unsuited for labor. David found himself again on the slope of a roof, repairing gaps that let in the rain. When he had finished that, he lingered on the docks, helping unload cargo when the next boat came in.

"You're being a sailor yourself, aye?" the ship's captain said to him that evening over a pint of thick, brown ale.

"Aye," David replied.

"And why are ye no' at sea now?"

David shrugged. "It's no' the place for me now."

"Well, there's a place for you on my boat whenever you decide to come back to the ocean. Because you will, you know. They always do, sailors."

"Aye." David drank deep of the nutty ale, wiped his mouth with the back of his hand. "My boat went down. I was near drowned." He wasn't sure why he'd decided to volunteer that information. Perhaps as a flimsy excuse to turn down the captain's offer of work.

The captain nodded sagely. "The sea nearly had you. She'll be calling you back."

"I'd be bad luck for you."

"Perhaps not." He studied David closely, measuring him. "Look for me when you're needing work."

"Aye. But for now I'll be going back to the island."

The captain's expression changed, his eyes narrowing. "The island? The one just offshore here, where you can see it when the sky's clear?"

"Aye."

The captain shook his head. "You'd be wise not to go back there. The seals . . ." He trailed off.

"It's selkies there, isn't it?" David's voice was a bit belligerent—he hadn't had a good strong ale in a long time, and it had gone to his head. "Is that what no one has been wanting to come straight out and tell me?"

"Aye," said the captain. "'Tis what they say. You must be watching yourself there, or one of them will come to you and steal your soul. They're beautiful, the selkie women. Once they've touched you, your soul belongs to the sea."

David nodded. He was too much a sailor, too much a Scot, to dismiss the idea. The stories of the mythical seals were in his blood, fed to him from childhood. Still, what was there to fear? So there might be selkies in the rocks. There was also Gilly, and he would not abandon her.

He had enough silver after a week to buy himself a shirt and trousers, new shoes, a dress and shoes for Gilly. He ached for her terribly, the need a living thing gnawing inside him. With the last of his silver, he paid his way back to the island.

He had no desire to see any of the townspeople. Not sure why he did it, he chose not to stay the night, instead slipping away from the docks, avoiding the town itself, winding his way up the hill without encountering anyone.

Dusk had fallen by the time he reached the cottage. It was

empty. He left his things on the bed and walked down toward the beach.

There would be little true darkness tonight. Only the gloaming, casting dusky shadows over the crags and cliffs, the shore. This was midsummer in this part of Scotland—in the winter there would be darkness in equal extreme. Now, the misty near-night allowed him to see the seals clustered on the rocks. One lay a bit away from the others, lifting its head high then shaking itself.

David stopped. He wasn't sure why. He stared at the seal then changed his path, finding a place behind a jut of the cliffs where he could watch without being seen.

The seal shook then stretched again. And then, as he watched, its skin split open and slid down, glistening. Gilly appeared from inside the black folds, naked, slipping out of the sealskin as if it were nothing more than a linen shift.

David's fingers clenched on the rock. He had known this. Somehow, he had known. This was why he'd ignored the warnings about the seals. But what had she done to him? Had she indeed ensorcelled him? Was that why he had hurt for her so much? Did it matter?

He watched for a few more minutes as, free from the sealskin, she picked it up, folded it and took it to a nook in the rocks where she slipped it away out of sight. He would be able to find that place tomorrow, in the light, he was certain. She slid her fingers through her hair, combing down the length of it, and started back toward the cottage. He turned and headed back up the hill, so that he would be there first.

Gilly had missed her sailor terribly. She had dreamed of him at night, remembering his touch, his kiss, the hard, beautiful lines of his body. But it had been a week. She had begun to allow herself to understand that he might not come back.

Ah, well. If he didn't, he didn't. It was the way of things for sailors to leave. She understood that. It hurt, though, a deep, dark pain inside her. Her mother had never said anything about that. She had said only to love them and to enjoy the loving while it was there. Nothing about pain when you let them go.

She had spent more time with the ocean over the past few days, letting its familiar rhythms drown her pain. The sea would always be there, whether the sailors were or not. It was her constant, her source, her mother. It took her in and bathed her, held her, let her be part of it.

The chill of the dusk bothered her not at all as she walked up the hill toward the cottage. She would go and lie in front of her fire to dry and wait again alone for her sailor to come back from the sea. If he ever did.

There would be another sailor. There always was. Someone else would wash up on her shore, someone else who made her body sing with desire.

But he would not be David Fraser.

The wind shifted against her face then, and she smelled smoke. A flash of fear shot through her and she broke into a run. Had she left the fire burning? She thought she'd smoored it before she'd left. Had she forgotten?

A few running steps brought her close enough to the cottage to see it. It was fine. She stopped. Smoke came from the chimney. Someone was there.

She ran again, her heart flying now into her throat. Was it too much to hope?

It wasn't. He was there, stirring up the fire, and when she came in he turned and held his arms out to her, and she ran into them and he kissed her, sweet and deep.

"I thought ye werenae coming back," she said, tears threading through her voice.

"I told you I'd come back," he said. "Did you think I'd lied to you?"

"Nay, laddie. I only thought that you're a sailor, and the sea had called you home."

She leaned back, reminding herself of the lines of his face. His dark eyes studied her. "What?" he said.

"You're a beautiful man, David Fraser," she said.

He smiled. "I love you, Gilly." The smile faded abruptly, as if he hadn't meant to say what he'd said.

She trailed fingertips down his face. "You don't have to. But thank you."

"What have you done to me, lass?" He laid a hand on top of hers, holding it against his face. "Is it magic?"

"Nay. I've no magic." She wondered at him, at the odd, searching look that had come into his eyes. "None that would hold you to me."

He let go of her hand, clasped her waist and just looked at her. Not sure what he was looking for, she met his scrutiny evenly. Something lurked in his eyes, something sharp and brittle. But suddenly it eased.

"Nay. You've no' ensorcelled me. If you had, you'd no' be so afraid you'd lost me."

"I cannae hold ye, laddie. Not against your will."

He smiled. Something inside her shifted; she realized then she'd been afraid. Afraid he'd changed his mind.

"Aye," he said.

He believed her. He knew she told the truth, that she'd used no magic to hold him to her. Just the magic of her eyes, her skin, her body. The magic of her.

The ache of missing her had come back. Even standing in

front of her, looking at her, it lay heavy in his chest. He had dreamed of her during his sojourn on the mainland, dreamed of touching her, holding her, having her. Though he had never felt such a thing before, that was no magic, nothing conjured of the sea. It was just desire. Just an ordinary, human thing.

He slid his hands around her waist, pressing against her back, bringing her closer. The deep brown of her eyes reminded him of the stories they'd told him on the mainland, of the seals, the selkie girls. They were dark, with dark, round eyes, eyes that enchanted a man. It didn't matter, not even after what he'd seen on the beach. She was Gilly. Nothing else.

But now he knew her secret. He would have her, and he would keep her.

He dipped his head and kissed her, soft at first, reacquainting himself with the taste of her mouth. First just her lips, the way they fit against his, the shape and texture of her full, woman's mouth. Then he pressed harder until she opened to him.

She was hesitant, uncertain still, so he led her, coaxing her tongue up against his until she began to play. She teased him then, touching and withdrawing, tapping her tongue against his. He could feel her smile against his lips.

Suddenly arousal gripped him like a fist, so hard it burned down through his chest, arrowing straight into his cock, which went so steely hard and aching he could barely stand it. No more teasing. No more playing. He wanted her. Needed her. Now.

His mouth went hard on hers then, demanding, and she made a small, startled sound as he pulled her up tight against him, clutching her. She made no effort to get away, not even when he lifted her, bending to pick her up and carry her to the bed. She just looked at him, right into his face, as he put her down on the blankets, her expression more curious than fearful.

She should be afraid, he thought. Even he was shaken by the intensity of his need. It had taken him over, pure lust pouring through his veins.

He tore at her clothes, dragging at her shift. He didn't even want it off her, just out of his way.

He wondered, vaguely, just beneath the level of his addled consciousness, what drove him. Animal need, or a specific need for her? Desire, or anger at the knowledge she hadn't told him what she was? Or had she, in her own way? She hadn't truly lied to him.

Still, the need came hard and fast, a need to possess her, to brand her. He wrenched her skirt up, yanked the shift over her head, threw it across the room. Then he grabbed her wrists and pinned them to the bed. Dipping his head, he kissed her hard. She was not a small woman but he was still bigger, stronger, and she was next to helpless under him.

His kiss was too hard, too rough, but she responded to it. She made no effort to escape his grip on her wrists. But as he drew back, catching his breath, she said softly against his lips, "David."

He opened his eyes and looked at her. Her face hid nothing from him. She was all openness and honesty and truth, her eyes wide and full of trust.

"David?" she said again.

The sound of his name, the question in her voice, brought him back to himself.

"You've no' lied to me," he said.

"Nay. But I've no' told ye all the truth either."

He stared into the damp depths of her dark eyes. "I know what you are," he said.

She showed no surprise, only smiled a little. "And you've come back anyway?"

"Aye. I'm a fool, it seems."

"Nay. 'Tis the way of things sometimes."

He shifted against her. His erection hadn't flagged, lust still smoldering in his groin. He only held it back for the moment, under a tight rein. She moved under him, opening her thighs so that his hips settled between them. He could feel the heat of her sex through the cloth of his trousers.

"Love me as hard as you like, laddie," she said. "I'm no' made of glass."

And she reached down to yank at his trousers, jerking them down off his hips. He just stared at her a moment, startled. Then the lust lurched in his chest and he set it free.

She was naked and open beneath him, so he did what his body called for him to do and shoved hard inside her, pressing her wrists down against the bed where he still held them pinned. She arched back and gasped a little. She was wet, but not as wet as he'd expected, and the friction of her not-quite-ready tissues dragged against his shaft, making him moan with the heightened intensity of entering her.

Still, he must not have hurt her because her hips lurched forward and up to meet his thrust, and as he withdrew her body clutched at him hard, squeezing on his shaft in a sharp convulsion and clenching even harder as he speared back in.

And he let go. Let the blind lust possess him, pinning her to the bed and pounding into her mercilessly. As aroused as he had been, he'd expected to finish quickly, but he went on and on, the rhythm going faster and faster, while the heat filled his groin, his pelvis, his scrotum, and finally exploded, hard and wet and spurting into her. He thought he howled with it, moaned or gasped or rasped some animal sound out through his throat, but the pounding in his head made it hard to hear.

Certainly she had cried out. There had been no pain or fear in the sound, just startled joy, but he hadn't felt the clenching rhythm of her release. She had perhaps risen and flown a bit, but he hadn't brought her to climax. No surprise there—he'd had no thought for her at all except as a place to slake the blinding lust.

She'd been willing, though, so it didn't matter. And it wasn't too late to remedy the situation.

He needed a moment though. Something had been wrung out of him with his orgasm, leaving him weak and empty. He let himself settle down onto her, careful not to make her bear all of his weight. When he let go of her wrists, she lifted her hands and slid them down his back, drawing him against her in a gentle embrace. He let his head sag to her shoulder and she turned her face a little until he felt her breath in his hair.

It was only then that he noticed the tears. His eyes were hot with them, and as he blinked they slid down his face. What was this for? Why was he weeping?

It was only the tears though, no sobbing, though a knot had clenched and then opened in the middle of his chest as if he had wept out his heart.

"I love you, Gilly," he said suddenly, and as before it came out without his bidding, surprising him.

She slipped her hand through his hair, cradling his head there against her shoulder. "And I love you."

They lay in silence for a long time. Her hand moved rhythmically over his hair, her fingers combing through it, brushing over it, occasionally sliding down past the fall of it to caress his shoulders, his back. Why did it feel so right here? Why did he feel like he could just lie here forever, cradled in her arms, cradled by her body? It was as if he were meant to be here, as if every event that had brought him to this place had been orchestrated, preordained. He belonged here.

But what did that mean? She'd told him already he couldn't hold her, that no man could. She had lied, though, because there was a way. She would be his.

She shifted under him, pushing a hand between their bodies. Realizing what she was doing, he lifted his head from her shoulder to look at her.

"Nay, lass. I'll do it for ye."

Her wicked smile made him go hot and suddenly, unexpectedly hard again. "Are you certain you'd no' rather watch?"

The idea intrigued him, aroused him and made him wonder again at the brash, beautiful boldness of this girl, his Gilly. He looked down the narrow space between their bodies to see her hand cupped over her mons. She really meant it. Her free hand rose, gesturing to him. He took it and she guided him, until he was kneeling between her open legs. Watching.

Her fingers disappeared into the dark, wiry curls between her legs. He watched her open herself, her first and second fingers spreading apart the moist, pink lips of her labia. It was hard for him to hold still—he wanted to touch her there, with his fingers, his tongue. Wanted to slide his own fingers inside, deep, and feel the heat and the syrupy wetness of her arousal. But he held still, just watching. If she wanted his touch, she would ask for it.

She was looking right at him, he realized, and when he glanced up at her face her eyes met his boldly, without hesitation or embarrassment. He smiled at her, and he knew he looked amazed and startled and flattered, and he didn't care. Didn't care if she saw that on his face, no matter how vulnerable that might make him.

Oh, but she had ensorcelled him, and no doubt of it.

His eyes went back to her fingers. She had lovely hands, he thought—he hadn't noticed it before. Her face, her breasts, the lush swell of her hips had consumed his attention—he simply hadn't registered the poetry that was the shape of her hands. Marred they were, from hard work, and they were large hands, but the bone structure was slim and lovely, with the grace of a bird's wing.

And now her fingers slid slickly over wet, pink surfaces he had touched, had tasted, but had never really looked at. It was a complex world there between her legs, with the differing textures, the varying shades of pink, the layers of soft, swollen lips. And the rising, hooded triangle of her clit, beaded now like a pink pearl beneath her fingers. She tapped it and it rose higher. He had never thought to do such a thing, but she kept it up for a few seconds, tapping softly then a bit harder, faster.

He turned his attention to her face, wondering what her reaction might be to what she did to herself. She had closed her eyes, her mouth a little open, her breath quickening. But she looked at him a moment after he looked at her, as if sensing his gaze on her. And she smiled.

Her free hand lifted to him. He met it with his own, lacing his fingers through hers.

She made a sharp, crying sound then, her back arching a little, and he looked back down. Her first two fingers had disappeared into her vagina, and she worked them in and out. Harder than he would have if he'd been doing it but certainly no harder than he'd forced his cock into her only minutes ago. Her fingers glistened with the weeping of her arousal, and as she stabbed unabashedly into herself, her hips lifted and pulsed, and her voice rose in a soft, humming murmur of growing pleasure.

He couldn't stand it anymore, couldn't stand to just watch her. With his hand still clasping hers, he bent over her. Her clit, untouched now, thrust hard and round from under its hood of tissue, and he set his mouth to it, sucked gently. She gasped and her hand clenched on his to the point of pain.

She didn't push him away, so apparently she didn't mind his moving out of the role of observer. He busied his tongue with her clit, tapping as she had done with her finger then rolling the tip of his tongue around it. He could feel the rhythmic movement of her fingers as she worked a spot high in her vagina. He registered that too for future reference.

He sucked her hard, his nose and his mouth full of the smell and taste, the musk of her, and suddenly she arched her hips up and cried out.

He wished he could have been inside her then, to feel the clenching pulsation of her orgasm on his cock, but he contented himself with the wrenching and shuddering of her body, the sound of her ragged, gasping breath. She drew her fingers free of her body and he caught her by the wrist, brought her hand to his mouth and sucked her fingers dry. Her arousal tasted like the ocean.

He lay beside her later, watching her until she fell asleep. She was soft and warm and beautiful next to him, and when he was certain she was asleep, he brushed a hand gently over her face, feeling the smooth, round softness of her cheek.

Then, silent, he slipped out of the bed.

He carried his trousers with him and pulled them on outside the door, not wanting to risk waking her. Then, fleet but careful, he picked his way down the hill to the beach, to the cave where she had left her skin.

It was still there. He drew it out, surprised at its soft suppleness. For a moment he just stared at it, at what he could see of it in the moonlight, barely able to believe what he saw, what he held.

This was his power over her. She had said he couldn't hold her, but he could. As long as this belonged to him, so did she.

He carried it up the hill, past the house, to a ridge of outcroppings almost as far as the edge of Hamish and Mary's sheep pasture. There he found a deep fissure in the rocks, and he slid the sealskin into it and covered it with stones and dirt. He would come back in the morning to be sure the camouflage proved sufficient. But he was certain she would never find it here, would never think to look.

Finished with his task, he straightened, brushed his hands together. Something nagged at him. Guilt, he was certain. He pushed it aside. If he didn't do this, he was sure to lose her. It was, as she would say, the way of her people.

He turned and made his way back to the cottage, back to the bed, back to her arms.

She woke spooned into his body, his heat surrounding her under the warm blankets. For a long time she lay still and content, listening to his heartbeat, feeling the deep, slow rhythm of his breathing against her back. One arm lay draped over her waist; she curled the back of her hand into his, feeling the rough calluses against her skin, the bigness of his hand compared to hers.

There was much to discover here. So many things about the touch and taste and textures of his skin that she had yet to learn. But he was deep in sleep, and the sun had found its way in through the windows at the front of the cottage. Gilly could smell the ocean.

She slipped out from under his arm. He shifted in the bed and made a sound, a sort of grunt that was more a change in his breathing than a vocalization. He didn't wake up. She found her shift, pulled it on and tiptoed out of the cottage into the morning sunlight.

The rhythm of the waves filled her ears, vibrated over her skin. It was as much a part of her as her heartbeat. It pulled her down the hill, toward the shore, the rocks where the seals sat. She followed.

She liked to swim in the morning. While David had been gone she had spent every morning in the water, often wearing her sealskin, sometimes as herself. The water was cold but she loved the feel of it and the danger when it dragged at her, begging her to come back to its depths. She had come to look forward to her mornings in the water, listening to it woo her and resisting its call. Someday, she had thought, someday I'll come back. But not now.

This morning, her excursion would be a risk, as it was possible David would awaken before she returned. But she wanted to feel the ocean water. She would go nude and human, so as to not run the risk of his seeing her sealskin.

She went to check on it, though, to be sure it was still safe. And there in the place where she always kept it, the crack in the rocks near the beach, she found nothing. It was gone.

She stood staring at the empty cranny, her body gone cold with fear. What had happened? Her first thought, crazed and frantic, was that one of the shepherd boys from over the hill might have come down to see the seals and found it. If that were the case, then her life had just been ripped up by the roots. With that thought echoing like a bell in her head, she stood, unable to move, unable to do anything but stare.

Then, suddenly, she realized the truth.

She looked up. Something had moved in the corner of her vision. David stood a few yards up the hill, watching her, and his eyes told her what he had done.

Her chest hurt with the thought. At least it hadn't been a stranger, but what was she to do now? She'd wanted to stay with him, she'd told him she loved him—had it not been enough for him? Did he only want not to lose her, or did he want to own her?

Dampness welled in her eyes as she looked at him. He met her gaze, but nothing on his face answered her questions. Finally, he turned, head down, and trudged back up the hill. She spun back toward the water, her face wet with tears.

6

THEY NEVER SPOKE of it. She would not ask him where he had taken the sealskin, and he would not admit to having taken it, beyond that moment on the beach, when he had seen her looking and had said nothing. She needed no further evidence that he had done it, and he needed no further proof that she knew.

After a time, it seemed more and more to Gilly that it didn't matter. She would have stayed anyway, and while she missed her occasional outings into the deeper parts of the ocean, missed the ease and grace of the seal's body, it came to haunt her less and less as the days and weeks went by. She had, she thought, traded the joy of her seal's body for the joy of sharing David's, traded her ability to swim in the ocean for the ability to swim in him, to lose herself there, to drown. Perhaps it had not been a bad bargain.

And he was good to her. More than good—he doted on her. It was hard for her to understand why he would want to stay. He was used to moving among people, and here he had only her. Surely he missed conversation and interaction, the bawdy loudness of a boat filled with sailors, the bustling noise of a village, the varied smells of shops and streets, of decks and cabins and high-waving sails. But he never spoke of it.

He went to the village from time to time, and occasionally even to the mainland, but he always came back.

It horrified her to think what might happen if one day he didn't return. She had no idea where he had hidden her seal-skin, and without it she could never return to the ocean. If he went away and chose not to return, or if he was killed, she might be forced to live out the rest of her life on the land. And she had no idea how long that might be. The seal-people lived a long time. A very long time. But without their ability to return to the water, perhaps not. She didn't know.

There were so many things, she thought, that her mother had never told her. Things Gilly now wished she knew. It seemed important, more important on days when she walked the shore, anxious for David to return from his latest outing. She trusted him, but sometimes she didn't.

One day he came back from the mainland with a soft bag filled with silver—earrings and bangles and a plain band for her finger. She turned the shining, lovely things in her hands, slid the ring on and lifted her hand for him to see it.

"Thank you, laddie," she said. He lifted his own hand to show her a matching band there.

"'Tisnae a marriage, not really," he said, "but perhaps it's as close as we'll come."

She nodded. Her eyes ached as if with tears but remained oddly dry. "When you leave—" She broke off, the words tangling in her throat.

He brushed his hand over her hair gently, smiling down at her. She loved his smile, the way it transformed the harsh lines of his face, making him look like almost a different person. "I miss you as well, lass. You know that. I only go because we cannae find all we need here on this island."

"It's no' that, David." She lifted her hand to his face, touched his lips. "What if one day you don't come back?"

He opened his mouth to answer then shut it, as if only then realizing what she was really saying. His eyes slanted sideways, no longer meeting hers, and he said nothing.

∽

After that he rarely left their side of the island and stopped going to the mainland altogether. He missed the outings, but she had a point. If something happened to him, then he had doomed her with his selfishness.

If he could have told her where the sealskin was, he would have, but he knew the rules. Once he had taken it, the nature of their relationship had changed. Now, as soon as she found it or he gave it back to her, she would leave him. Slip into her other self and disappear into the ocean, and he would never see her again. That was the way of it in the legends, and he had no reason to doubt their accuracy. He would watch her bending over the fire or making some simple meal and try to convince himself that she would stay with him no matter what, but then she would look up with her large, limpid, dark brown eyes, so like the eyes of the wild seals, and he would be reminded of her otherness. She was only his now so long as he held control of her magic.

But what if something did happen to him? He had to find a way to make this right. He loved her too much to leave this between them.

Finally one morning he left her sleeping in their bed and walked up the hill. He made note of the exact path, of landmarks, of twisted trees, outcroppings, the direction of the sun, the slope of the hill. In front of the hiding place in the rocks, he stopped, oriented himself thoroughly then walked on until he reached Hamish and Mary's farm.

Mary gave him an odd look when he asked for paper and a quill. "Aye, of course," she said. "And what are you needing it for?"

"I'm just needing to draw a bit of a map," he said reluctantly.

She quirked an eyebrow at him. "A treasure map?" she said, teasing.

"After a fashion."

Mary gave him paper, quill and ink, and he sat down and carefully sketched the pathway up the hill, putting in the landmarks he'd noticed, supplying a compass rose in the corner of the page for orientation. Once he was satisfied, he waited for the ink to dry, then carefully tore off the first third of the page. There was just enough on that portion to make it obvious it was part of a map, but not enough to orient the person using it. On the back, he wrote a note.

> *Gilly, my love. If you are reading this, it means that I have died, or I have not returned from the village or from the mainland. I ask you to think on me always kindly, as I have loved you with all my heart. Take this paper to Hamish and Mary at the top of the hill, and they will give you the rest. Go back to the sea with my blessing.*
>
> > *With the deepest affection of my heart, David.*

He folded the pieces and sealed both of them with wax, then held the larger piece out to Mary.

"If she comes here looking for it, give it to her, as it will mean I am dead," he said bluntly.

Mary frowned. "I'm no' understanding you, lad. Is it a sort of will?"

"Aye, in a way." She still hadn't taken the paper from his hand. "Please. It's that important."

Finally, Mary nodded slowly and took the sheet of paper. "I'll be taking good care of it."

"And if something should happen to you, I'd ask that you leave it to someone you can trust, and make sure Gilly will be able to find it."

"All right, lad."

He took a slow, relieved breath. "It's grateful I am to you, then." Impulsively, he kissed her on the cheek. She blushed a bit then cupped his face in her hand.

"You're a good lad, I'm thinking," she said. "You make me wish I'd been able to bear a son."

He smiled. "You make me wish my mum hadnae died when I was but a bairn."

Blinking a bit, she patted his cheek. "Off wi' ye now, and take care of your lass."

He couldn't tell if the solution pleased Gilly or not. She smiled when he gave her the folded parchment, but it was a sad smile and gave him little reassurance.

"For if I die," he told her. "Or if I go away and dinna come back to ye."

She only nodded and put the bit of paper away in a drawer. He resolved never to speak of it again.

After that, life went on much as it had before. He had attended properly to his responsibility to her, and so that pall had left them as far as he was concerned. She still went to the shore though, to sit and look out at the sea. Sometimes the seals would come up to her, and he would watch from a distance as she stroked them like dogs. Sometimes he thought she spoke to them even, and he wondered what she said.

Gradually, the days grew shorter, the wind from the sea

colder. Snow fell, and fell thick, leaving them stranded in the small cottage for three days before the storm let up enough for David to dig them out. It didn't matter—they had firewood and peat, a bed and blankets and each other.

Gilly remembered the previous winter as cold and unpleasant, with the ocean icy and the cottage never warm enough to suit her. She had tried one year to migrate with the seals, but after so long in her sealskin she'd had a hard time coming back to herself and it had frightened her.

But this winter she was far from cold. It was never cold under the blankets next to David. If a chill breeze dared waft into the cottage and touch her, she would move closer to him, and he would roll toward her, even asleep, and pull her into him. His heat was more than enough for the both of them. And in the mornings, when the chill in the air was too much for either of them to want to leave the warmth of the bed, she would more often than not find his hands traveling her body until she was on fire with need, and he would roll her under him and slide inside her, and she had never in her life found a more satisfactory way to spend a winter.

In the middle of February, a warm breeze caught them by surprise, melting the snow and ice and tempting Gilly to the shore. But when she rose from bed she found herself dizzy and sick, and by the time she reached the rocks she could do little more than sit with her head in her hands.

She had left David asleep in bed, but it wasn't long before he came up behind her and sat on the rocks, pulling her gently against him. "What is it, lass?"

Lacking the energy to speak, she only shook her head, but the movement sent her spinning into nausea. She sank into him, letting his body support her. His hands stroked her gently. Her skin seemed too much alive, too sensitive, so that she could barely stand his touch, but at the same time she needed it just to keep from collapsing.

"You're sick," he said, and promptly picked her up and carried her back to the house.

He waited on her throughout the morning, bringing her broth and plain bread, and by the afternoon she felt almost normal again. But the next morning the sickness was back, wrenching and uncomfortable, and it was then that she realized what it was.

David wasn't far behind her. "'Tis a child coming, lass," he said that evening when, feeling less nauseated but painfully tired, she allowed him to knead the bread and lay it by the fire to bake. "You'll have to trust me with the chores for a time."

He smiled widely at her, and she couldn't help but smile back because his happiness was infectious. But it left her quickly, for this meant that once again everything had changed. David, of course, would not know this, and she would have to explain it to him. She didn't want to though, for this, the growing of a daughter within her, meant nothing more or less than the beginning of the end.

The third morning she dragged herself from bed at dawn and, in spite of the wrenching sickness, made her way to the seashore. Settling onto her favorite rock, she sang until the pink of the sky had changed to blue. By the time she had finished, her head was spinning, her limbs weak and aching. She would never be able to make it back to the house. But when she turned away from the open ocean she saw David standing a few yards away, his brow creased in concern. When her eyes met his he came quickly to her and once again carried her back to the cottage, to lay her down on the blankets and add peat to the already-warm fire.

"You'll no' be doing that again," he told her. "You endanger yourself and the wee one."

"I have to," she managed.

He spun on her, his eyes so fierce beneath drawn-down brows that for a moment she was afraid of him. "You have to go to the ocean and sing? Why?" His voice was as sharp and fierce as his eyes.

To tell him would be to violate every rule that had been impressed upon her from the day she could understand her mother's words. But she couldn't hide this from him. She wondered suddenly if her mother, who had kept all the secrets, had ever truly loved any of the men whose daughters she had borne. "I need her," she managed.

His expression softened a little. "Your mother." His quick understanding surprised her.

"Aye."

"All right, then. Tomorrow morning I'll be taking you. 'Tis too much for you to go alone."

So he took her, the next morning and the next, and every morning for the next three weeks, when March came in with a great blast of snow that trapped them again in the cottage.

For five days this time they were forced to stay inside while the wind howled around them. Gilly slept through a great deal of it, the child taking more of her strength than she had thought possible. David lay quietly with her, stroking her hair, rubbing her back. He spoke little these days. She knew he was concerned, but perhaps he didn't know how to ask her whatever questions plagued him.

On the fifth night, the wind finally quieted. Gilly, drifting into sleep, heard her mother's voice. "I've heard ye, wee one. I'll be there soon." The next morning she stayed in the warm bed while David went to dig away the snow in front of the door.

"You'll no' be going to the rock to sing today," he told her when he came back in.

"Aye," she answered. "'Tis all right. She'll be coming soon."

∞

Gilly's condition concerned David more and more as the days went by. He hadn't spent a great deal of time with pregnant women, but he'd visited his sister once when she was carrying her third son, and she hadn't had nearly the discomfort Gilly was having. Of course, he knew the early part of a pregnancy was often the most difficult, but still something seemed wrong. He should talk to her, he knew, but he was so afraid of what the answers might be that he couldn't bring himself to ask the questions.

"She's coming, you say?" he finally ventured, about a week after the March snowstorm had ended.

"Aye," said Gilly. She seemed a bit better today, sitting up in bed sipping broth. He'd tried to tempt her with more substantial fare, but she had declined with a shake of her head.

"She's taking quite a long time about it."

"She has a long way to travel." She reached toward the bread and cheese he'd put on a plate and set next to her in the bed. It gratified him to watch her eat it in small, careful bites. Perhaps she was getting better.

"When she comes—" He broke off. She looked up at him with her wide, moist, dark eyes. Something like fear had come into them. He looked away from her, finding a spot on the floor to hold his attention. "When she comes, you'll be leaving me, aye?"

Her voice came soft and trembling. "I don't know."

Slowly, he looked up at her. The fear in her eyes had turned to sadness, and she blinked back tears.

7

WHEN GILLY'S MOTHER arrived, David saw her first.

He had left Gilly in bed, still sleeping. She slept so much these days, as if she couldn't get enough rest. Something in her seemed to be slipping away, and he didn't know what it was or how to stop it. Perhaps the child demanded too much of her, but she seemed such a braw lass. He couldn't imagine something as natural as a pregnancy could actually hurt her. Or kill her.

Walking down the hill toward the shore, he was absorbed in these thoughts and the pain they brought when suddenly he realized he wasn't alone. He stopped, looked toward the ocean and saw her.

Even from this distance, he knew immediately who she was. What other tall, dark-haired woman would be walking toward him, up from the edge of the ocean? He moistened his lips, suddenly nervous. Should he go to her or wait? His feet didn't seem to want to move, so he waited.

As she approached him, he assessed her, almost in the same way he might size up an enemy. She was nearly as tall as Gilly, her long, dark hair streaked with silver. She wore a lightweight shift, much like the one Gilly favored. He had to wonder where it might have come from, if she'd only just emerged from the sea after abandoning her seal form. There was magic in these people, more than just the shifting from human to seal. When she came close enough that he could see her eyes, he saw that magic in them and it startled him. Gilly's eyes were so open, so clear. This woman carried the weight of more years than he could imagine, and of magic that came as naturally to her as breathing.

She stopped a few steps away from him and scraped her gaze up and down him. When she spoke, the words were Gaelic, in an accent and a dialect he barely recognized.

"You're the one, are you not?"

It took him a moment to understand what she'd said. "Aye," he stammered, also in Gaelic, though not the same as hers. "I suppose I am, at that."

She seemed not to have the same problem with comprehension. She nodded. "Take me to my daughter."

He turned and walked back up the hill, leaving her to follow. When he reached the door to the cottage, he looked over his shoulder to see her right behind him, her dark eyes narrow and evaluating.

"She was sleeping when I left," he told her. "She may still be." He laid his hand on the door to push it open, but her fingers touched his shoulder, stopping him. He looked back at her again.

"Do you love her?" she asked.

"Aye."

She nodded and drew her hand away. David opened the door.

Gilly was sitting up in the bed, wrapped in the heavy covers and leaning toward the low-burning fire. She looked up and smiled as David came in, then she saw her mother. Tears sprang to her eyes.

"You've come," Gilly said in the same strange Gaelic her mother had used. The older woman came to her, sat on the bed and took Gilly in her arms. David pushed the door closed behind him. Gilly wept on her mother's shoulder and David suddenly felt as if he shouldn't even be here. There was magic between mother and daughter, and he had no business being near it.

He took a seat in the rocking chair on the other side of the room and waited.

⚭

They talked together for a long time, the odd Gaelic turning into a muddle not unlike music. David caught a word here and there, but the dialect was so different than what he knew that their quick, easy conversation proved beyond him. He heard his own name once or twice, heard the word for "baby" and a few others he recognized, but not enough to string them together. But there was little laughter between them, and Gilly's tears came in slow, silver waves. Her mother seemed focused and grave.

Finally, seeing that the fire had gone down, he left the house to bring in more wood.

He came back a few minutes later with an armful of sticks and found Gilly's mother bent in front of the fire laying peat on the flames. He laid the sticks on the hearth, his shoulder brushing against the woman's. She looked at him sharply.

"You've taken it, haven't you?" Her voice was sharp as well, and he registered the tone before his brain managed to interpret the words.

When he realized what she'd said, his mouth hardened and he straightened. With a look at Gilly who still sat huddled on the bed he went back to the rocking chair.

The old woman's gaze followed him, her mouth thin, her eyes flinty. David settled into his chair and looked straight back at her. He had no desire to be forced to defend himself. Especially since he knew he couldn't.

She seemed to realize he had trouble understanding her because when she spoke again the words were slower, clearer. "You've ensorcelled her, lad. It was wrong of you."

He set his jaw and didn't answer.

"Mother——" Gilly began.

"Don't defend him, girl." She still spoke slowly. This part of the conversation was meant for David's ears, and she was going to be certain he could follow it. His hands clenched on the arms of the rocking chair as he forced himself to be still and listen. "You, David Fraser, you took what did not belong to you. Return it."

"I'll not return it. I can't. If I give it back to her she'll leave me."

The old woman's eyes flashed at him. "That's right. She will. And if you don't give it back to her, she'll die. And the child as well. Your little girl. She'll have dark hair and brown eyes and you will kill her if you don't let her mother return to the sea."

David pushed to his feet, temper flaring. "You lie. You lie because you want me to let her go. I won't. She's no' wanting to leave me."

The woman held his hard, flinty gaze for a moment then turned back to Gilly. Gently, she said, "I've told you what you need to know. The rest is for you to work out." She went to her daughter, gently kissed her forehead. "I wish you luck. I do think that he loves you."

"He does," Gilly said softly.

"Then perhaps it will be well."

She walked to the door then, brushing past David on the way. Her eyes burned through him one more time, then she left and closed the door hard behind her.

∞

Gilly knew the truth of what her mother had said. Could feel it as real as the child inside her. The girl grew now, so that Gilly could feel her soft, swimming movements. The water within her echoed the water of the ocean, and her child swam within it.

And sickened there because Gilly could not swim as well.

She did her best, eating the broth David brought to her, as much bread and cheese as she could manage. But she needed the water around her. Needed her sealskin, and the sea.

She wondered about what her mother had said. Was it true? Would she really be compelled to leave him if he returned her sealskin? She knew the legends always went that way, but had it been the choice of the sealwomen or a true compulsion? She wouldn't know until he gave it back to her, and then it would perhaps be too late. Certainly she would have to return to the ocean to bear her child, but afterward would she not be drawn to him?

She couldn't imagine that she wouldn't. He had become like air and water to her, necessary for life itself. She couldn't imagine willingly leaving him and never returning. Could she ask him to come with her? She couldn't imagine asking him that either. Couldn't imagine asking him to make that kind of sacrifice for her.

Outside, night had begun to fall. David came to sit next to her on the bed, brushed a big hand over her hair. "How are you feeling, lass?"

She forced herself to smile a little. "Not well, I'm afraid."

He blinked a few times, rapidly, then looked away from her. His brows drew down and his eyes went distant. After a time he turned his attention back to her, his expression strangely fierce. Then it softened and he bent to kiss her. "I'll be back, lassie. Dinna miss me greatly."

She watched him as he left the small cottage, her heart sinking. He was going out for wood, she thought, but somehow she knew this was not the case. Holding her hands out toward the fire, gathering in the warmth, she could do little but wait.

When he came back he had sticks, and he laid them in the basket next to the fire then squatted there, looking into the flames, forearms braced on his thighs, fingers woven together. She watched him, measuring the breadth of his shoulders with her eyes. Could she memorize him now, before it was too late?

He bowed his head, his dark hair spilling down to hide his face from her view. For a long time he just sat that way, the orange light from the fire playing over him while she looked at his white shirt straining against the wideness of his shoulders, clinging to the groove of his spine. She wanted to go to him, touch him, feel the warmth of his skin through the linen, but she had no strength.

Finally he pushed himself to his feet and turned toward her. "Gilly, lass," he said, his voice barely a whisper. "If you leave me, do you think you'll ever be coming back?"

She swallowed. "I don't know."

"Would you? If you could?"

"Oh, aye. If I could I would. If I could I would stay with you until we both wither and die."

He smiled a little, one tipped-up corner of his mouth tipping up a little farther. "I love you, Gilly. You know that, aye?"

"Aye. And I love you."

He nodded. "'Tis all I needed to hear. All I needed to be sure of."

He went to her bed then, bent, slid his arms under her, blankets and all, and lifted her. So this was what it was to be, she thought. Pushing her face against his shoulder, she inhaled his smell, concentrating. She wanted to remember this. The pressure of his arms, his easy strength maneuvering her through the door, his hair falling against her face, his smell filling her nose and mouth. Her eyes went hot and she blinked to stave off the tears.

Outside, the sunset burned orange through the sky and the ocean, the distant waves tossing back the light like flickering flames. Suddenly she could smell only the ocean and pushed her head hard against him, desperate to keep his smell close to her. It was no use. The sea, its sound, its rhythm, its sight and its smell, had filled her every pore. Her body yearned so deeply for it, the longing drove everything else away. She shuddered in his arms.

He drew her a little closer, kissed her hair. He took her to the flat rock where she had often sat to sing and settled her down there gently as the wind took her hair and whipped it out to its full length.

A dark mass lay on the rock next to her—the sealskin. Almost afraid to touch it, she looked up at him. "Are you sure?"

"How can I not be, lass? You're dying, and our child with you." He paused, blinked again and she saw the glint of tears in his eyes. One fell, crystalline in the orange light of sunset. "Put it on. Go." He stood and turned away from her, his shoulders set, head low. "Go."

An emptiness had opened in her, just below her heart. She

had never felt so wounded, so dark inside. How could she possibly leave him? But he was right, and even if he wasn't, the pull of the ocean had become too hard inside her to ignore. If she did, it would wrench her heart from her.

Leaving David would as well.

She reached for the sealskin, touched it, let its soft folds fall over her hands. "David—" she started, but he said again, "Go," and started to walk back up the hill.

She watched him go. She could have called him back, but she knew he would not have come. Tears fell hot on her face then suddenly inside her the baby lurched. Reaching for the sea.

Gilly watched David until he opened the cottage door and went in. She wanted to remember forever the lines of his body, the wide shoulders and narrow hips, the cant of his head as he paused just outside the door, as if he might turn back and look at her one more time. He didn't, though, and so she had no memory of his face from that moment. She would have to dig a little deeper for those textures, those lines, those colors. It was already becoming difficult for her to remember anything at all of the land, over the relentless call of the pounding ocean.

She turned away then from her last memory of him and lifted the folds of the sealskin from the rock and let it fall over her body. The change came slowly then in a lurch, and she felt the child within her exult with it as she slid softly into the cold, surging ocean.

8

DAVID STAYED IN the house for several days. Four, maybe five—he lost count somewhere. He felt numb, broken. The tiny cottage seemed vast and empty without Gilly.

Finally, he came back to himself enough to realize she wasn't coming back. He'd known this, of course, but it took a long time to absorb it. He kept expecting to hear her singing on the rocks by the ocean or see her walking up the hill, the wind pulling at her long, black hair. To roll over in the middle of the night and find her lying next to him, soft and willing.

On the fifth or sixth night he dreamed of her, of her softness, her taste and her smell, the shape of her hands on his body. He woke aroused and weeping and decided he'd had enough. It was time to go.

He packed what few things he owned as well as all the food left in the cottage and a few things Gilly had left behind. In a small chest near the fireplace he found jewelry made of shells, pearls, a few pieces of coral. He found one of her shifts; it still smelled like her and he folded it into his own clothes and took it with him.

After making sure the fire was completely out, he trudged up the hill, through the sheep fields, to Hamish and Mary's house. Mary answered the door when he knocked. She took one look at him and held out her arms, and he walked gratefully into her embrace.

"It'll all be well," she said, patting his back. "Dinna fash, lad."

She took him inside and brewed tea, which he accepted gratefully. He hadn't had tea in a long time. It tasted good, the warmth filling a little of the emptiness inside him.

Mary watched him for a time as he quietly sipped from her fine china cup. She waited until he had finished the tea before she said, "She's left you?"

"She had to. 'Twas the babe."

Mary's eyes widened a little. "I'm so sorry, lad."

"Aye."

She smiled sadly and got up to pour him more tea.

She had forgotten how wide and open the ocean was. In her human form she had found words inside her mind to describe it. In this form there were only feelings, movement, sensation. She missed the words, but the feelings overwhelmed her.

The child loved it. She could tell by the way it moved inside her. Gilly began to gain a stronger sense of her daughter as the baby swam and rolled and kicked within her womb. Her movements echoed Gilly's, matched the rhythm of her swimming as she fought or rode the currents.

She swam for a long time before she remembered David. The change, the utterly consuming presence of the ocean, had driven her memories down deep, in a low current where she couldn't reach them. When they finally returned to her, in vague images and sounds, she realized it was because she had healed somewhat, rejuvenated by the water.

When she remembered she wished she hadn't. It was easier

to let the ocean currents take her, to let them carry her from time to time to the shore, to live in that rhythm, than it was to be reminded of what she had been forced to leave behind.

Could she go back? If she did, she couldn't stay, she knew, because she needed the ocean around her right now, because her daughter needed it to live. But something inside her needed David. She hadn't been able to say goodbye to him properly. She'd been too ill, too desperate for the sea. It wasn't fair. Whatever the rules of her people were, they should have allowed her at least the chance to say goodbye.

She had to try to get back to him, if only for a few hours. It wouldn't be long enough to hurt either herself or the child, but it would be long enough to end things with David the way they should have been ended.

If she could go to him. She wasn't sure yet that she could. But it was worth it. Worth the effort, worth the risk.

She swam until the currents eased, until the shape of the water told her land was near. The island where she had lived was still some distance away, but she could start her preparations here. Pulling herself up onto the land, she began.

David stayed with Hamish and Mary for several weeks, helping with the sheep, making repairs to the pens, the barn and other outbuildings and generally making himself useful. They seemed to appreciate his presence, though he spent hours on the hill, looking down toward the cottage, and when he was home he lapsed often into silence and memories.

One night he came in from bringing in the sheep to overhear them talking by the fire.

"The lass, she's ensorcelled him," Mary said. "Taken his soul, perhaps, with her into the ocean."

Hamish scoffed. "Nay, she's only taken his heart. He'll find it again soon enough when another lass looks soft at him and smiles."

"Nay. 'Tis more than that. She was of the seal people, and you know how their ways are said to snare a man."

"He'll be all right," Hamish said again, more firmly this time.

David took that moment to walk into the room, making noise now so they could hear him. Mary gave him a sympathetic look.

"Are you well, lad?" she asked.

"Aye." He thought perhaps he should say something else, but nothing came to mind.

"Are you needing anything else then?"

"Nay. I'm to bed." He turned away then paused, rubbing the back of his neck. "Thank you. For all you've done."

Mary smiled. "Sleep well."

He nodded. For a moment he hesitated, still feeling as if there was something more he should say. But there was nothing.

There was little room in Hamish and Mary's house, so David had made up a corner for himself in the barn. The smell and presence of the sheep bothered him not at all—he'd spent the night in much less pleasant circumstances shipboard. Here he had a pile of sheepskins to lie on, a good, heavy blanket to lie under. It was warm and there was a roof over his head. It was enough.

Here, in the silence as he tried to find sleep, was where it was hardest to turn his thoughts away from Gilly. He could almost feel her next to him as he lay there, drifting off. It didn't get any easier. He worked hard in the fields, trying to exhaust himself so he could fall more quickly into sleep, but it rarely worked. Closing his eyes, he tried hard to think of nothing, to let his weariness pull him under.

Which it did, finally, but still the images haunted him. She walked in his dreams, along the rocks, her black hair and white shift blowing behind her. The colors were pale, faded, old, the sea gray, the sky a worn shade of blue. He watched from a few yards away, unable to move. So beautiful. What he wouldn't give to touch that beauty again . . .

She turned to look directly at him. "Come to me," she said. "Come to me now."

He bolted awake, breathing hard. She was there. Somehow he knew. He pushed up out of his bed of sheepskins and ran.

His feet went out from under him halfway down the hill and he slid a good distance before regaining his footing. But by then he was close enough to smell smoke. She was there. She had come to the cottage and put a fire in the fireplace and she was there waiting for him and he got back to his feet and ran down the hill as fast as he could.

The smoke was indeed coming from the cottage's chimney. Blue peat smoke, drifting on a light breeze. The same breeze touched his face, drying tears that had rolled down his cheeks that he hadn't known he'd shed. He half-ran, half-stumbled down the hill, staggered to the open door of the cottage. A light was on.

She was there. In the bed, the blankets drawn up to cover her breasts, her shoulders bare. She looked vital, alive, not wan and drained as she had the last time he'd seen her. The ocean had done her good.

He stopped in the doorway, hands braced in the frame. "Gilly?"

She smiled. "Aye, laddie."

"I didn't know you could come back."

"Neither did I, until I tried."

"How long—?"

"I'm not knowing, so come to me now before the ocean calls me home."

He went. She let go of the blanket to lift her arms to him, to draw him to her.

Her smell surrounded him, drowned him. Her body felt different in his arms, fuller, softer. Truly the ocean had healed her. Given her what he could not.

"I love you," he whispered.

"I love you." She breathed her answer against his lips then kissed him, soft and deep, until he could barely remember his own name.

Pulling her in to him, he slid his hands down her back, reveling in the smooth softness of her skin. It was hard for a moment to remember this was real, not a dream or a figment of his imagination. She really and truly was here, in the bed they had shared, in his arms.

The swell of her stomach pressed against him and he curved his fingers over it. He could feel the movement within, a soft rolling, swimming motion. His hand tightened a little against it and he looked into her face in wonderment.

"Your daughter," she said.

"You're certain 'tis a girl?"

"'Tis always a girl, with us."

He didn't have time to think about that. All he wanted right now was her. To love her the way he should have been allowed to before he had been forced to let her go.

He bent his head to kiss the swell of her stomach, felt the child moving against his lips. Then he let his hand slide down that vague curve, below, to touch the soft hair beneath, to open her gently with his fingers.

She was hot and damp and ready, but he toyed with her, wanting to hear her intake of breath, her soft gasp, wanting to feel her shudder. Shifting over her, he caught her breast in his mouth, tasted the hard pebble of her nipple. She tasted different somehow. The curve of her breast seemed larger as well.

It wasn't fair. He should be able to share this with her, to watch all the changes her body would make as the child grew within her. He should be able to hold her as she labored and watch his daughter enter the world. Instead, he would be allowed a few hours to make love to her and then he would have to let her go again.

She arched into him, crying out as he pressed his fingers deeper into her. He drew her breast deeper into his mouth, pulling, suckling, trying to forget that this would be the last time. Her hands clutched at his back, her fingers digging into him as if she would force him to her, hold him forever.

He wanted it to be slow, wanted to make it last, but he was so hungry for her it was all he could do to hold himself back. Then she reached between them, closed her hand over his cock and pulled him toward her.

Fighting her wasn't an option. He slid his fingers out of her, let her direct his hungry erection into her. Her hips shifted against him as his glans touched the heat of her vagina, the movement bringing him in deep.

"God," he gasped, unable to hold back his own voice. She was so hot, so deep, so ready for him. He held as still as he could to keep from spilling himself right there.

She seemed to understand, as she held still as well. Then, when some of the needy tension had left him, she pushed at him, rolled him over.

On his back, looking up into her face, he closed his hands around her waist as she moved on him, clenching her body hard on his cock, rocking her hips against him, making the rhythm she wanted. He matched it, lost in the sensation of her sex pulling at his, lost in the depths of her body. She tossed her head back, her dark hair flowing behind her, so long it brushed against his thighs.

Suddenly she stilled, her body arching even farther back. He tightened his hands on her waist, holding her, supporting her as she gave herself up to her climax. Her vagina clenched and pulsed on him, and he could hold back no longer as sensation piled up in his pelvis and he had to let it go, let himself spill hard into her, crying out as he did, and broken in the knowledge that it was too soon.

But she looked back down at him then, smiling into his face, and he smiled back because he couldn't not. She was beautiful. She had been his.

"I love you," he whispered. "Know that always, lass, and be sure the ocean knows as well."

She lowered herself to his chest, kissed his throat. "Aye, my laddie, and that I will."

The bulge of her stomach had hardened and moved a little between them as she shifted to make herself more comfortable. He curved his fingers around it, feeling the soft swimming of his daughter, knowing it would be the last time.

She was gone in the morning. He'd known it would happen, but it was still a jolt, a numbing blow to his heart. But it wasn't as bad as it had been the last time. At least now he had been able to say goodbye.

He lay in the bed alone for a time, absorbing the smell she'd left behind in the blankets. Finally, hungry, he got up and put out the fire.

Maybe he would be able to smile again now, he thought as he trudged up the hill. At least now he knew she loved him, that she would have stayed if she could. It didn't make it any easier though. Didn't make him miss her any less.

In Hamish's barn he gathered up his things, tied them into a bundle. Then he walked across the field to the house, to say goodbye to Mary.

She was in the kitchen, kneading bread dough, and looked up as he came in. She took in the expression on his face, the bundle of clothes over his shoulder, and smiled sadly.

"You'll be off then?" she said.

"Aye. Off to the mainland. 'Tis time to let go."

"I'm sorry, lad." She came to him, embraced him, kissed his cheek. "We'll miss you."

He nodded. "Thank you, Mary, for all you've done."

"Hamish is in the field. He'd be glad for a word before you go, I'm certain."

"Aye."

David found Hamish and said goodbye to him as well. The old man said little, but David had a sense he would be missed. It was all right. It was good to know someone cared for him. It had been a long time since he'd felt that from anyone besides Gilly.

It was a few days before the boat went out to the mainland. He spent it working at the inn. When the boat arrived, he bought passage, and on the mainland he looked up the captain who'd offered him a place in his crew. Three days later, he was back at sea.

Where he belonged.

9

THE DAYS AND weeks and months bled into each other, spent on deck fighting the sails or the other sailors, or spent on shore loading or unloading cargo. They were old and familiar rhythms, ingrained in him from years of habit. It was almost enough to make him forget.

Almost, but not quite. He dreamed of her sometimes at night, the images misty and elusive. In dreams he could remember her face, her body, her touch, more clearly than he could in daylight. Part of him just wanted to forget her because perhaps in forgetting her he could let go of the pain.

Captain Sullivan took him aside one evening after David had spent the day overseeing the catch.

"What's wrong with ye, lad?" the captain asked.

The question surprised David. "Nothing."

"'Tis the lass, aye?"

David frowned, offended. "If there's been something lacking in my work, I hope you'd tell me, though I cannae imagine what might be lacking as I've worked myself hard and well for you these months I've been on this ship."

The captain cocked an eyebrow at him. It occurred to David that this was quite possibly the most he'd spoken to the captain since he'd signed onto the ship. He'd been taciturn, perhaps too much so, focused on his work and on forgetting.

"Aye, and that you have. But the men fear you, which isnae always a good thing."

"Why would they fear me? I've made no threats against them."

"You speak little to them or to me. You seem as if you're somewhere else more often than not. You lean on the rail at night and stare out into the sea as if you look for something." He paused, studying David's face. David forced himself to look back, discomfited by the captain's scrutiny. "We all know what happened to you, lad. That you nearly drowned. If the ocean's calling you back then go to it, but I'll ask you to no' take my ship with you."

David said nothing. It wasn't the ocean that called him back, but he would tell no one of Gilly. She was his, his memory of her a precious thing he would share with no one.

The captain waited, and when he found no reply forthcoming, he slapped David gently on the shoulder. "Perhaps next time we touch land, you should take some time, stay at port until our next visit. It might do you good."

David nodded, though he sincerely doubted that would be the case.

Gilly carried her memories of her last night with David into the depths of the ocean, past the places where the real seals could go, to the dark deeps where her people reigned. The child grew steadily within her until her body seemed little more than an extension of the baby, a vessel for the child's growth and birth and little else.

She found her way to the secret places, the seal people's country, where no human being had ever set foot unless a seal woman had changed him. They were all women here, except for those very few men who had accepted the change.

It was a difficult choice to make, she knew, because once a man had been changed he could never go back to the human world. Only the women could take the seal form and roam the ocean. The men were bound to the seal people's world, here in this place that was not quite land and not quite ocean. Those she knew who had come here didn't seem to regret their choice, but could she ask that of David? Would it be fair?

Would it be fair not to?

She came to the shores there and shed her skin, standing on two feet for the first time since the night she'd made love to David, on that night that seemed almost a dream to her now. Her balance was strange, thrown off by the weight of the child inside her.

It wouldn't be long now. She knew, somehow, that the baby would come within the week. Whether her daughter communicated that to her, or whether her body knew, she wasn't sure.

She also sensed, somehow, the presence of her mother. Once her legs felt steady under her, she set out to find her.

It didn't take long. Gilly remembered, vaguely, the place where she herself had been born and had spent the first twelve or thirteen years of her life. It was a cottage of sorts, of stone and driftwood and seaweed, held together as much by magic as anything else. And her mother was there, cooking dinner.

Gilly ran into her embrace, happy to see her again. Her mother laid a hand over the swell of her belly, felt the child move inside and smiled.

"He let you go," she said.

"Aye." And suddenly there was nothing else to be happy about, and she fell against her mother, weeping.

When the tears had passed, they sat down and Gilly told her mother what had happened—that David had willingly let her go to save her life and the life of his daughter.

"It's a rare man that will let us go without our having to deceive him," her mother admitted.

"I love him," Gilly said. "I don't know if I want to go on without him."

Her mother nodded wisely. "You could, of course. Don't deceive yourself into thinking the loss of a man means the end of your life. But I know how you feel."

"You've felt this?" The thought surprised her. Her mother had seemed always to be happy without a permanent mate, going from sailor to sailor, occasionally coming back to this place to give the seal people another daughter. Had she too had her David Fraser?

"Aye, lass. I felt that way about your father."

"What did you do?"

"I went back, after you were born, to see if he would come with me, be changed, live here where we could be together."

"What did he say?"

"I never got the chance to ask him. By the time I'd birthed you and returned to his shores, he was gone."

"He left?"

"Aye. He left and he drowned. The sea took him where I could never touch him again." The older woman's eyes sparkled with tears, which she blinked back quickly. After a moment she added, "He was a good man, your father."

Gilly absorbed this. Finally, blinking back her own tears, she said, "I went back to David."

Her mother seemed surprised. "You did?"

"Aye. For a last night with him. A few hours. I wanted him so much—" She broke off. "He let me go. Again."

"I wasn't certain of him when I saw him before." Her mother's voice was soft now, reflective. "But if he's done this for you—I'm not doubting now that he loves you."

"Aye. He loves me. I've no doubt of that at all."

"Then you'll go back, and you'll ask him, and perhaps he'll come to you." She laid a hand gently over the large bulge of Gilly's stomach. "After the baby's come."

"After the baby's come."

Gilly's daughter was born in the faded early morning three days later. Gilly labored for hours, tired and sweating, wrenched with pain, until finally the small, wrinkled form was laid in her arms, gaping, and Gilly put the little girl to her breast.

"Why can we not give birth in the seal form?" she asked her mother later. Her whole body ached with the effort of having given birth. "Seals seem to suffer so much less."

"'Tis a mystery," her mother told her. "I've not the answer." She brushed a hand gently over her tiny granddaughter's head. "It does seem unfair though, aye?"

"Very much so."

She fell asleep that night with her daughter curled up asleep in her arms, warm and soft, her little mouth open, her tiny eyes lost in dreams. Gilly dreamed as well. Vivid dreams of David. When she'd been in the ocean she'd had a hard time remembering even what he looked like, but it came back to her now, intense, beautiful. His face, his body. His hands touching her, the taste of his mouth. Even his voice, weaving through her dreams. She woke with tears on her face.

She would go to him. As soon as she could leave the baby behind, she would cast herself into the ocean and find him, ask him if he would come to stay with her, be with her forever.

It didn't occur to her to think what she might do if he said no. Perhaps because she simply couldn't imagine it.

⌒⌒

The next time they stopped for cargo Captain Sullivan suggested again that David take a shore leave, but when the ship set sail again, David was on the boat. Throwing himself back into his work, trying not to think about Gilly, where she might be, if she might ever come back, or if his daughter had been born yet.

He began to dream about her, the dreams more vivid than any he'd ever had. She came to him in his sleep as if making up for the fact she couldn't come to him in his waking world, and there she loved him, rolled him, made him shake and moan and tremble. It was almost more than he could bear.

He took to walking the decks at night, almost afraid to go to sleep because there were times when the intensity of the dreams frightened him. In the dark, he would lean over the railing and look down at the waves and wish for the sight of a seal.

⌒⌒

Gilly swam. It was always hard to tell the way back from the seal people's country to the land of men, but she knew she went in the right direction. Her body felt sleek and lithe, recovered from the travail of childbirth. She missed her daughter, the tiny child she had yet to name because she wanted to see first if her father wished to have a hand in naming her.

She was close, she knew, after several days of swimming. She could swim longer than any human, of course, but also longer than any seal. They were more than half magic, the seal women, and the birth of her first child had unlocked more of that magic. She could swim now in human form, if she chose, not having to always depend on the seal part of her to help her find her way through the waves.

It wasn't long then—or was it? It was hard to tell the passage of time—when she found herself on a rocky beach on the western coast of Scotland. She knew somehow that this was the town on the mainland, near the island where she had met David. He would be here.

It saddened her that he was here, and not still in the cottage on the island. She wasn't sure why—there was no reason for him to stay there after she had left. He had a life of his own to reclaim, and that life demanded that he take to the sea. So this coastal town, with the boats moving in and out of its docks, was a logical choice.

Would he sense her presence as he had before? Or had their connection been broken by time and distance and the growth of her magic? There was only one way to find out. She settled herself on the rocks on the shore and waited.

As the sun began to burn orange down the sky, he came. She watched him pick his way down the hill, through the rocks, toward the shore. There was a dazed expression on his face, as if he didn't know for certain why he was here, why he was coming to this place on the shore. Then he saw her, and his expression changed to shock, and he picked up his pace, half-sliding down the rock-strewn slope.

She stood as he came to her, met him with open arms. He engulfed her in his own embrace, lifted her and spun her around, cradling her against his chest. "Gilly," he whispered against her ear. "Gilly, my Gilly. You've come back to me."

"I cannae stay, David," she said as he set her back on her feet. "I've come only to ask you a question." She couldn't keep her voice from trembling, shaken with uncertainty as she was. He looked down into her face, frowning in concern.

"What is it, Gilly? What is it you're needing to ask me?"

"I cannae stay," she said again. "But you can come with me."

His eyes widened in shock. Hope sprang warm into them then faded. "Come with you where?"

"To the land of my people. To the seal people's island."

His hands, which still held her upper arms, tightened a little. "Where mortal man can go and never return."

"Aye. 'Tis a place of magic, and once a mortal has been touched, he never can go back to the world of men."

"You cannae ask this of me, Gilly." His words stabbed through her heart. They had come too quickly, without even time for thought, and the fear trembling through his voice shattered her own carefully nurtured hope into pieces.

"Lad, it's the only way we can be together. Would you think on it, at least? There's no need for you to decide today." But those words came from desperation because if he didn't come with her now she knew he never would.

He studied her face. The desperation in his eyes made her heart ache. "I cannae," he finally said. "I'm sorry, lass."

Her lips tightened and suddenly it was hard for her to look at him. What had happened to the love he had declared for her? Had it all been a lie?

But perhaps it was truly too much to ask. After all, how many other men had declared their love to a seal woman and then made the same choice to let her go? She'd hoped he was different, but in the end she had to realize he was, after all, only a man.

"Do you wish to name your daughter?" she said then, barely able to force the words out.

"She is well then?" He seemed interested, at least, perhaps even a little excited.

"Aye, she is well. Hale and healthy and beautiful."

A corner of his mouth twitched up a little, almost making a smile. "Name her as you would then. I've no right."

Gilly blinked back tears. He was letting go of even that then. She took a step backward, out of his arms. "I'm leaving you then, David. This time it's forever."

He blinked rapidly a few times then nodded. "I love you, Gilly. Never forget it."

She only nodded, turned and walked away from him, back into the black and roaring ocean.

10

HE MISSED HER terribly, and there was no denying the pain that consumed him, day and night. Captain Sullivan took to watching him closely, afraid perhaps that he would make a mistake that would kill other members of the crew. If he killed himself, David had the feeling no one would be surprised. Least of all himself. But he had no intention of taking anyone else with him.

The weeks passed, painfully slow, day after day adding ache to his already shattered heart. He had been bright and happy once. He remembered that. Missed that. It seemed like a dream to him now.

He had nothing, he realized one day, staring out at the sun-sparkled ocean. His mother gone, his father drowned so many years ago David no longer remembered him. There were brothers and sisters, but he hadn't seen any of them in so long he was no longer certain where to find them. And Gilly gone, and with her his daughter, whom he would never meet.

In his bunk that night he lay awake, listening to the rhythmic singing of the waves as they slapped against the side of the ship. It was a calm and quiet ocean tonight, black and vast and sparkling with starlight when he had last seen it, before he had come to bed. The snoring of sailors at times overcame its quiet rhythm. He closed his eyes and laid his ear against the wall by his bunk until he could hear nothing but the waves just on the other side of it.

What would it be like to be lost in that? To give up his life to the ocean? He had worked on the sea all his adult life, had lived within its influence since he was born. If he truly decided on death, he would give his life not to a knife or a noose but to the waters.

With his ear against the wood, his mind adrift in the sound of the waves, he fell asleep.

He woke partway through the night when the sound of the water changed. They were moving out of the deeper ocean, toward the shallows, toward land. Still, they would not reach shore for several days. Wrapping his blankets more tightly around his shoulders, he drifted back to sleep.

In the shallower water, there were seals. They came to him, and though he somehow knew this was a dream, somehow he also knew it carried truth.

She was there. Brown and sleek and beautiful, and in her wide, brown eyes he saw her human half, his Gilly.

He smiled in his sleep, the first time he had smiled in a long time. In the dream he reached for her, but she moved away, sleekly through the water. And turned to look back.

"Yes," he mumbled, and started awake.

He stared into the darkness of the cabin as reality slammed back down around him. Reality with its cold and damp and the stench of unwashed bodies packed too closely into a too-small space.

"Yes," he said again, his voice firm but quiet. He shoved his blankets aside, pulled on a pair of trousers and half-ran up to the deck.

The sky spread black and wide over the ship, spattered

with stars from horizon to horizon, utterly empty yet full to the brim. He felt much the same way.

He ran to the deck rail, slammed into it. The smell of the ocean seemed suddenly overpowering. He closed his eyes, let it fill him.

Where was she? Was she truly there, out on the ocean in the thick, black night? With his eyes closed it seemed he could sense her, smell her almost—but no. It was a deeper, more mysterious sensation than that. It settled over him until he felt it like sea-spray on his skin, then it reached into him and touched his heart . . .

He opened his eyes. There, in the darkness, a seal. Starlight illuminated the sleek, wet curve of a head upthrust from the easy waves. Wide, brown eyes blinked at him, damp and limpid.

"Gilly," he breathed.

"David! David Fraser!"

The voice came from behind him, harsh and authoritative. Captain Sullivan. David didn't turn—he barely even registered the sound of his own name. He put one foot up on the bottom rail, then the other.

"David!" The captain's voice came harder now, commanding. David turned a little.

"Dinna touch me, Captain," he said evenly. "Dinna stop me."

"What do you mean to do?"

David smiled. "'Tis the ocean, Captain. She's called me home."

The captain said nothing. David stepped to the middle rail. The captain made no move to stop him. David turned back toward the ocean, looked out to the dark place where the seal had been. She hadn't moved, her wide eyes still regarding him through the darkness.

"I'll no' stop ye, lad," said Captain Sullivan. "'Tis the way of things, and I'll no' risk my ship or my crew for you."

Not looking at him, David nodded. "It's been a pleasure sailing wi' ye, Captain Sullivan."

"Go wi' God, lad."

David pushed himself up to the top of the rail, his eyes locked to the seal's, and let himself fall.

He managed to straighten before he struck the water. Hands extended, he cleaved the water like a dolphin. His breath rushed out of his lungs as the dark ocean clenched him like a fist of ice. If this was death, it would be over soon.

Down, down and down, deep, cleaving the ocean, into the cold and the darkness. The icy water covered and swallowed him. It seemed to go on forever.

Had she really been there? Had it only been his imagination? Had he indeed thrown himself into death?

Did it matter?

Then something touched him. Something sleek and smooth and familiar. He remembered this, from after the gale.

Gilly. It had to be.

He reached for her and held her, barely conscious now, not cognizant enough to tell if she was woman or seal. All he knew as he slid into darkness was that she was safety, and haven, and love.

He woke to warmth. It was the first thing he noticed before he came completely into wakefulness. He was warm and there was softness over and beneath him. It felt good.

Then he heard the sound. A soft, contented mewling. A sound of life.

He opened his eyes. Was this real or a dream? It was too vivid to be a dream. Real then. He was still alive.

"David." Her voice whispered to him from a few feet away. "David, lad."

Tears sprang to his eyes and he turned his head. "Gilly?"

She was there, sitting in a rocking chair, human and real and lovely. Her dark hair tumbled down over her shoulders and in her arms she held a baby. His daughter.

David sat up, blinking. Gilly smiled at him, and her eyes too were full of tears. She rose from the chair and came to him, sat next to him on the low bed where he lay.

He reached up to her as she sat, took her in his arms and held her there, the baby soft and small between them. Looking down into the little girl's face, he saw himself and he saw Gilly and he smiled.

"Ah, but you're a pretty thing," he whispered, smiling. His heart had been empty, but now it was full again. He looked up at Gilly. "So this is the place, aye? The place I can never leave?"

She nodded, uncertainty in her eyes. He looked away from her, taking in the room, the oddly colored walls that seemed to be made of driftwood. The ocean whispered in the background, distant and yet always close. A fire burned in a fireplace, and the blankets were soft and warm. He wondered where exactly they were—an island or a magical place beneath the ocean, or some combination of the two, or even something else entirely.

There would be time for those questions later. Right now the only answers he needed were in Gilly's eyes, and he looked into them and smiled.

"It seems well enough."

She smiled her relief and gently laid his daughter in his arms. "I havenae named her yet."

"We'll name her together."

"Aye." She looked down into the baby's face then back up

into David's. "Why did you come? What made you change your mind?"

Tucking the baby carefully into the crook of one arm, he lifted his other hand to trace the curve of Gilly's cheek. "I realized I had nothing to lose." There was a tear on her face. His finger found it, brushed it away. "Except you."

She bent toward him, put her head against his shoulder. With one arm around her and the other supporting his daughter, he closed his eyes and breathed happiness.

He needed nothing else.

Voyeur

SHILOH WALKER

1

ASHLYN SHUDDERED, A hoarse moan falling from her mouth. Her elbows gave out and her upper body collapsed on the bed. Behind her, Kye panted roughly while he pumped in and out of her shivering body. Looking down, he watched as he slid back inside the tight glove of her anus.

Ashlyn's fingers circled madly around her clit, and her knees started to quake. "Aw, hell. Kye, harder. Hard and slow," she hissed, her breath catching in her lungs as his thrusts went from short and quick to long, hard, and slow.

As always, the feeling of him buried inside her ass bordered on near pain, but each time she thought she couldn't handle it, her body clamored for more. The first climax caught her in its fist, and gushed from her vagina to soak her busy hand. Even as her body spasmed around the invasion in her butt, she ordered harshly, "Don't stop yet, Kye. Give me more."

He grinned and clamped his fingers harder on her hips, pushing her almost completely off before burrowing back in to the hilt, her agile fingers grazing the sac of his balls before returning to rub her clit.

Shuttling in and out of her tight little hole, he felt his own climax building at the base of his spine. Kye forced her hips down and dug in a little harder, angling his hips until he felt the tremors start inside her body again.

Just as he shot off inside her ass in vicious spurts, she screamed long and low, her anus clamping around his cock as she came a second time.

Black dots danced in front of her eyes as his hot semen pumped inside her butt. Her arms buckled and Kye fell against her as he rode her body down to the floor before he collapsed and rolled to his side, bringing her with him.

Some time later, he asked, "Who would you like to ride while I screw your ass?"

She stiffened, and buried her face in the pillow. They had moved to the bed after cleaning up and she had been drifting off to sleep.

It wasn't an unusual question, at least not from Kye. He seemed determined to share her with somebody, determined to slide inside her ass with tiny, invading thrusts while somebody else lay beneath her, fucking her in a more traditional manner.

As thrilling as the idea seemed, she wasn't about to let it happen. She knew herself too damn well and suspected if the time for such a treat ever came, she'd probably run scared. Ashlyn was not the adventurous type, or at least, she didn't think she was.

Anal sex was certainly something she had never considered. Kye had practically begged, and she still hadn't given in. It had taken him months to talk her into.

And hell, the first time she had let Kye give it to her in the ass, she had been more than a little tipsy. And the second time. "But by the third, and fourth times . . . she had come to crave it.

But another man in the bed? Not likely. She'd feel like a deer in the headlights—caught, fascinated—and then she'd turn into a rabbit and run like hell.

"Lay off it, Kye," she muttered, wanting to fall into the waiting maw of oblivion. With the exception of the past hour, the whole day had sucked. And tomorrow was going to be just as bad. The pediatric office where she worked had turned into hell on earth. Temporarily. One nurse on maternity leave. Another sick. And everybody just *had* to get in that day. Or the next. But only after four o'clock.

She snuggled into her pillow and yawned, the demands of the past few days catching up with her.

"Come on," he cajoled, fondling her breast as he propped himself on his elbow.

"Kye, it won't happen." With a sigh, she pushed up until she sat, and drew her knees to her chest. "Maybe I do want to try it, once. But I'm neurotic enough that it will have to be somebody we know, somebody we can trust. And I'd like it to be somebody I don't personally know. An anonymous stranger I know we can trust, how likely is that? It would also have to be somebody I'll never have to see again. I'd probably die from embarrassment. Facts, disturbing, distressing, embarrassing facts that I just can't get past, but hey, that's life."

Tugging her down next to him, he considered that while he rubbed her back. "Go to sleep," he murmured.

2 *Three months later*

KYE'S HANDS WERE busy on her ass while he nibbled on her neck. Burning candles were scattered about the hotel room, the flickering light turning her pale skin to gold. She wore a silk robe and nothing else.

He was still dressed in a silk shirt she had bought that he rarely wore and a pair of khakis that showed his tight butt to perfection. Ashlyn's head was reeling from it all—coming home from work to have him stuff an overnight bag into her arms and usher her out to the car before she had even changed out of her scrubs.

Driving to this beautiful hotel nestled on the river and checking into a sumptuous suite. He had drawn her a bubble bath, she remembered, as his mouth closed over the hot point of her nipple. Urged her into it and washed her back, her hair, everything, in a gentle soothing manner that had aroused, and comforted at the same time.

And then he had left her alone, with a quiet order to relax. He'd left the robe in a gift-wrapped box. She had pulled the fine, rich silk over her soft, scented body while a goofy smile curved her mouth.

Her body looked quite luscious, she had thought as she smoothed the silk over her nipples, her gently rounded belly and curvy hips. She teetered between a size twelve and fourteen and took it as a matter of fact that she was, and would always be, a twelve something. With her broad shoulders and hips, she'd probably look anorexic in a size eight anyway.

Now, he tugged open the robe, sliding one hand down the length of her body to uncover her, but he left the silk on her shoulders. "Close your eyes," he ordered, sliding one thigh between hers, lowering his head to nibble on her shoulder.

Her lids drifted closed and her head fell back as he stroked and caressed, rubbing his cock against her belly. Of an equal height, Ashlyn and Kye were eye-to-eye, mouth-to-mouth when they stood facing each other. Right now, his mouth was cruising its way down her chest to lock onto her nipple with gentle teeth, as she arched her back over his arm. A sigh shivered out of her and she rubbed her hips insistently against his.

"Kye, please," she whispered, reaching for his trousers only to have hands close over her wrists. Big hands. Unfamiliar hands. Her eyes flew open and she stared into Kye's gaze while a big body pressed against her back.

Lowering his head, Kye whispered, "I know him, have for more than half my life. But you don't. And you won't ever have to see him again."

"No," she whispered as those big hands glided up and cupped her breasts, dragging the silk over the nipples, plumping them together, tweaking the hard points. A hard, long cock pressed against her spine and she caught a glimpse of a golden head swooping down to bite her along the side of her neck.

Kye grinned at her, hot and wicked. "No?" he repeated, sliding one hand down, into her wet, hot pussy. "Your little kitty just got wetter, Ash. Really want me to make him leave?"

As he asked, his fingers left her dripping passage and both hands gripped her hips, urging her to turn around and face the man who had been fondling her breasts.

Her eyes stayed stubbornly straight ahead, which had her looking at his chest. It was covered by a nubby Aran sweater in some dark color. The candlelight made it hard to tell, but it was probably navy. That chest stretched the fine wool and rose up and down as he breathed.

One of those big hands came up to cup her face as he dipped his head and covered her mouth with his. Behind her Kye cuddled his cock against her silk covered backside, his hands stroking along her sides and hips as he nuzzled her neck.

The stranger—an anonymous stranger she didn't ever have to see again—seduced her mouth, nipping at her lip, gliding his tongue in to taste her, leaving before she could make up her mind to turn her head or kiss him back.

And he knew how to kiss. Between the two men—her husband and this stranger—her knees buckled and she started to slide, only to have those big hands catch her under the arms, one thigh going between hers to brace her weight with his. Behind her, Kye continued to rock his cock against her butt.

"Am I staying or going?" the stranger asked, his voice deep, rough, with a lyrical accent. *Irish. Oh, damn. He was Irish.*

Finally, *finally,* Ashlyn opened her eyes and looked up at him. He was *gorgeous,* almost too beautiful to be real, with a foxy, narrow face, large, intelligent, hot eyes that almost burned as he returned her stare. High cheekbones, almost hollow cheeks, and a mouth . . . hmmm, what a mouth.

Big broad shoulders strained against the dark wool of his sweater, matched by a broad chest before tapering down to a long narrow torso. Heavy thighs—strong thighs—she knew, remembering how it had felt just seconds ago as she rode one when he caught her weight.

"You got a name?" she asked, her mouth going dry as she stared up at him.

"Connor," he said, his hand stroking and kneading her breast.

"What do you want, Ash," Kye whispered in her ear. "I've known him most of my life. I trust him, with you, with this. He's a good guy, healthy and single. And you won't ever have to see him again." He nudged Connor's hand out of the way and wrapped his arms around her while she stared into the handsome, golden face in front of her. He had light eyes, probably blue and that golden hair fell almost to his shoulders.

Cuddling her against him, Kye said, "Or I'll ask him to leave and I'll let it go. I want to give you this—watch this. But it's your choice. Either way, it's your choice."

"Watch?" she repeated.

A grin tugged at his mouth and he said, "Yeah, watch. Watch you ride him before I take you in the ass. Watch while he plays with your nipples, and sucks on your clit." In a hot, smoky voice, he murmured, "Watch you suck on his cock while I eat you up. Then you can suck on mine and he can see just how good you taste." A hand drifted down, gathering moisture from her folds before bringing it up and painting her lips with his wet fingers.

Then he ate at her mouth, sucking and licking the cream he had rubbed onto her mouth.

"Yeah, I want to watch," he repeated after he lifted his head. "And you want it, too. You're almost ready to come just thinking of it."

Her body was hot, wet, and quaking at the thought of taking them both inside her. Before Kye had introduced her to the pleasure of anal sex, she had never before imagined it. But since he had . . . yeah, she had thought of it, in dark, wicked fantasies she never would have admitted, if Kye hadn't first suggested it over a year ago.

With her hands keeping Kye firmly against her middle, she stepped forward. A small grin curved Connor's mouth, a chiseled mouth that would have put Val Kilmer's to shame. One hand lifted, palm up and waiting. She put hers in it and let him draw her up against him.

While Kye's hands went to take her damp hair down, Connor lifted her hand to his mouth and pressed a kiss to it. "If you change your mind, I will leave," he promised, trying to ease some of the nerves he saw in her eyes. If it had just been nerves, he would have left.

But there were hot little licks of excitement there as well, darkening those eyes in that heart-shaped face. He had been sitting in a chair in the corner of the room—hidden by the shadows—watching as his old friend kissed and stroked his wife.

She was adorable and sexy all at the same time, with her dark hair piled on top of her head, her body covered by the red silk of the robe. Beneath it, he imagined she had a soft, round, woman's body, with full, heavy tits, round hips, a firm but soft ass.

As he lowered her hand, he stepped forward until her soft, scented body was pressed between his and Kye's. Then he dropped to his knees in front of her and tugged apart the edges of the robe that had fallen back to cover her.

Yeah, a woman's body, Connor thought, leaning forward to nuzzle her belly as Kye's hands stroked and kneaded her breasts. This was a first for both of them, as well. Connor had been more than a little shocked when Kye had mentioned this to him on his last trip to the States.

Shocked and intrigued. He had seen pictures of Ashlyn,

and there was something almost catlike about her, something feline in her small, smug smile, about her up-tilted eyes. She was sexy and inviting, and he had wanted her from the minute he had seen her picture.

But she belonged to one of his best friends, one of his oldest friends.

Shocked, intrigued.

Intrigued enough, that he had agreed to something he had never given thought to before.

And now, as his teeth closed over the hot little point of one rosy nipple, he was thanking his lucky stars he had agreed. A sexy little moan escaped her lips and Connor chanced grazing his knuckles over the patch of hair between her soft pale thighs. Drops of moisture were already beading in that downy thatch like pearls.

Her knees buckled and Connor supported her weight as she slid down to straddle his lap.

Kye propped his shoulder against the wooden entertainment center and stared, his cock tight, full, pulsing at he watched Connor bury his hands in her hair and drag her head back, eating at her mouth while his hips surged, pressing his cock against the wet folds between her thighs.

Her hands clutched at his shoulders, and her legs crept around his waist to lock behind his back, opening herself to him, purring when he started to rock and rub his shaft against her.

He kissed his way down her neck and shoulder, across her chest until he could feast on those tight, puckered little nipples. Through the heavy material of his jeans, Connor could feel her, feel how hot she was, how wet she was.

Kye went to his knees behind her, and Connor remembered he wasn't alone with this woman. Remembered the man behind

Ashlyn was her husband and he had more right to be here, that he was the one who was sharing his wife. So he shifted his legs, shifted the panting, hot little bundle in his lap until Kye was once again pressed against her butt. Lifting his head from her wet nipple, Connor met Kye's eyes over her shoulder. "The bed?" he suggested softly, afraid to speak too loudly, to move too suddenly.

Kye nodded and rose, helping Ashlyn to her feet, nuzzling her neck and wrapping his arms around her, fondling her breasts while Connor stood.

Kye eased her onto the bed while Connor stripped, palming a rubber from his pocket and tossing it to the table before joining them. Ashlyn was seated on the side of the bed, her hands busily undoing Kye's shirt while Kye worked the belt and buttons of his trousers. Loathe to do it, Connor settled behind her, letting Kye go back to kissing and suckling his wife's pretty tits while Connor stroked and soothed her shoulders and spine as he cupped her body with his own.

He wanted to be in Kye's place, sucking on those sweet breasts, tracing his hands over her quivering, soft thighs. That is, until she squirmed against him.

From this position, Ashlyn's ass was pressing on his rock-hard cock and she kept squirming against it. He shoved back with a groan, his fingers digging into her hips as he thrust against her, a bead of moisture leaking from the tip of his cock.

They ended up with her straddling his hips as he nuzzled and bit and sucked on those pretty little rose nipples and the heavy white globes of her tits.

Kye's hands buried in her hair and he tugged her away from Connor—pushed her down until she could wrap those full lips around his cock. Connor shifted until he was propped against the headboard, watching as she sucked his friend off, his hand going to his own cock, and stroking it absently as he wished he was the one kneeling there with her in front of him, taking him deep in her throat.

While Kye might have mentioned her doing the same to him, Connor didn't see it happening. She wasn't going to wrap those lips around his cock and take him deep in her mouth. She was too damn skittish, too nervous. And damn if that didn't turn him on even more. She was hot and hungry for this, no doubt of that, which Kye had promised. But she was also jumpy, flicking him nervous little glances, her face flushing each time she looked at him.

Except for now. She was a little preoccupied with nibbling and sucking on her husband's cock, something she was turning into a work of art, from what Connor could tell.

Moments passed and then Kye's body stiffened. He came in her mouth with a groan and she swallowed, lifted her head and kissed his belly before turning her eyes to Connor.

Some of the nerves had left her eyes—now they held heat, and an endearing shyness. Her gaze drifted down to glance at his cock as he stroked it with an easy, sure hand. Her mouth parted and her tongue slid out to wet her lips, her lids drooping while her body started to lean his way. His hand slid up, briefly closing over the fat head of his cock, his thumb catching the moisture there and spreading it around, making the tip gleam.

His eyes closed as he had a visual of her mouth on him, sliding up and down, pausing to lick and suck on his sac. His whole body stiffened at the image and his cock jerked in demand as Connor resisted the urge to guide her mouth down to his aching flesh.

Ashlyn's breathing sped up as she watched Connor's hand

work his cock in sure, unselfconscious strokes. His penis was big, long, and thick, rising from a thatch of golden hair. The smooth head of his shaft was ruddy and gleaming from the pre-come he had spread around, the shaft itself thick and straight. She wanted to feel those hands on her, and suspected he would be just as confident handling her body as he was his own.

Her gaze lifted to study the rest of him, lounging on the bed in all his naked glory. And talk about glory. His shoulders, just as broad as they appeared under his sweater, gave way to a sculpted, muscled chest, naked of any body hair, before tapering down to a narrow waist and flat belly where a fine line of blond hair grew, arrowing down to his cock.

Giving in, she went back to watching what intrigued her the most, his hand on his cock.

She wanted to taste him, she admitted to herself, licking her lips.

Glancing at Kye, she shifted and lay down on her stomach between Connor's thighs, turning her body so that Kye could stroke and caress, guiding his hands to the wet curls that covered her mound, moisture from her body gleaming like pearls on the short curly strands of her hair.

Then she turned her attention back to Connor, her attention and her mouth. He bucked in surprise when her lips lowered and engulfed half his cock in one swallow. "Aw, fuck," he gasped, one hand going to tangle in her hair, his eyes staring down in dazed delight as she slid her lips up and down his cock, one hand wrapping around the base, while the other stroked his balls. He held up her long curled locks of hair, staring at her profile, shuddering as he watched her take him in again, her lashes a dark fan against her ivory cheeks. Her mouth, swollen and red, slid wetly over his shaft and she paused at the head to nibble and swirl her tongue around him.

She glanced at him before turning her attention back to the task at hand. Kye stroked her clit, shifting her lower body so that she could open her thighs for him. Then he hardened his tongue and stabbed inside her waiting vagina, drinking down the musky cream before using his teeth on the hard little bud just atop her slit.

And Connor had a front-row seat. His gaze tracked back and forth between what she was doing with her mouth and what Kye was doing with his. He watched, noting what had her hips rolling forward, what had her strangling a gasp while she deep throated his cock. Her breath caught and Connor felt it as it drew his length just the slightest bit deeper into her mouth before she pulled off and threw back her head, gasping and climaxing with a weak little cry when Kye started to thrust two fingers back and forth inside her, twisting his wrist slowly as he entered her, rotating it back as he pulled out.

He watched and ached, and remembered, because he was next. Connor wasn't leaving now, wasn't leaving this room without tasting everything this hot little woman had to offer.

Between her very talented mouth and the very hot show, Connor lost control and came inside her mouth, groaning as she swallowed his cock and his semen down before her head fell onto his thigh and she stiffened and bucked her hips as a second climax rolled through her.

"My turn," he muttered as Kye moved away. Without a glance at the dark-haired man, he lay between Ashlyn's quivering thighs, cupped her ass in his hands and lowered his head. Still shaking, still sensitized from Kye's hands and mouth, she shrieked when Connor drew his tongue up the wet slit, lapping up the moisture from her climax, closing his eyes and savoring it.

Kye rolled to his side, lying crossways so that he could put his mouth to work on her torso but still watch everything.

Connor paused, raising his head to stare up at Kye, his pale eyes going dark with lust, with need. "She tastes like heaven," he muttered, his mouth wet and gleaming.

"Eat her up," Kye offered. "You won't have this chance again."

Ashlyn's face flushed with embarrassment—with pleasure—before she sank her teeth into her lower lip as Connor did just that, eating her up with greedy, thorough strokes of his tongue. He stabbed repeatedly at her wet aching cleft with his stiffened tongue, rotating his thumb against her clit until her hips rose and fell against him. Shifting a little, he nibbled and sucked on her clit, rubbing his tongue in circular motions against the hard bead of flesh.

Kye bit and sucked hard on her nipples, lifting his head he replaced his tongue with his hand so he could watch as she exploded again. A pleased smile curved his mouth as she fell apart beneath his hands, beneath Connor's mouth. He had given her this, he thought, quite pleased. That dazed, blind look in her pretty eyes—the flush that tinted her face and torso a faint rose—her heaving breasts as she gasped for breath. He had given her that. Her lids lifted and she stared at him with hazy, hot eyes as a pleased little purr fell from her lips.

And they were just getting started.

He stilled his fingers, turned them to soothing strokes as her breath shuddered out of her lungs. When Connor lowered his head, ready to burrow his tongue back inside her wet folds, Kye stopped him, holding him back with a hand on his big hard shoulder.

"We've got all night," Kye said mildly when Connor snarled at him.

But only tonight, Connor thought darkly. *At least for me.*

He wanted her, his friend's wife, for his own, and he wasn't certain if one night was going to be enough. "Y'got the rest of your damned life, mate. I've only tonight." But he shifted, coming to lie down on the other side of her, his cock stiff as a pike and eager to slide inside that hot little pussy.

Ashlyn's lids fluttered open and she stared at the dark, handsome face of her husband, into his beautiful dark eyes, at his high cheekbones—a gift from his Native American blood—at the black hair that fell straight as rain to just above his shoulders. "I love you," she said thickly, cupping his face in one palm.

Connor's gaze fell away, well aware of his intrusion, as Kye lowered his head and bussed her mouth gently, lovingly, as he murmured his own love. The jealousy that curled in Connor's gut startled him, enough that he almost got up and walked away. God, he wanted that—that connection, that certainty that your love was returned.

Feeling isolated, and slightly shamed, he started to move away when her hands caught his.

Ashlyn rolled to her knees, stroking her hand down the length of his torso, her eyes meeting his for a long moment before returning her gaze to Kye. "He's right; we only have tonight and I don't want to waste a second of it."

She shifted to straddle his thighs, catching Connor's cock in her hand as Kye came to cuddle against her back. He had retrieved a tube of lube at some point and she felt his movements as he spread it across his cock, smeared it between the cheeks of her ass as he stroked her, guided her into position over Connor's hips.

He was bigger than Kye, which was no surprise, being as he was close to a foot taller. His cock was longer, and thicker, and she eyed him a little nervously as he guided it inside her. The fat head stretched her tightly and she bit her lip and hesitantly started to work his shaft into her body. His hands came up to grip her hips and he rocked and thrust his way inside. She fell forward bracing her elbows beside his head, positioning her ass for Kye as Connor rolled his hips, burying his cock to the hilt.

She shuddered, moaned. He moved his hips in tiny little thrusts, so that the head of his cock rubbed against the mouth of her womb. With a shift of his thighs, he opened her further for Kye's penetration.

Kye pressed against the tiny rose hole, barely brushing it for now, waiting until it started to spasm. "Make her come," he told Connor. "I'm not fucking her ass until you have her moaning."

Connor stared up into the heart shaped face just inches from his. Her eyes were glazed, pupils dilated. "She's ready now," he said softly, continuing to roll his hips against hers, loving the little flutters and ripples as her body worked to accommodate his.

"Make her come." Kye pressed his thumb against the rosette, smiling as she moaned hoarsely. "She's close." He reached between her thighs with his other hand, reaching around where Connor had entered her until he could press against the hard little knot of her clit.

Connor used his hands to lift her a little higher, well aware of what Kye was doing while Connor's cock eased in and out of Ashlyn's tight little sheath, knew Kye was stroking and plucking her clit. He could feel it as he pushed back into her creamy warmth and couldn't help but be startled at how erotic it was to fuck a woman while another man played with her body.

"Ashlyn," he whispered, hoarsely. He wanted her to see *him* when she came, wanted her know he was the one inside her.

Her eyes met his—blindly, a little dazed—and he groaned when she lowered her sweet little mouth and kissed him. The tastes of each other's body lingered in their mouths and she whimpered as he bit her lower lip. Then he grasped her hips, pulled out, and drove into the heart of her.

Again . . . again—faster and harder—until she shattered above him with a hoarse little scream, bearing down on him while her vaginal walls milked him, dragging him much closer to orgasm than he was ready for.

Kye braced her hips and eased inside her anus as she rode the wave of the orgasm, feeling her flutter around him, the ripples from her belly echoing through the tight little sphincter so that he felt it as surely as she did.

"Easy," Kye crooned when she instinctively flinched away from the double penetration. "Easy, baby."

Still shaking from the orgasm, she collapsed on Connor's chest, staring up into his hard face, a will of iron keeping his body still as Kye worked his own cock inside her. Connor could feel it, could feel Kye's cock through the thin wall of flesh that separated them, felt her tighten around him as Kye started to work his cock in with slow, tiny thrusts and Connor couldn't help but wonder. "Does it hurt?" he asked roughly, reaching up to stroke her cheek. Over her shoulder and back, he could see the curve of her ass high in the air, held in place by her stiffened knees.

Kye was working his cock in slowly, waiting for her to accommodate him before easing further inside. She was stretched taut around Connor's shaft and the muscles of her anus were tighter than normal, fighting his slow intrusion.

The reddened flesh of her rosette stretched tightly around his cock and he groaned as he got past the tight ring of muscle there, gripping his flesh like hot, warm living silk. She whimpered deeply in her throat, a tiny pain-filled sound and he felt her body's slight, instinctive recoil from his possession. She had done that a number of times when they had first started this kind of sex play and he suspected it was hurting her a little.

But she was so wet, the cream from her vagina was apparent even to Kye. He could feel it, smell how hot and eager she was. The air was perfumed by the scent of her lust, so he continued to thrust inside with tiny, forward motions.

"A little. At first, but then . . . her eyes fluttered closed and she flinched as Kye seated himself inside her ass, all the way down to the base.

"It's hurting her," Connor said, starting to pull out. "Back off."

"She likes it," Kye muttered, holding his position. "Ashlyn, do you want me to stop?"

"Don't you dare," she hissed, lifting her head to glare at him over her shoulder. Then she turned to look at Connor. "It always hurts, at first. Just a little." She rolled her hips as best as she could with Kye stuffed inside her ass and Connor buried inside her pussy all the way to the womb. She'd never felt so tight, so unbelievably full.

Something caught her eye, and she glanced sideways. Saw the unopened rubber on the bedside table. Her hesitation was minimal. And then she turned back, feeling Connor inside her, skin to skin, his cock snug against her vaginal walls.

"Feel good, Ashlyn?" Kye purred, rolling his hips against her, smiling as it sent a shiver quaking down her spine.

"Kye . . . Kye, please." She arched back, pushing against him. Ashlyn cried out when he pulled back, teasingly, keeping her from taking his entire length back inside. "Damn it, Kye, stop playing with me and fuck me!"

"Are you ready?" he asked, timing his slow thrust to match Connor's. It was enough to have him coming on the spot as he drove back inside her, feeling Connor's cock as it left her dripping pussy. Then as Kye pulled out he could feel Connor driving back in, the sensation sending a shudder down his spine.

Connor raised his head and he set his teeth in the curve of her throat, using that grip to hold her still while he slid inside the tight clasp of her body.

"Please," she gasped, rolling her head to the other side, giving better access as Connor continued to hold her flesh in the grip of his strong, even teeth.

Kye planted his knees and started to ride her, shuttling in and out of her ass, hard, slow, and deep. Connor released her neck when she started to lift her head—staring up into her heavy-lidded eyes, watching as her tongue darted out to lick at her lips.

"Connor, will you . . ." Her cheeks flushed and her eyes dropped away. Her whole body quivered.

"Fuck her, Connor," Kye finished for her as the ability to speak clearly left her. "That's what she wants."

"Ashlyn—"

"Connor, please," she gasped, twisting, trying to ride his cock, but unable to move well with Kye digging his cock into her ass.

"Want me to fuck you?" he asked, the words falling from his mouth in that lyrical accent, so that it sounded like poetry. Maybe he wanted to tease her a little, but he also wanted to make sure this wasn't hurting her. "You're so tight, so tiny. Are ya certain, now, you want me to fuck you?"

"Yeah," she panted. "Fuck me," she pleaded, feeling a climax just beyond her reach.

She was stuffed so full of cock—both front and back—she

couldn't possibly reach down to stroke her clit, couldn't help bring the climax any closer. "As my lady wishes," Connor purred, quite satisfied that it would be his face she saw when she found the climax she was so obviously seeking. "Just let me look at you while I do it. I like the look of you."

She kept her eyes trained on his as Kye and Connor started to move in tandem, a reverse echo of the other's movements. Kye would fill her as Connor retreated, then Connor would thrust into her wet passage as Kye pulled back outside the tight grip of her ass.

"You're so pretty," Connor crooned, his voice low and gruff, as he pumped and rolled his cock in and out of her body. "I want another taste of you, Ash."

Kye chuckled breathlessly as he rode her ass, filling her, leaving, then filling her up again. "Con, my friend, we should have made a souvenir video of this. Then you could see it from my view.

"Her ass feels like silk when you're inside it. She's so tight around me, you have to . . . aw, damn . . . so tight, you have to work it in slowly or it hurts her too much. Then you're inside and she's tight and soft and hotter than hell. You'd fill her so full, she'd probably taste your come in her throat."

Ashlyn was beyond speech, whimpering mindlessly, rubbing her nipples against Connor's broad chest, as he fucked her pussy and Kye fucked her ass. Connor's hand joined Kye's on her butt, pulling the flesh apart, holding her completely open as they rode her hard.

It hit her like a monsoon, knocking the breath from her, and sizzling through her body like an electric shock. Both her anal and vaginal muscles locked down on the invading flesh.

Kye groaned and went off inside her, pumping her ass full of semen, filling her in hot, wet jets.

The orgasm took Connor by surprise. He'd been determined to make it last, to draw it out, but her vagina had viced down on him and tore it from him before he realized it was happening. He bellowed beneath her, closing his hands on her thighs and flooding her with a hot gush, plunging repeatedly into the hot, tight depths of her vagina.

Kye collapsed against her, his weight bearing her down harder on Connor while the climax dragged on, tearing through him almost viciously. As their weight settled on Connor, he guided her body to the side so that she was cuddled against his torso, and spooned from behind by Kye.

"Oh, shit," Ashlyn mumbled after long minutes had passed. Her own fluids and their semen trickled down to dry on her thighs as she shifted, slowly sitting, then turning so that Kye's body cupped hers, propping her up.

Looking down at herself, and then at her two partners, she said, "We need a bath."

Connor remained sprawled on the bed, tempted to leave, unable to do so. Kye and his wife had retreated to the bathroom while he stayed where he was, fighting down the jealousy that was eating his gut.

She wasn't his.

She wasn't ever going to be his.

That hot, wild woman with the shy eyes and clever mouth would never be his.

And until tonight, he hadn't realized that she was what had been missing from his life. Until tonight, he hadn't realized that anything had been missing.

As the shower turned off, he rolled to his side. Spying his jeans, he grabbed them and tugged them on moments before the door opened and Kye and Ashlyn tumbled out—wrapped in the heavy cotton hotel robes—giggling like teenagers. He left them open, his soft cock uncovered and still damp from her as he strode past them, determined to shower and get the hell out.

When he stepped from the shower, Ashlyn was waiting for him, Kye standing behind her, watching her with hot eyes as she dropped to her knees in front of Connor.

"How can you share her like this? She's your wife. Does it not bother you, to see her doing this to another man?"

Kye met his eyes as Ashlyn took his cock into her very talented mouth.

Slowly, his mouth curled up in a smile and he shrugged, saying, "I'm giving her a fantasy, something she's dreamed of but would never ask for on her own." The answer was the same as it had been when Kye had first presented the idea that had been brewing in the back of his mind, the same one he had given to Connor as Connor stared at him as if he had lost his mind.

Wrapping his hand in her wet hair, he braced his back against the tiled wall. Groaning with pleasure as she deep throated him, shuddering when she pulled away to nuzzle and lick at his balls.

His head fell back against the tile, but he kept his eyes open, watching their reflections in triplicate from the mirrored walls. He could see the curve of her ass as she serviced him. With a flick of his eyes, he could see her face in profile, see as her lips slid down his cock. She paused as she came to the head and swirled her tongue over it, nibbling gently before taking his length inside her mouth again.

From the doorway, Kye watched before coming up behind Ashlyn, kneeling down, sliding his hand between her legs to fondle and play as she fondled Connor's heavy, hard penis.

She paused when she felt Kye's familiar hands stroking over her, paused and lifted her head, turning her body and catching his mouth with hers. Connor dropped to his knees behind her while she kissed Kye and ran her hands down the darker man's rib-cage to grip his ass while she lowered her head to his groin and took his waiting cock in her mouth.

Staring down at her ass, thrust high in the air, Connor saw why Kye had wanted this position. The tight little hole of her ass beckoned. Her vagina had been made for that kind of penetration, yet she gloved him so tightly. What would it feel like to have the puckered little rosette open up and take him?

He knelt behind her and bumped his cock against her ass, brushing and stroking. Ashlyn's body quivered and a whimper fell from her lips as she paused to bite delicately at Kye's balls. Connor repeated the motion, smiling when she quivered again. Every brush, every press against her anus made her moan and shake.

"I've made her come just by doing that," Kye said roughly, panting, taking her head between his hands and holding her still so he could plunge his cock in and out of her mouth at his pace, which grew frantic in mere seconds.

A muffled groan escaped her as Kye flooded her throat with hot jets of come, and Connor continued to rub his cock tauntingly against her ass. "Damn it, baby, I think you're going to empty me before the night is over," he muttered as she sucked on him like a straw, drawing the last few drops of fluid from him.

Kye eyed Connor over the naked expanse of her back, one black brow raised. Guiding her back up, he pressed a kiss to Ashlyn's mouth, and rose, easing her body back against Connor's before he left the room. "Are you enjoying your fantasy, Ashlyn?" he murmured, rocking against her butt, stroking his hands over her sides, her thighs, to graze over the wet curls before cupping her breasts and rolling her nipples between his thumbs.

She swallowed, savoring the taste of Kye's come in her mouth before she rolled her eyes to meet Connor's. "Hell, yes," she answered, her voice ragged and hoarse. Kye returned, watching as Connor palmed her breasts, rubbing his cock against her ass, eyes narrowed in pleasure—in need. He joined them, catching her face in his dark, work-roughened hands and plundering her mouth.

Her head fell back with a sigh of surrender as he moved from her mouth to kiss and nip along the cord of her neck. "How sore are you?" he asked softly, lifting his head to look at her.

"Just a little," she replied, relaxed against Connor's chest, amazed at how easy, how natural it felt to be with these two men—together. Rolling her head on his shoulder, she pressed a kiss to Connor's neck, straining to brush her mouth against his jaw. His wet, golden hair fell across her face and neck when he lowered his head to meet her lips, kissing her with a startling hunger.

Kye leaned closer, whispering in her ear while Connor ate at her mouth like a man starved. "Think you can take another round?" Kye asked. Lowering his hand until he could circle his thumb around her clit. "I think Connor's wanting to switch around."

She tensed, pulling her mouth from Connor's to look at Kye. But he knew her well and cut off her hesitancy simply by rubbing her just the right way, sending her mind spiraling out of her body. Just a glide of his finger inside her wet vagina, a pass of his thumb over her swollen, throbbing clit while Connor rocked against her bottom.

"Just go slow," Kye told Connor, pulling Ashlyn up until she was straddling his hips. "She'll tell you if it's too much. She'll tell you how to do it."

"*She* hasn't told me she wants to do it," Connor growled as Kye offered him the lube he had used earlier.

"If *she* didn't want to try," Ashlyn interrupted sardonically, "*She* wouldn't still be in here." She took Kye inside in one quick thrust, a little hum of pleasure escaping her. "Do what you were just doing, put some lube on and I'll do the rest. I'll do it this time."

Connor hesitated, but he slowly took the tube of lubricant, squeezing it into his palm and smearing it over his cock until it gleamed under the bright lights. He squirted more into his hand so he could coat her anus with it, eased the tip of his finger inside her hole, preparing the tight ring of muscle there for his entry. She pressed her brow against Kye's, looped her arms around his neck and waited until she felt the broad head of Connor's penis press against her ass. Kye continued to roll and thrust inside her, pressing his thumb against her clit and whispering in her ear, "You're so tight, so sweet. When he gets inside your ass, he won't ever want to leave. Heaven knows, I never want to."

He continued to croon into her ear, distracting her with words and his shaft so she wouldn't get apprehensive about what was to come. He knew she was usually a little sore after anal sex, and suspected that taking Connor's cock inside wasn't going to be quite as easy as taking his.

Connor was taller than Kye, bigger, and it took a few moments and some shifts in position before she could take both of them. She started taking little increments of Connor's shaft as Kye rolled and flexed his hips, rocking his own cock inside her slowly, using his thumb to circle over her clit in slow, teasing circles.

At first, all she did was bump her anus against the head of his cock, while he used his hand to hold it steady. And then she started to slide herself down on him. Kye's hands came up to grip the cheeks of her ass, opening her as she slid down a fraction, working the head of Connor's cock into the tight little rosette.

Connor's breath was dragging out of his lungs, a fine sweat coating his body as she took him. Slowly. So damned slowly he thought he would die before she got him in. When she had him half-way seated inside, she gave a short little scream of frustration. "Damn it, I can't—" she panted shifting, twisting, trying to get in a better position.

"Pull out, Kye," Connor ordered, bracing her weight by putting his hands under her thighs. As soon as Kye withdrew, he rose, holding her weight, holding her half impaled on his cock.

Moments later, he pressed his back to the wall and spread his thighs wide, keeping her cunt low enough so that Kye could resume his position. Ashlyn hung helplessly with Connor half impaling her on his cock, her wide-spread legs opening her wet folds.

Connor could see it in the mirror and he lowered his head to purr in her ear, "I've never seen a woman so ready to be fucked, never in m'life." His accent had thickened as the lust consumed him. "Aw, darlin' girl, aren't you a sight?" He held her weight easily with his body, staring at the reflection until her gaze met his.

Kye hesitated, his attention caught by what he was seeing—Connor's big hands supporting Ashlyn's thighs, holding her up just with his grasp, leaving her wet and open, small drops of her cream seeping from her body, the lips of her sex red and swollen. Her breasts were heaving as she gasped for air, her nipples puckered tight and hard. After taking a long moment to enjoy the picture, he enthusiastically took his position, burying himself into her hot, silky little sheath with one hard thrust. Sandwiched between them, unable to move, Ashlyn whimpered as Kye filled her repeatedly. Connor stayed stubbornly still, holding himself back.

"Do it," she whimpered, trying to twist away from his restraining hands so she could work herself down further on the hard length of him.

"I don't want to hurt you," he muttered, shuddering from restraint. It wasn't easy. Fuck, he could feel it as Kye rode her, feel it as he pummeled her hips, and drove his cock inside her. There was a maddening brush against his sac every time Kye drove in as Kye's balls bumped his. Each thrust caused her body to tighten around Connor and he knew he was going to go mad and lose it right there.

"I want you," she whispered her head falling back against his shoulder as Kye's head ducked, his teeth catching a nipple and biting down hard enough to hurt—hard enough to leave a faint mark around the skin of her nipple. And she gloried in it. "All the . . . way . . . inside," she panted. "Just fuck me . . . okay?"

With a roar, he used his hands and drove her down until he was fully seated inside her snug, hot, tight little ass, causing her to shriek and writhe helplessly in his arms.

It was different from being inside her pussy, tighter, the skin seeming smoother, almost softer somehow. Definitely hotter.

He found his rhythm and matched it to Kye's so that she was being fucked simultaneously, as she had been earlier in the bed. They pressed her between them and fucked her endlessly, mercilessly.

His control flew out the window as her muscles rippled around him, working to accommodate him. And he forgot Kye's words, *"Just take it slow."*

He took her fast—hard and fast—the first orgasm tearing from him before either Kye or Ashlyn had reached their peak. As he spewed inside her hot little hole, he kept pumping in and out, his cock still as hard as it had been when he began.

God, he'd had some good fucks before, some good nights when he'd spent most of the time screwing, but never like this. Never needed a woman as desperately as he needed this one.

He felt like he was digging his cock into hot, wet, rich, *living* silk that moaned and responded to his every thrust. So good, so unbelievably good.

A keening moan fell from her lips and she whimpered. Some part of his brain whispered that he was hurting her, had to be hurting her, but Connor really didn't give a damn. She was coming now, clenching around them in tight, hot little pulses that set Kye off. Kye climaxed inside her with a groan— pressed in to the hilt—letting her milk his orgasm from him.

But when Kye pulled away, Connor didn't stop, he bore her to the floor—to her knees—and continued to fuck her ass, dragging another one of those keening moans from her.

Kye sagged to his knees in front of them and Connor wrapped his hand in Ashlyn's hair, dragging her head up and forcing her face to Kye's softening cock. "Suck him off, little girl. Make him hard again, make him come. Now, it's my turn to be watching," Connor ordered, shoving her head up and down as she opened her mouth to take Kye's soft, wet penis inside.

Kye stared at Connor with wary eyes—at the animalistic need that was written naked on his face—but Connor didn't even notice as he watched her head start moving in rhythm with his hard, pounding thrusts. He had lost himself inside her body before, knew how easy it was for him to do so, but apparently she had caused his civilized friend to lose a little bit of himself as well.

Connor kept going until he pulled another climax from her—until she had licked all her cream from Kye's now pulsating cock—until another climax started to tighten her body. He could recognize the signs now. Her muscles would start to flutter around him in little seizures that gradually grew in strength.

"It's too much," she whispered, lifting her head from Kye. "Too much, damn it. Can't take any more."

"You will," Kye said, shoving his cock back inside her mouth. "You want it." It was written all over her, there in her flushed face, in the tight, beaded nipples, in the submissive way she held her ass for Connor's deep penetration. His own balls drew tight against his body as he watched that long, hard dick ride her ass, as he watched her plump, swollen lips close over his cock before she tried to turn her head aside.

But the hand fisted in her hair wouldn't allow it. Kye took over, gripping her head as he had earlier until he was fucking her mouth as surely, as ferociously, as desperately as Connor screwed her ass.

When she started to come this time, Connor planted himself inside to the balls and refused to move until the quivers stopped. "You aren't coming yet. There's more," he purred, stroking the white mounds of her ass, leaning over to lick a wet path up her spine.

She started to pull her mouth from Kye to curse at him, but Kye grinned—just a little evilly—and clamped his hands on her head, refusing to let her stop. "Keep at it, baby," he said, meeting Connor's eyes over her naked back. "Suck me. Suck me

off. I want you to; I want to shove my cock down your throat
and come while he butt fucks you."

Connor still refused to move, watching instead, concentrating on watching as she deep throated Kye—as she paused
to nibble on the head of his cock before sliding her mouth
down the length of him.

After a time, Connor started to thrust again, pulling out
and burrowing back in, using long, slow strokes that had her
writhing around him. Each time her head started to slow,
Connor would stop.

Taking pity, Kye took over, fucking her mouth—filling her
mouth and throat with his cock so she could stay still. It was too
much for her to suck on him with Connor buried in her ass.

He was big, and he was hurting her in a delicious sort of
way, so that each time he retreated she followed with her ass
until his big hands forced her to be still. He lowered his chest
until he was cuddling against her body, so he could whisper in
her ear, "You've had your fantasy, Ash. Now we'll have ours."
His voice was a low, purring rumble in her ear. "He wants to
watch me take you like this, while he shoves himself down
your lovely little throat. And I want to fuck you like this, in
your hot little ass until you come again and again, until you
can't even remember your name," he finished, watching while
Kye pumped in and out of her mouth. Her eyes rolled to
stare into his and Kye grabbed her hair, turning her gaze—her
attention—back to him.

Kye's cock in her mouth was a familiar, well-enjoyed thing.
She knew how to drag out his orgasm, knew how to make it
short and quick.

But the men weren't letting her do it her way. They controlled her with their hands, with their bodies, until she could
only do what they wanted.

And she liked it.

She wasn't submissive, but she gloried at being controlled in this manner. A strong, confident woman in the outside world, she should have been shocked at how much she enjoyed them ordering and controlling her body—taking their pleasure—while withholding hers.

But she reveled in it. Reveled in how Connor's fingers dug into her hips when she tried to ride his shaft—reveled in how Kye's hands tightened in her hair in warning when she tried to turn her head from his pulsating cock—reveled in how Connor filled her with hard, fierce digs of his huge cock.

Holding her at his mercy, Connor reamed her ass hard, taking a dark pleasure when she flinched a little at his near-brutal assault on her anus. "Such a good little fuck," he murmured, bending over to whisper praise into her ear. "So tight, so hot. Would you like to come now?"

She nodded as best she could while Kye forced her to take his cock all the way in, until her mouth could touch where his shaft joined his body. She started to gag and tried to relax her throat so he could do it again.

"What do ya think, mate?" Connor asked, his voice rough and tight as he watched how her anus would narrow when he pulled almost all the way out—the way it would stretch open around him when he drove his cock all the way in. "Should we let her come?"

Kye grinned, and said, "Might as well. The sooner she recovers, the sooner we can start again."

Again? She thought helplessly as Connor continued to ride her hard and rough, with none of the gentle hesitancy he had shown at first. Could she possibly take this again?

Hell, yes.

Connor shoved her hips down lower so he could bury his

cock inside her anus in hard, deep thrusts, grabbing her hand and forcing it down until she could fondle her swollen clit. "Go ahead, Ash. Play with it." He shifted a little higher and pulled out—all the way—watching as her anus closed completely, then driving all the way back in and shouting out a ragged, "Aw, fuck," as she opened back up to take him eagerly—the pink hole widening and accepting him, closing around him like an eager little mouth to eat up his heavy, surging cock.

She screamed around Kye's cock, mingled pleasure and pain clawing through her. "Want it harder?" Kye asked, feeling what it had done to her. "Fuck her harder, Connor." The words left him in a series of rough pants as he did the same, fucking her mouth harder than he ever had before. He could feel her throat close around him, trying to reject his invading shaft and it felt like glory.

Ashlyn didn't want it harder—it already was too much—but she couldn't say anything because Kye's hands held her head trapped, and his cock filled her mouth so that she couldn't speak.

Stop it, please, ohdamnit'stoo MUCH! Ithurtsithurts—

And Connor took her harder—harder and harder and harder—until she started to come. Long, vicious spasms filled her belly, spiraling outward until she could barely breathe around the cock in her mouth.

And as her orgasm hit this time, it knocked her out, sending her flying off into the blackness while both men started jetting off inside her at the same time.

They took her into the large, enclosed shower—both of them—cleaning her bruised, aching body with gentle hands. After cleaning the come and small traces of blood from her thighs and buttocks, Connor went to his knees in front of her, gripping her ass tenderly with his hands as he opened her swollen folds with easy strokes of his tongue.

Kye took her breasts, soaping her nipples and rinsing them clean before taking first one and then the other in his mouth.

There was no way she could come again, she thought cloudily.

No earthly way.

But they did it.

There in the shower and again on the bed, first with her straddling Kye while Connor watched. And then with Connor putting her beneath him and easing his way inside her swollen tight pussy.

This time with Connor it lasted nearly an hour—with him taking exquisite care, coaxing tiny little orgasms from her exhausted body before bringing her to a larger, mind shattering one as he flooded her body with his hot semen—as Kye watched from inches way, stroking his cock until his own climax erupted and come trickled down his cock and belly.

Connor collapsed to lay his head between her heaving breasts, staring at Kye with dull eyes. "Once I regain feeling from the neck down, I'll be moving," he said tiredly, feeling utterly drained, utterly spent.

Ashlyn hummed, a low thrumming purr deep in her throat, squirming out from under him until she could cuddle against his side, one arm draped low over his back. Kye pressed up against her from behind, his arm hooking over her hips. "No," she said simply, rubbing her cheek against his bare shoulder.

"No."

Kye pressed a kiss to her tangled hair, adding his weight to hers.

"Sleep," she muttered.

Connor laughed and said, "I've not the life for anything else, darlin'."

Within seconds, they all slept.

When she woke in the morning, Kye still slept beside her.

But Connor was gone.

3   *Three Years Later*

TEARS BURNED HOTLY in her throat as she stared at the coffin covered with flowers.

Kye was gone, killed by some mother-fucking, drunk-driving bastard as he walked to his car one night after work.

He had held on until she had gotten to his side, held on until he could stare up into her face, and hear her tell him she loved him one last time.

He had mouthed the words back to her, the unbearable pain from his battered body darkening his eyes to black. The lids of his eyes had drifted closed, and in despair, she fell against the bed.

". . . don't cry. Please, don't," he had whispered. "Love you, baby. God, always loved you. Don't cry. Don't cry. Love you." The words had fallen from his mouth in a hoarse plea while his face spasmed in agony.

And then he was gone, the internal injuries so severe death had been a blessing. His spine had been shattered from the waist down by the impact, and the internal bleeding had been massive.

Yeah, the death had been a blessing for him. The nurse inside of her knew that. He had been in agony and none of the morphine or Demerol or various other opiates they had pumped into him had touched it.

And for her, she supposed. That's what the logical part of her mind knew and accepted. She never could have watched him suffer through it. Each spasm that had gripped him had ripped through her as well. But the other part, the part that was only complete after she had found Kye, that part despaired. The ever-present tears burned her eyes, but she stubbornly refused to let them fall. If she started to cry, she wasn't sure she'd be able to stop.

He was gone.

"Ashlyn."

She whirled at the familiar lyrical accent. God knows, she had heard it often enough in the past three years. Just about every other time she tumbled into dreams with Kye's arms wrapped around her.

That voice, the one she had heard only one night, was almost as familiar to her as Kye's had been.

He stood behind her, his handsome, almost angelic face ravaged with grief. But he met her eyes squarely. "I came as soon as I heard," he said gruffly, moving up to touch his hand to the smooth metal of the coffin. "But if you aren't wanting me here, I will go."

"No. He was your friend, and you were his. I . . . I'm not ashamed of what happened. I think maybe I expected to be. But that's neither here nor there," she said, her voice hoarse and rough from all the tears she had shed.

Brokenly, she whispered, "He killed him, Connor. He took my beautiful Kye from me, destroyed his body, smashed him into pieces. And he sits in a jail, alive and well. And Kye is in . . . *there.*"

"*Oh, God, I can't take it,*" she moaned, starting to fall to her knees, one hand pressed to her mouth.

Connor caught her against him and eased her to the floor, thanking God that Kye was still in the private viewing room. His own throat was knotted shut with grief. He'd never see his childhood friend again—never see the laughing, smiling man who had loved his wife enough to give her a fantasy most women would never have.

Never see him again—never hear him laugh and tell a dirty joke.

Ashlyn sobbed in his arms while he rocked her body back and forth, stroking one hand down her black, silk covered back.

He'd have the bastard's bloody balls on a pike—that was certain.

Nothing would ever bring Kye back, but the bastard would have to pay. And five fucking years for manslaughter weren't enough. A friend of his, an American lawyer, had told him in disgust that five years was sometimes optimistic for vehicular manslaughter.

Some sort of justice could be found, or bought, with enough money. Christ knew, he had more than plenty.

But he wasn't sure what to do for the woman who cried in his arms, her heart breaking.

Wasn't sure what to do for himself—he hadn't even had a chance to tell Kye good-bye.

Or tell him he was sorry for how he had pulled back. Or explained why.

Of course, the bloody bastard probably knew.

Knew that Connor had fallen head over heels in love, in lust with his wife that night.

It was too late. Too late to tell him anything.

Staring in stony silence at that flower-covered coffin, Connor rocked the grieving woman in his arms, back and forth, stroking his hand up and down her back, rubbing his cheek against her soft dark hair.

"Who called you?"

"Da. My father. You knew, didn't you, that Kye's father was Irish? Moved here after he met Kye's mother?"

"Yeah, I knew," she said, taking the handkerchief he offered to wipe her eyes and blow her nose. Clutching the expensive silk in her hand, she settled back against him.

"Jacob called Da, and Da called me. I found out last night and spent the entire night in the air over the Atlantic."

"I found your number in his book. At least, I figured it was yours. I called, but some lady who sounded like Mrs. Doubtfire told me you were unavailable. I didn't want somebody else telling you."

"Da found me. They loved him too, Ma's heartbroken. They will be out here in the morning, I'm thinking." He paused, pressed his lips together until he was fairly certain he could go on without crying himself. "When will they lay him to rest?"

"Day after tomorrow," she said, swallowing the knot in her throat. *Rest? He was thirty-three years old. It's not time for him to rest,* she thought dully. "How am I going to live the rest of my life without him there, Connor? There's a part of me missing now, and it's in that coffin with him. How am I going to do this?"

Catching her face, he turned her until he could stare into those soft hazel eyes that had haunted him. "By remembering the last thing he'd want for you is to lay down and join him in the grave," he told her honestly. "Is that what you think he wants you to do?"

"He doesn't want anything from me. He can't. He's gone," she bit off, stiffening and jerking away from him, rising to her feet.

"He's not. He's just not here any longer," Connor disagreed, surging easily to his feet to stare at her while she paced the room in long, angry strides. "We're Irish—Kye and me—both of us believe in something beyond death. Don't you?"

She stopped and stared at the coffin. "I don't know. I think I used to."

"Even if there is nothing else, nothing beyond the life we have now, do you think Kye would be pleased to hear you saying you can't go on without him? Do you think he would want that?"

When she didn't answer, Connor said, "I know he wouldn't. So what you do is, take it one day at a time." Slowly, unsure of his welcome, he moved until he could lay his hand on her shoulder, rubbing it in gentle soothing strokes. "And the pain will ease. You will find a life beyond him."

She shuddered, her head slumping down. "I miss him, Connor. He hasn't even been gone a damn week and I can feel it inside me, that hole that being with him filled. It's empty," she said, her voice breaking. *"I'm empty."*

"I know. I miss him, too."

∞

It was hell, being dead.

If it had been just . . . nothingness, it wouldn't suck so bad.

If he hadn't been able to hear, see, smell. Remember.

The pain had been indescribable. But he'd rather face that again, than what he was facing now.

He couldn't move beyond her.

And she was breaking his heart.

Kye watched impotently as Ashlyn sobbed herself to sleep. Again.

He had watched as his coffin was lowered into the ground—

watched as Connor had driven Ashlyn home—as he led her to the bedroom and urged her to rest.

He had watched as she lay there crying silently so Connor wouldn't know she was awake, and hurting.

And now, he was stuck there. Watching. Again.

"Ashlyn, please stop," he murmured, pounding his head against the barrier that stood between them. The one that allowed him to see, hear and smell her, but kept him from reaching out and touching her.

Touching anything.

And he was stuck here, unable to go away, unable to go on to whatever happened after death. He had always believed in heaven, but being stuck in this limbo made him wonder.

She continued to cry, her face buried in a pillow, muffling her sobs.

The fury exploded through Kye and he punched against the barrier, roaring as the rage coursed through him. Over and over, until his hand hurt and throbbed and his throat was hoarse from yelling.

You could feel pain after death.

And then he sagged, limp and exhausted, until he knelt on the floor, his brow pressed against the barrier. "Ashlyn," he whispered raggedly.

"Ash."

A week later, she sat in the apartment they had shared, surrounded by his clothes, his books, his stupid video games. Connor sat across from her, silently boxing up what she turned over to him, rarely saying a word.

After that first day, he'd said as little as possible, stayed in the background, stepping forward only if she couldn't do something herself, offering assistance, a silent shoulder, and a comfort she hadn't expected to find, least of all, with him.

It should have been awkward, right? She had met him only once, on that hot night three years ago. A night that could still make her body wet and tight with remembered pleasure.

So why was it so easy for her to be with him?

Other than the fact that her body hadn't gone into hibernation, even if her heart was trying to. Watching him gave her a hot little thrill low in her belly that shamed her.

Kye not even gone a week and she was aching for another man. Aching, hell. She needed him so bad it was like an empty hole in her gut.

But Ashlyn shoved it aside, turned it off.

And she accepted his help graciously, gratefully—accepted his silent, comforting presence while she did what he had said, what Kye would have wanted. She took it one day at a time.

"I think this will do it," she finally said, using a roll of tape to seal off one last box. To her right was a pitifully small pile, all she would keep of him. A few shirts, a necklace she had given him—a silver replica of the golden Celtic knot he had given her the day they married—hoards of pictures—a couple of books. A thousand-and-one memories.

"You don't have to get rid of it all just yet, Ash," he told her, his heart wrenching at the pain in her soft, hazel eyes.

"I can't keep it here," she said simply. "Seeing his things, day after day, will only hurt. He's gone, and keeping his favorite video games won't bring him back. Was there anything you wanted?"

An hour later, she walked him to the door, her hands tucked into the back pockets of her jeans. The boxes were loaded in the back of his truck, boxes of books, videos, clothes.

"I can come tomorrow, if you like," he offered.

She shook her head. "I'm going back to work. The sooner I do, the sooner . . . the sooner I do," she finished lamely, unsure of what else to say. The sooner she'd feel better? The sooner she would start to heal? How did one heal an empty gaping wound in the heart?

He nodded, brushing his fingers against her cheek. "I'll be around," he said before leaving, his head tucked low against the cold winter wind.

Kye watched in disgust as Connor walked away from the apartment, behaving like a fucking gentleman.

"Come back," he muttered.

"Come back and make her stop crying, make her stop hurting," he snapped, pacing at his spot by the window, watching helplessly as Connor drove away. "You're dying to get inside her again, so do it."

Kye just wanted the pain in her eyes to ease.

It broke him to pieces to watch her, hurt and lost and lonely.

Because on the few times the pain started to clear, the invisible thread that bound him to her lengthened, and he was able to drift. Drift closer to a place where he couldn't see or hear her. Where he wasn't tormented with the sight of the beautiful body he couldn't touch, with the scent of the skin he had come to crave. Where he wasn't torn apart as he watched her cry herself to sleep at night.

Where he was safe and warm and happy.

She was why he was stuck.

Until she let him go, Kye's soul wasn't going to let go of Earth. Or her.

"Besides," Kye said wickedly as he watched Ashlyn settle down on the couch and flip listlessly through the channels. "It would be something that was actually fun to watch."

He moved closer, until he was as close as he was able to get. The barrier kept him from coming closer than a couple of feet. Settling down on the glass-top coffee table, he folded his legs Indian style and stared at her.

Sharp, bright pain ripped through him when the tears once more filled her eyes.

Stupid, miserable bastard, Connor thought to himself. She just buried her man, and you're wanting to crawl up her skirt.

Driving away to the furnished condo he had rented, he tried to shake off the frustrated desire. Tried to think past the guilt that wanting her was causing.

Tried to settle his mind.

Because somewhere, sometime, in the past miserable days, as he watched one of his oldest friends laid to rest, he had made a decision.

He was going to give her time to get past it, and then he was going after her.

He would have her, and damn anybody who got in his way.

The one person who could have kept him away—who had kept him away—was gone.

And if Connor knew Kye at all, Kye was smirking down at him from somewhere, telling him he'd better be thanking his lucky stars Kye had brought them together.

For now . . . for now, he had to wait. Had to lash this burning need down, keep her from seeing what he wanted.

4

KYE WATCHED WITH a grin, feeling something light enter his heart. This was new. Over the past few months-how long it been? Three months? Six? He didn't know, but over time, something inside Ashlyn had started to shift, to lighten.

It was odd, how he could sense her moods so acutely now.

And the pain that had been starting to lessen wasn't clouding her eyes today.

Nope. Her eyes were clouded by pure and simple need. His heart pounded slow and heavy as he watched her step from the shower, and smooth oil on her skin until it was gleaming and soft.

Ghosts were perfectly capable of getting a hard-on.

Kye had become vastly familiar with the phenomenon. Of course, he wasn't able to come, which only made the whole business unbelievably frustrating. He couldn't reach out and touch her, couldn't kiss her, couldn't love her body.

Oh, but he could easily become aroused. Just watching her gave him a stiff dick.

She had turned the showerhead to massage and cried out in the shower while he watched, his hand stroking absently up and down the length of his cock as she whimpered and moaned.

He had whispered, "That's not gonna satisfy you, baby. You need a man."

Kye's eyes narrowed as he watched her step into a pair of thong panties, followed by a pair of very skimpy shorts. Fuck-me clothes, he realized, as she topped it off with a push up bra that did amazing things for her lush tits. The T-shirt she pulled on was thin and tight and showed the lacy bra quite clearly.

"Why, wife, you're looking to get laid," Kye mused as she painted her toenails a little while later. Murderous, bloody red on her toenails and her finger nails. Her mouth was slicked with a deep wine red, her eyes darkened and lined until that mouth and those eyes dominated her entire face.

He followed in her footsteps as she paced nervously up and down the hall of the little house she had bought. Just goes to show that ghosts didn't necessarily haunt houses. Some haunted people.

He flopped down on the couch as she continued to pace barefoot, rubbing her arms, stopping periodically to check her reflection in the mirror.

"You look tasty," he told her, even though she couldn't hear him. "I'd love to do you myself. If I could."

She was muttering under her breath, her eyes wide and dilated, her tongue nervously wetting her sexy little mouth. Under her bra, her nipples were hard little peaks that pressed into her shirt. The shorts stopped just below the curve of her ass and were tight—tight enough that he imagined the seam at the crotch was biting into her soft wet flesh. A picture of nervous sexual tension.

"Watching is going to have its advantages," he said as he saw Connor pull into the drive. "Maybe I can't fuck you, but I can watch him do it."

Her mother would have been scandalized, Ashlyn knew. Completely, totally scandalized.

It was August, more than six months since Kye had died.

And she was dying of unrequited lust.

Connor had never really left.

Oh, he flew back and forth to the States on business, but the art gallery in Ireland was mainly run by his younger brother now, while Connor concentrated on the one he had started here in the States. An Irish gallery, full of art and crafts by friends and family, and his own work.

He had remained, she knew, because of her, out of loyalty to Kye.

But he was treating her like she was his damn sister.

And Ashlyn wasn't sure how much longer she could handle it.

After that one single night when Kye and Connor had shared her body, something for Connor had worked its way into her soul. There had been nights when she had ached to be pressed between their two surging bodies again.

And while Kye was gone—forever gone—Connor was here. And the need inside her belly was a constant, burning ache.

Staring at her reflection, she tried to decide whether or not she was being too blatant.

The short, snug shorts weren't too obvious. Bullshit. But she was decently covered, and while she looked ready to get laid, she didn't look like a slut. And after all, it was hot. The short, sleeveless tank top was thin and white and while she had been tempted to go braless, she decided that was too tacky.

So she had donned a push up bra that matched her thong panties and secured her hair in a loose, casual ponytail. She looked sexy, no doubt about it, but casual and not so blatant that it would bother either of them if Connor decided to ignore the invitation.

It was possible that he just wasn't interested, and she would hopefully be able to tell by the time the day was over. Before she embarrassed herself and stripped naked in front of him, begging him to take her.

She wasn't cut out for celibacy.

But she wasn't really into casual sex either.

An anonymous fuck might solve the immediate problem, but not very likely. She wanted Connor, in her vagina, in her throat, in her ass.

In her life.

She left the bedroom of the house she had bought a month after Kye had died. The little condo had been too full of memories, too full of Kye.

And this little house nestled on the hills of Floyd County, Indiana, overlooking the rolling Ohio River, was perfect. It felt like home to her, even before she had moved the first stick of furniture in.

In the backyard, there was a lazy hammock where she could read the day away and large oak trees that shaded the ground from the intense summer heat.

And the extras—the large master bath with dual shower-heads and a sunken tub—the large hot tub in the back yard— the fireplace she had spent so many lonely nights beside, reading, or just thinking.

The doorbell rang and she paused—pressing a hand against her belly to soothe the butterflies there—then she opened the door, smiling at the man who stood there waiting for her.

Always waiting for her, it seemed.

Connor's breath stopped in his throat, trapped in his lungs. When she had called and asked him to come over, he hadn't even let himself hope it was for anything other than friendship.

Not that he hadn't come to value that in her. She was a damn fine friend—funny, honest, with a biting humor that echoed his own.

But he was dying, bit by bit, every time he was around her without being able to touch her, every time he stifled the burning need he felt for her. He loved her, had been in love with her probably before he had ever met her, when he had seen a picture Kye had shown him.

Something about her eyes had called to him. And, after all, he was Irish, he believed in destiny, in love at first sight. Of course, he had never imagined he'd fall in love with a woman who didn't love him back.

Staring at her now, in a brief, snug pair of shorts that left her long, smooth legs bare, at the beautiful tits barely restrained by her white shirt, he couldn't stifle it. Couldn't hide it. Couldn't hide the raw, burning need in his gut, or the ache in his heart.

And when he met her eyes, he saw what he felt echoed in hers.

He reached for her just as she reached for him and they fell against each other, mouths seeking while their hands tore at their clothes.

He stripped the shorts down her thighs and jerked her shirt over her head, but didn't bother with anything else. She popped the buttons on his shirt and clawed at his belt before freeing his rigid, aching cock.

"Hurry," she panted as he lifted her, turned and braced her against the wall.

Shoving the shiny material of the thong aside, he drove into her, burying his cock inside her body, inside her wet pulsating sheath. Her head fell back and hit the wall as a cry fell from her lips.

"Bloody hell, Ashlyn," he muttered, staring down at her face—the half blind need that glazed her eyes, her full, red-slicked lips parted as she gasped for air. The hot press of her breasts against his chest, the hard little points of her nipples against him, all drove him closer to the brink as he shuttled his cock in and out of her body, groaning as her tight wet tissues closed over him like a greedy fist.

He rode her hard, flooding her body with his semen before she had a chance to come. She cried out a protest but he stifled it with a hot, hungry kiss against her mouth, still taking her hard and deep, his cock as aching and full as it had been before he had even touched her.

He was nowhere near done yet. He had more than three years of need built up inside him and it wasn't going to be over just like that.

He dropped to the floor, pulling her with him, and he continued without breaking stride. She was tight, as tight as he remembered, and wet, her own cream mingling with his come as he worked her up and down his erection, as he shifted a little higher so that each thrust brought him against her clit.

He wrapped the back panel of her thong around his fingers, jerking it up so that the material bit into her ass, pressed against her sensitive rosette.

She shrieked, arched up against him, and tried to pull him completely inside her body.

But he had taken the edge off, and now he wanted to savor. Lowering his head, he used one hand to lift her breast so that he could reach it with his mouth. He sank his teeth into the plump mound of flesh while he rode her hard and slow.

Rising onto his knees, he grabbed her legs and shoved her thighs wide, her knees up, so he could watch as he worked his erection into her waiting, wet body.

God, she had missed this, missed feeling a man inside her, missed feeling a man's skin next to hers. Her fingers dug into the carpet beneath her as he dug his cock into her, as he shoved her closer to climax. He was big, so big and thick and long . . .

Every driving thrust forced her to take his cock so deep inside the delicious pain in her loins blended with a pleasure so profound she thought it would kill her. She could feel the thick head of his cock as it breached the mouth of her womb, feel it as he passed over the bundled nerves deep inside her wet cleft, but he seemed to be deliberately withholding the contact that would allow her to come.

Of course she wasn't above begging. Or demanding. "It's been so damn long, don't make me wait," she whispered.

"You Americans," he teased, catching her earlobe and biting down gently. "Always so impatient."

"Impatient, hell. Damn it, Connor, let me come," she gasped out. "Please, please, please!"

He lowered his head to purr in her ear, driving her legs to her chest as his weight shifted. "If I do that, it's gonna take me with ya, darlin'. I donna wan' this ending so fast," he whispered raggedly.

"Make me come," she cried, straining upward, clenching her vaginal muscles deliberately so that she milked his cock teasingly. "Damn it, Connor," she panted as he pulled out just shy of hitting that spot inside her body. "Let me come. God, I've needed this."

"Needed it?" he murmured, kissing her silkily before telling her, "You don't know what need is. Need is what happens when you hunger and ache for a woman for years, ache and need to the point that nobody else will do.

"I've been wanting to fuck you since I left that hotel room, and I thought I'd never have you again." He rolled his hips, releasing the thong to slide his fingers upward until he could soak up some of her cream, returning to smear it on her anus and slide one finger in.

"Waiting to taste you," he murmured, bending his head to eat at her mouth. "Waiting to slide my cock inside your talented little mouth, inside your hot little pussy, inside that tight, tiny hole." As he spoke, he forced his finger in up to the knuckle. He rocked against her in tiny thrusts as he said, "Do ya know, darlin' Ash, that I'd never fucked a woman in the ass until you? Never knew what it was like?

"And I haven't done it since, and let me tell you, I've worked up a powerful need for it," he finished as he started to withdraw and plunge deep, while he pressed his finger upward inside her ass.

"Let me come," she pleaded, her head rolling restlessly against the floor. "And you can fuck me how ever you want."

He purred low in his throat and asked, "D' ya promise?"

"Damn it, yes. I swear . . . shit!"

He had pulled out and rammed back in, out and in, hard, glorious digs that hit that spot each time, and on the fifth brutal stroke, she climaxed, clamping down on him and milking his orgasm from him. She screamed as the orgasm caught her in its grip, as he leaned forward and bit down hard on her nipple while his other hand closed painfully on one cheek of her ass, the thong stretching and pressing ever tighter against her anus.

He flooded her vagina again, in spurts of liquid fire that had her shuddering.

∞

Kye watched with hot eyes as Connor shoved her up against the wall and drove his cock into her body. Kye could see it as he pulled it out, wet and shining with Ashlyn's cream. A ripple of need rolled through Kye's belly as Connor plunged back into her, dragging moans and screams from her throat.

He watched as Connor bucked against her, his eyes closed in agonized pleasure as he came. At least, Kye assumed he was coming. "You better not plan on stopping just yet, buddy," he muttered, intense frustration ripping through him. But instead of stopping he took Ashlyn to the floor and rode her hard, shoving her thighs high and wide.

"Shit," Kye muttered, dragging his jeans open and wrapping a hand around his cock, pumping furiously. From his vantage point by the window, he could see as Connor's thick cock left Ashlyn's cunt, ruddy and wet and glistening—could see as he pushed it into her slowly until she was whimpering and straining against him.

"Shit," Kye repeated as he felt something he hadn't felt in months. A climax building at the base of his spine. His hand worked furiously at his hard dick while Connor whispered and murmured to Ashlyn.

She lay beneath him, begging and pleading, screaming when she came—again and again—under Connor's long fingers. One big hand went to cup her ass, and one finger . . . yeah, he was finger fucking her ass.

Just as Connor roared, Kye felt the come spurt from him, burning his hands and belly as it coated him.

∞

After a long, hot bath, she cuddled against him. A sigh of pleasure rippled through her.

"You sound fairly pleased," Connor murmured, idly combing his hand through her damp hair.

"Hmm," she purred, nuzzling the smooth skin of his chest with her nose.

Smoothing his hand down her back, he cupped a round white buttock, slid his finger against the crack and said, "I'll be even more pleased in a bit."

She cocked her hips up, rubbing against his finger. From beneath the pillow, she grabbed the tube of *Wet* she had put there while he finished in the bathroom. "Hmm, me too. I think, in, oh, say five or ten years, I may be satisfied enough to go an hour in your presence without wanting you."

As she spoke, she sat up, flipping open the cap and pouring a small amount of lube into her palm. Connor watched—his eyes heavy lidded with lust—as she rubbed the lubricant on his turgid cock. "I'm needing more than five or ten years, darlin'. Ah, keep that up, why don't you?"

She slid her hand from the head of his cock, down to the base, back up again in a slow maddening rhythm while she covered his length with lubricant, pausing to tickle his sac with her fingers before getting more of the clear substance and applying another slow, lingering layer.

She grinned at him and slowed her strokes. "But if I do, you may not be any use where I want you," she teased, lowering her head to lick the tip of his penis.

"I've been hard since I saw you again, Ash. You jacking me off won't even take the edge off," he groaned, lifting his hips against her tight hand. He lifted hot blue eyes to stare at her, eying the way she perched by his hips, the sway of her full breasts as she moved, the tumbled red locks that fell around her shoulders, and splayed over her breasts, teasing him with brief views of her red, peaked nipples before shifting to hide them again. "I could stay here a bloody month and still be needing ya insanely."

But he rolled away from her, spying the lubricant and pouring some into his hand, warming it in his palm before smoothing it onto his fingers so he could prepare her ass. While he rimmed her anus with his fingers, he positioned his body so that he could use his other hand between her thighs and thrust his fingers into her wet depths while nuzzling and suckling at her erect little nipples.

She panted and strained against him, and as soon as he could feel her climax coming closer, he turned her onto her hands and knees and mounted her from behind. He brushed against her little hole, while his fingers sought and found her clit, hard and swollen, in her folds.

He could see it, in his mind's eye, that first time, how her anus had spasmed when she was ready, and he waited, rubbing and bumping against her until the edge of that tiny opening started to flutter against him.

Smearing the *Wet* on her rosette, he started to ease inside her, working his hard shaft in slowly, while she planted her hands and knees, her head hung low, like a pliant mare waiting for a stallion. The picture appealed to him, appealed to something inside him that enjoyed controlling and dominating her.

He crooned his praises while he stroked her ass and eased a little deeper, a little harder, grunting in pleasure when she started to rock back against him. "Hmm . . . Ash, oh, darlin', you're so tight, so hot. Are you wet inside, baby? It feels like it from here, so wet we probably didn't need anything other than you," he purred as he started taking her in long, slow strokes that had her arching against him.

Weak mewls left her throat as she strained harder against him each time he pulled out. "Connor, please," she gasped, rocking back.

Those long, slow strokes were driving her mad. She needed it fast and hard now, and she told him so.

"But I'm not ready for this to end," he told her, continuing at his own pace. "Fast and hard, and you'll start to come, then I will, and it's over." While he talked, he watched as his flesh joined hers, as her little asshole stretched so tight and hot around the head of his penis as he pulled out before shoving back into her, a little harder, dragging a weak cry from her lips. Her narrow passage was wet for him and eager, gripping his cock like silk while he watched his length disappear inside her. Each time he withdrew, she followed, seeking his cock, trying to keep him from pulling out. Her spine bowed up as she shuddered, as the inner walls of her ass clenched and convulsed around him.

She felt hot and cold at the same time, her body quaking around his intruding cock, shivering as he impaled her fully. A little harder, a little deeper with each stroke until she was screaming hoarsely with every thrust.

"Good, so damn good," he rumbled as the quivers started inside her ass. They grew stronger and stronger until the flesh gloving his cock felt like it was seizing around him.

When she bucked up high, screaming, he caught her around the waist, pinning her torso against his while he shoved her weight down, forcing his shaft in as far as it would go. And stayed there while her body viced around his, his semen flooding her.

They remained upright like that, panting, with her still

impaled on his now softening cock, his arms holding her tightly against him. Silently, he mouthed against her hair, *I love you.*

And he stiffened when she sighed and settled comfortably against him, murmuring, "I missed you, Connor. After you left, I missed you. So much, it hurt."

He eased them down to the bed, stubbornly keeping his half hard cock inside her anus. But before he could find a reply, she cuddled against him, humming in pleasure, before dropping into sleep.

Kye felt like a fucking voyeur but he'd be damned if he missed out on this. "This is the most fun I've had since that last night with you, darlin'," Kye drawled as he watched Connor smear lubricant on her waiting ass.

"It's almost as much fun to watch you fuck as it is to do you," he said. "Well, maybe. You need to tie her up sometime, Connor. Slap a pair of cuffs on her wrists and she'll be your slave. Willingly."

He groaned, moving closer, not realizing he had crossed that invisible barrier until he was standing by the bed, close enough to touch. "Oh, shit," he whispered as he watched Connor ease two fingers inside her tight little pussy, pressing his thumb against her rosy anus, probing until the muscles relaxed and welcomed his intrusion.

"God, that's good," he muttered, dropping to his knees to better see as Connor started to butt the head of his cock against her rosette. "Come, baby. Let me watch."

Kye's hand had sought his own swelling penis and was cupping his balls as he jacked himself off, watching in dazed, hypnotized pleasure as Connor started to ream her ass, slowly and almost gently.

He could see cream as it oozed down the lips of her sex to fall on the bed. He missed the taste of it, missed feeling her soft skin against him as he ate at her sex. One last time, he thought helplessly. *I want one last time.*

He grunted as a drop of precome started to leak from his penis. Connor was fucking her hard now, shoving her hips low so he could fill her hard and deep.

Ashlyn was writhing and shuddering underneath his hands, her butt up-thrust and quivering. Kye grinned tightly when Connor's hand smacked sharply at her ass and the semen jetted from his body.

Kye's eyes widened in shock as a wet spot appeared on the sheets, spreading and spreading as his come soaked into the sheets.

"Oh, shit," he muttered.

It was there, wet and rapidly cooling, as real as the come that had soaked Ashlyn's ass and started to leak out to dry on her bottom.

And the two on the bed never even noticed.

∽

"Looks like you've ended up in the right place."

"Kye?"

"Who else would it be?" he asked, his voice amused as he sat on the edge of the dresser, watching while Connor sat up, dried come and sticky lube on his soft penis. Ashlyn remained curled in sleep.

"I'm dreaming."

"Maybe," Kye said, grinning. "But that doesn't mean I'm not talking to you, mate."

"How can you be?" Connor asked. "You're dead." But he was staring right at him, at his golden skin, glowing faintly, as though he was lit from within. He could see that longish raven-wing hair that

fell around his sharply cut facial bones, the warm, humorous, dark eyes and his wide, full mouth that seemed almost too damn pretty to belong to a man. How many times had Connor teased him about his almost pretty looks? How often had he ragged him about the hair that he stubbornly refused to cut?

Slowly, dumbly, he repeated, "You're dead."

Kye's eyes sobered and his mouth straightened. "I know. Dying does hurt, buddy. Don't think it doesn't. But it wasn't as bad as it could have been. Leaving her, I mean. I knew you'd be here."

"You know, don't you?"

"That you love her? Yeah, I know." Kye sighed, reaching up to run a hand through his hair in a familiar gesture. "I knew it that night. I didn't know what to do about it, though. Kept hoping you'd get over it."

He eased down off the dresser and came to stand beside the bed next to Connor, and stood staring down at his sleeping wife. "Don't know why. I never got over it," Connor admitted. Kye eased down, until he could sit by her head and stroke her hair.

Connor could see it, see the way her hair moved and shifted, falling through Kye's dark fingers before he would scoop it up again. "You still love her," he said. Only his voice wasn't out loud. It was only in his head.

But Kye heard him.

Turning his head, he grimaced, and said, "Till death do us part. Death parted us, but it hasn't stopped the love I feel."

Well, fuck me, Connor thought helplessly. It was just as hard for Kye now as it had been—as it was for Connor. Two men, in love with one woman.

But now Kye was dead.

"And you're not." Kye continued to comb his hand through her hair. "Don't pull back on my account," he said, staring down at the curve of Ashlyn's cheek, leaning his head down until he could buss her soft, smooth skin with his mouth. "She needs you."

"I can't . . ."

"Don't—okay, Connor? God, she's so beautiful," he murmured, lifting a lock of hair to his nose. "I've been trying to get through to you for months, ever since I died. I can't cross over, you know. Not yet."

"Cross over? You mean . . ."

"I'm stuck in limbo. Don't know why. Hopefully it's almost over. It hurts, being able to see her, smell her, but not touch her. Not talk to her."

"Why haven't you talked to me before now?"

Kye shrugged and said, "I've tried. Haven't been able to." He rose, turning to face Connor, seeming somehow larger in death than he had been in life. They stood eye to eye and Kye raised a black brow. "Are you going to take care of her, Connor?"

"If she'll let me."

"Do it," Kye ordered, his eyes glowing and hot, authoritative. "She'll fall in love with you. She already needs you."

"I need her. I love her. But I won't force my way into her life, mate. For any reason."

Kye smiled sadly, as he turned back to study the woman on the bed. Her mouth puckered and shifted in her sleep, as if she were seeking something. He could feel the need, the lust, the love coursing through his body, and wondered, if she opened her eyes could she see him? Touch him?

"I forced you into her life, Connor. Remember? You've been inside her ever since, and she's been inside you."

"Regretting it now, are you?"

Kye laughed, the happy, wild laughter that Connor remembered so well. "Regret it? Hell, no. That was every bit as good for me as it was for her. Not as good for you, in some ways, I know. Knowing she was leaving with me, that she was mine.

"But," he said, shrugging. "Now she is yours. Take care of her." Leaning forward, he hugged his friend hard and whispered, "You were always a friend, Connor. One I was proud to have."

"*Kye, wait . . .*"

But he was gone. And Connor went tumbling back into sleep.

∽

When he woke, he wondered if it had really happened.

He curled around Ashlyn, his heart pounding, his eyes stinging. Her sweet little ass pressed against him as he wrapped his arms around her, holding her tightly against his body. Lowering his face to her silken hair, he let out a shaky breath as a tear managed to escape and roll down his cheek.

Damn you, Kye.

This is not how things were meant to be, mate.

And he could almost hear Kye's dry voice asking, *How in the hell do you know?*

∽

When Ashlyn's eyes flew open, it was dark out. She wasn't sure what had woken her. Connor was sprawled against her from the back, his face buried against her hair. It was silent, save for the hum of the fan beside the bed.

Swinging her legs over the edge of the bed, she peered around her in the dark room. When her eyes landed on the door to the bathroom, she shrieked.

Or at least she thought she did. Her mouth opened but no sound came out.

And then she felt exceptionally silly for doing it.

It was Kye. Only Kye. The love of her life.

"Hey, beautiful," he murmured, unhooking his ankle from behind his leg and moving out of the doorway, walking until he was standing right in front of her. Close enough to touch.

"What took you so long?" she asked. Then she frowned, and pressed her fingers to her still mouth. Her lips hadn't moved.

"'S okay, I can hear you," Kye said, reaching out and pressing one finger to her full lower lip. "I think maybe it is so you don't go waking anybody else up." Slowly, he knelt in front of her, staring at her as if memorizing her face.

"Don't know if you're going to remember any of this, darlin' girl. I'm here to tell you good-bye."

"I figured that out," she said, a sad, heartbroken smile trembling on her lips. "I've been waiting. And hoping. Kye . . ."

"Shh, beautiful," he crooned, dropping to the floor before he took her hips and eased her naked body down on his lap. His blue jean-covered lap.

God, he feels so real.

"I am real," he told her softly. "You aren't dreaming this. I am here, I am touching you." Jealousy flared in his eyes. "I'm sitting here with you naked on my lap and I am smelling Connor all over you." A brief smile came and went on his mouth.

She flushed, feeling the blood rising from her chest, up her neck, until her face flamed. "Don't," he whispered roughly, cupping her cheek. "I don't want you to stop living. If you had lain down beside me after I died, I would have never forgiven you for it. Or him—for letting you. Connor was right about that."

Her eyes widened, remembering that conversation in the private viewing area of the funeral home, months earlier. "You saw . . . ?"

"I've been watching and trying to talk to you ever since it happened."

Watching . . . ? Guilt, shame, pain all pooled in her belly, a vicious cramp seizing her.

"Don't," Kye ordered through clenched teeth, one hand fisted in her hair and forced her face back up to his when she would have looked away. "Don't. You're alive, damn it. Alive. You're supposed to be making love, going to work, eating supper. You're supposed to be living. Don't feel like you shouldn't." With a wry smile, he said, "Hell, this

has probably been the most fun I've had since that fucking car hit me."
Gently, he stroked a finger down her cheek. "It was good, watching
you. Almost as good as being with you myself."

"If I'm supposed to be living, why do I feel so guilty? And why
are you here? Aren't you supposed to be somewhere else? Or are you just
lingering on earth to watch me screw?" she asked acidly, dashing one
hand across her damp cheeks.

God, she could feel the after effects of hard sex on her body, muscle
aches, dried come on her thighs, and she was sitting in her dead hus-
band's lap.

And unless she was mistaken, he wasn't . . . unaffected by her
naked body.

With a sigh, Kye said, "I can't pass over, Ash. I've tried. I'm
stuck here for some reason, and I'll be damned if you add to this hell
by feeling guilty." With one finger, he lifted her chin up until he could
stare into her eyes.

"I've always loved you," he whispered gruffly, lowering his mouth
to hers. "You made my life worthwhile. Without you . . ."

"Life would have been empty," she finished when his voice halted
abruptly. "You were my life. If it . . ."

"Don't stop saying what's on your mind, Ashlyn. Not to me—not
to anybody."

"If Connor hadn't been here, I think I would have lost myself," she
said honestly. "He's been so good to me. Such a good friend."

"A friend? Is that how you treat your friends? Damn." A quick-
silver smile lit Kye's face, the familiar one she had loved so well. "He'll
be even more, if you will let him. Don't let me get in the way of that."
Pulling her close, he kissed her gently. "God, I wanted, want, so much
for you. A long, happy life. Kids, grandkids. Connor can give you
that."

"I don't love him," she said, a sob sounding in the air. "I love
you."

"I'm dead, baby. I'm gone, dust in the ground. Please, for me. Go on, live your life. The one I wanted to share with you. I want that. I need that." Kye's eyes were wet—with desperation—with sorrow—with grief. "Ashlyn, if I don't know, in my heart, that you'll be okay, I'm gonna be stuck here. I can't pass over with things unresolved. And you were the only thing in my life that mattered."

"I don't love him," she repeated, a knot in her throat." I can't!"

"You will," Kye said with simple certainty. "He loves you already."

Before she even realized it, he was on his feet and she was in the bed, with him leaning over her, handing her over to Connor's waiting arms. In sleep, Connor wrapped his arms tightly around her, as if he had missed her presence in the bed.

"Be happy. Live your life, Ashlyn," Kye whispered, lowering his head, pressing his lips to hers in a sweet gentle kiss. A tear spilled from his eye, just as one leaked from hers. "For me, Ashlyn. If you won't do it for yourself, then do it for me."

The last thing she saw, felt, remembered was his lips, brushing hers one last time.

In her sleep, she turned in Connor's arms, seeking his body, his warmth, as she sobbed in her sleep.

Kye was still reeling from the shocks he had just received. First, when he had spewed his come all over the bed. He had been immaterial for so many weeks—no substance—no ability to touch or be touched.

And then he had reached out and touched Connor, rousing him from a sound sleep.

Then he had touched Ashlyn.

Spoken to both of them.

And some instinct inside him whispered that his time here had come to an end. He was running out of time.

⚭

Ashlyn awoke to a sensation she thought she would never feel again. Pressed between two hard, surging male bodies. Connor's long length was pressed against her back, where he had fallen asleep.

In front of her was Kye.

He was slightly glowing, slightly transparent.

And solid.

She gasped, reached out to touch him, to be sure, even though she could feel him pressed up against her body, hard and tight and firm. "Kye?"

"Hey, beautiful," he purred, grinning that cocky, arrogant grin that managed to be little boy sweet at the same time.

Then his grin faded and his face swooped down, his mouth closing over hers like a man starving. She was dimly aware of Connor's body stiffening behind her, dimly aware that he was no longer asleep.

Her moan died in her chest and she threw her arms around him, rolling atop his so very solid body. Connor remained lying on his side, watching with blank eyes.

"Kye," he muttered, reaching up to rub his tired eyes with a shaky hand. The loose, liquid feeling that spiraled through him wasn't shock though. It was joy, pure and simple. But the joy faded slowly as he took in the faint glimmering form of Kye's body, the near translucence to his skin.

And his eyes blanked again as confusion raced through him.

Blank eyes, until Kye rolled Ashlyn back between them and whispered, "One last fantasy, beautiful. One last time." Over her shoulder, Kye looked up and pinned Connor with hot, hungry eyes, his face stark and harsh and full of a desperate need.

Ashlyn gasped when she was flipped to her back and ravaged by both men. Kye's mouth went straight for her pussy,
while Connor focused his attention on her breasts and neck
and mouth. As Kye parted her with his tongue, she screamed,
shocked and startled, as she flew straight into orgasm, ejaculat-
ing into his mouth as he ate at her.

"Missed you, missed this more, Damn it, Ashlyn, do it
again," Kye muttered roughly, pulling away to blow a cool
puff of air on her swollen clit before burying his face against
her a second time.

Kye controlled them this time—both of them. He shoved
Ashlyn so that she sat between Connor's spread legs, Connor's
hand cupping and massaging her breasts as Kye returned to
lap up the juice that started to trickle from her. His hands were
everywhere, massaging her ass, lifting her hips, plucking at her
nipples until she cried out.

Snatching her from Connor, he tumbled to his back and
guided her mouth to his hard swollen cock. And when Connor
started to rub his dick against her exposed entrance, Kye snarled
and pinned her beneath him so he could again fuck her orally.

Starving. He had been starving for her and was being
offered one last banquet.

When he finally lifted his face from her cunt for the third
time, his mouth and chin were wet from her climax, and her
tissues were swollen and sensitive from his teeth and tongue.
Rising to his knees, he pulled her up, effortlessly, draping
her across his lap as though she weighed nothing. Some new
strength flooded him and he lifted her easily, holding her above
his cock, her vagina dripping her juices all over it. Then, staring at her, he dropped her, forcing her to take his entire length
in one brutal stroke. When he was fully embedded, his eyes

drifted closed and he shuddered. "Beautiful," he whispered, holding her tightly against him, reveling in the euphoria of being buried inside her one last time.

His eyes flew to Connor who knelt on the bed, only inches away. Gutturally, he said, "Just me this time. This time, she is mine."

Connor only stared and nodded, his own erection hard and pulsing. Closing his hand around his flesh, he stroked it as he watched Kye and Ashlyn.

"Later," Kye whispered in her ear, shuddering as her wet slick sheath squeezed his cock. "Just me, this time. Look at me."

Her hands lifted and cupped his cheeks so that they stared into each other's eyes as he rocked her slowly into climax, a wash of hot fluid filling her only moments after she cried out in pleasure.

His cock stayed hard and firm as he pulled it out of her, lifted her off and guided her head down until she eagerly took the fat swollen head of his penis in her mouth and sucked him down. His hands closed over her head, buried and twisted in her hair while he muttered, "You always knew how to suck, baby.

"Oh, shit. Do that again," he ordered when she swallowed his length down her throat. Turning eyes that burned to Connor, he whispered, "Fuck her, Connor."

She was wet from her own climaxes and from Kye's, and it felt hotter than normal for some reason. Shoving his cock inside her roughly, Connor groaned and grunted as her overly sensitized sheath starting to convulse around him. "Harder, harder, fuck her harder," Kye was rasping out as she deep throated him and shot him closer to climax. "Give it to her harder, until she can't see."

And to her, he kept saying, "Suck it, baby. Take it in your throat like you're taking him in your pussy. Like you're going to take me in your tight little ass. I'm going to fuck your ass, beautiful. Hard and slow, until you're begging me to stop."

Ashlyn groaned, trying to lift her head. She could barely breathe. And she wanted to see Kye, wanted to stare at the skin that glowed a soft mellow gold in the dim room. But his hands kept her head low, kept her working on his cock while Connor pummeled her from behind.

Talk about simultaneous orgasms. All three came at once. She closed tightly around Connor, her pussy going into spasmodic clenches as Connor's seed flooded into her vagina and he roared out her name. Kye's come filled her throat as he gasped out, "Beautiful."

But when she pulled away and collapsed, exhausted, to her side, Kye shoved her thighs wide, startling her when he started to lap Connor's seed from her thighs before turning his attention to her throbbing cunt.

Connor stared and swore softly when his cock started to twitch, then throb as Kye ate and drank from her pussy. "Trying to kill me, he is," he mumbled, rolling until he could close his hot mouth over her hard pouting nipples as she thrust them high.

"Kye, stop," she whispered when his tongue laved roughly against her swollen clit.

Connor laughed when Kye ignored her; he could hear Kye's eager, hungry sounds as he sucked and licked at the cream she gave him. "He can't, darlin' girl. You're so tasty," he purred, one hand going under her thigh to rub into the fluids that soaked the cheeks of her ass, her anus, and the sheets beneath her. Then he slid the two fingers inside his mouth and licked them clean before returning to suckle at her nipples.

Her eyes fluttered closed and she whimpered as Kye speared his tongue inside her, stabbing repeatedly before working on her clit with his teeth and tongue. "Kye, I can't," she pleaded even as her hips lifted invitingly.

"You'd better," he replied before lifting her up, and placing her astride Connor. "Because it's time to do a little double penetration. I have to fill your ass with my cock again, beautiful. I have to."

And so he did, smearing lube all over her ass, rubbing her anus, probing with his finger until she was bucking and squirming against him. With that uncanny strength, he lifted her, holding her steady while Connor rolled to his knees so he could work his cock inside her tight little vagina, so swollen and sensitive from being ridden all night.

"Poor baby," Connor murmured, working his shaft inside her, feeling how tight and swollen she was. "Are you sore?"

"Yes," she gasped, quaking when Connor used one hand to shove her breast high so he could close his teeth around her hard, tightly beaded nipple.

Releasing it, he reached down and grabbed her ass, fondling and massaging the firm white globes as he whispered, "You're so tight. And even though I've been fucking you most of the day, I feel like I can't get enough of you." He kissed his way down her face and neck, sinking his teeth into her flesh and biting when he was all the way inside.

She felt Kye's fingers probing the tight pink rosette, then the thick head of his cock. He started to work his cock into her anus, shuddering as the tight ring of muscle relaxed just slightly, allowing him to slide inside a bare inch. Connor's hands closed tightly over the cheeks of her ass, spreading her wide and open. "Thanks, mate," Kye said with an unsteady laugh as he thrust a little further, until half his cock was buried inside her. The faint glow that still emanated from his body cast faint shadows on Ashlyn and Connor. Leaning back, he watched as he forced a little more of his length into her anus. The pink hole stretched wide and tight around his penetration, the skin of her ass so pale and white and lovely against the darker gold skin of his body.

Her nipples ached and the oddly tight, hot feeling was spreading throughout her loins, until she was shivering and shaking with combined hot/cold feelings. Connor's mouth closed over one nipple, taking it gently between his teeth and pulling it long and tight away from her body before releasing it.

From behind her, she heard Kye rasp out, "Fuck it." And that was all the warning she had before he fucked her, ramming his length into her and pulling out before doing it again, and again, and again, and again until she was screaming and begging for more.

"Harder! Harder!" she screamed mindlessly, clutching at Connor's shoulders while she rode him, while Kye rode her. When she lifted off of Connor, Kye pulled down, leaving her rectum almost completely, and when she dropped down on Connor's impaling dick, Kye would ram his cock back inside her.

"Harder," Connor muttered harshly. "Fuck her harder. Fuck me harder," he ordered Ashlyn grabbing her face and eating at her mouth savagely. He nipped at her lip, hard enough to hurt and then he sucked at the tiny bead of blood as her tight, wet pussy shot him closer to oblivion. "The best little fuck," he gasped, smacking her sharply on the ass as he started to pump his aching cock inside her.

She climaxed, but begged for more. More of Kye's rod in her ass, even though it hurt. More of Connor's cock in her vagina, even though she ached.

Connor's seed flooded her, but he, too, needed more. More of her hot, pulsating little pussy—more of the breathy moans and wild screams that fell from her tasty mouth.

And Kye continued to pound into her, even after his climax faded, until his cock was hard and firm and long once more, filling her ass completely. *He* needed more of everything—more of her sweet cream in his mouth as she ejaculated—more of her pleas and demands for more.

And he knew time was running out.

So he fucked her slowly, then harder, gently, then roughly until her waning body stiffened and bucked and arched in the circle of their arms. When she started to sag, he lowered his head to whisper in her ear about how tight and hot she was, how good her ass felt around him, or to order Connor to play with her clit or her nipples.

He lowered his head and set his teeth into the soft fleshy mound of muscle atop her shoulder, biting, moving to another spot, marking as he screwed her ass, shoved her a little closer to the edge. "I'd like to tie you up, standing in the middle of the room, with your arms stretched overhead, so you're helpless. While we take turns fucking you," Kye whispered. "We wasted three damn years and we'll never get them back and now we only have tonight."

She whimpered as his hands closed over her breasts, his thumbs rolling her nipples, lifting them to Connor's mouth. Her head fell back against Kye's shoulder, one arm clutching Connor to her, the other wrapping behind her to hold Kye close.

"You like that, eh?" Kye asked. "You like the thought of him watching while I eat your pussy? It *is* tasty—hot and creamy and yummy. Do you like the thought of me making you eat his cock? You want some cock in your mouth now?"

She started to shake her head no, she just wanted this to continue.

"*I* want some cock in your mouth," Kye told her, whispering directly in her ear. "I want to watch you suck him off while I fuck you senseless."

But he only closed his hands over her hips, whispering, "Not yet, not yet, not yet!" With an agonized groan he climaxed, flooding her ass with hot wet seed while she screamed blindly—Connor's teeth sinking into her nipple, Kye's into her shoulder—stuffed full of cock and unable to move; pinned between two hard bodies. And she felt Connor's come jet off inside her vagina, flooding her womb.

Dark stars and rainbows filled her vision, and she went limp, slipping into unconsciousness for a few brief seconds. When her eyes opened, she was lying on her side, facing Connor, Kye draped over her shoulder, his face pressed against hers. "I love you," she told him quietly.

He grinned—sad and bittersweet. "I know. But I think it's time to move on. Both of us."

And then he started to fade. Panicking she struggled out from between them, to turn and grab him. When she reached out, her hand went right through him. He grimaced, solidified only briefly, long enough to reach out and catch her hand.

"It's okay, beautiful. It *will* be okay," he promised.

And then he was gone.

Ashlyn buried her face against Connor's chest and sobbed.

The sun was edging up over the horizon as Connor stood by the bedside staring down at Ashlyn's sleeping form. *Time to move on,* Kye had said.

It finally dawned on him that he had to move on as well. Ashlyn wasn't letting go of Kye. After she had cried herself to sleep last night, he had made the decision to go back to Ireland.

Maybe in a few years . . .

"Don't, mate," he told himself, pressing his palms to his eyes and rubbing.

Quietly, he tugged on his clothes and found his keys.

Should he leave a note? he wondered as he pulled his boots on.

Say good-bye?

She'd figure it out sooner or later.

A deep tide of self-pity washed over him as he left the house. As Connor drove away, it damn near drowned him. Bloody hell, he loved her. Loved her so much it was damn near killing him, being so close, spending the night holding her while she cried for Kye.

He was going to be noble about this if it killed him.

He was going to step away, step aside, while she took some time to heal.

Hell, she didn't love him, now did she? Had she ever said so? No.

Hell, she wasn't ready to love him yet. Probably never would be. She had yet to let go of Kye. Not that he held that against her. Kye had been the kind of man most people would never know—kind, loving, honorable through and through, a good man, a good friend. Connor had never known another friend like Kye, and knew he never would again.

How could he expect her to let Kye go when Connor could barely do it?

Ashlyn might need Connor, but she still loved Kye. And that wasn't going to be changing any time soon.

And he wasn't going to fool himself into believing she would come searching for him.

Ashlyn awoke to the sound of the door closing quietly behind Connor.

She lay alone in the middle of the tumbled, tangled sheets, her body aching and sore. She groaned when she rolled up to her side at the edge of the bed.

It was so quiet.

Completely silent.

Reaching up, she rubbed her hand against her breast, feeling the slow steady pounding of her heart.

Alive.

She was alive.

And she wasn't going to lie down beside Kye and die.

"Not my time," she whispered softly.

But she figured she knew what time had come.

Sunset found her standing at an old cemetery nestled in one of the numerous valleys of Floyd County, Indiana. The marble headstone said so little about Kye, his name, his date of birth and his date of death. *Beloved.* And he had been beloved, to her, to his family, to his friends.

But it said so little. Nothing of his life.

Nothing of the joy they had found in each other—nothing of the love—nothing of the fun—nothing of the life they had shared. Nothing of the emptiness his death had left inside her.

The gaping hole in her heart was by no means healed. But she also didn't feel as if she were slowly, and endlessly, bleeding to death inside. It no longer hurt so badly to think of Kye.

He was okay.

And she had gotten to say goodbye.

Maybe now it was time to see what else she could find in her life.

She knelt down, settling on her heels in front of the stone, laying a white rose down on the grass. "I loved you," she whispered quietly.

A soft gentle breeze drifted by and she smiled.

"I'll find what it is you wanted for us. And I'll remember you, every day. But I won't stop living."

She waited a few days to let her aching body recover. Gave her spinning head time to settle. Let her wounded heart take a breather.

But when she went after Connor, he wasn't there.

The house was closed up.

He had turned his booming new business over to the very hands of his very shocked office manager.

Gone back to Ireland.

After waiting for her all this time, he had gone back to Ireland just when she had started to realize exactly why he had been waiting.

Ashlyn stood on the sidewalk in front of Celtic Concepts, the trendy little shop of Irish art, music and lore that Connor had started and had flourishing in less than five months.

The shop he had left behind.

She was shaking and trembling and angry.

And hurt.

Both her heart and her pride.

Just like that?

She paced back and forth on the sidewalk while the new shopkeeper stared at her through the windows, watching her with worried eyes, as the pedestrian traffic flowed around her, some giving her a curious glance, others muttering in annoyance as she blocked their passage.

Couldn't he have given her a little more time?

Then she stopped.

Maybe he hadn't realized she needed it.

Maybe he hadn't realized that she needed him.

5

IT TOOK THREE weeks.

Three long, lonely weeks while she waited for her passport and cleared her schedule at work. Well, maybe cleared it wasn't the right term.

They hadn't wanted to give her time off.

So she had quit.

After all, Kye's life insurance policy had covered her very nicely. Even after paying for the little house in the Knobs, if she wanted to spend the next twenty years at home, she could.

Working out two weeks notice, she packed and planned and pouted. Ashlyn alternated between being angry and hurt. Between sulking and brooding.

What if she was wrong? What if Kye had been wrong?

Maybe he didn't really love her.

And what if she got there, looked at him, and realized she didn't love him?

She laughed at herself. She was already in love with him and had been for quite some time. Maybe even since that first night, maybe it had started to grow then.

∞

Now she stood with her feet on Irish soil, staring at the River Shannon, her hands cupping her elbows in the cool air. Even though it was well into August, it was cool. Probably only in the fifties this early in the morning.

Her eyes were gritty from lack of sleep. Her body stiff and weary from trying to sleep during the flight. *Should've brought some Xanax,* she chided herself. And she was seriously starting to question her sanity.

Now what?

Find him, the saner part of her insisted. *You sure as hell didn't come this far just to turn back, did you?*

Maybe. She had a wide streak of cowardice in her, and it was rearing its ugly head.

Wimp.

Definitely should have brought some Xanax. Maybe she could have shut up the voices in her head.

Ashlyn forced her feet into motion and plodded back to her hotel. She needed a few hours sleep.

Then she'd try to find her way out to his house.

This has to be the wrong place.

Ashlyn stood outside her little rental car, which, thankfully, was still in one piece after driving on the left side of the road. The little narrow, winding paths that served as *roads* here. And the roundabouts.

Oh, the roundabouts.

Maybe she was still stuck on one of the roundabouts and had driven herself straight into an unconscious state and she was dreaming.

That huge, towering stone structure in front of her couldn't possibly belong to Connor. If so, she was seriously out of her league.

A man who owned a house like that wasn't going to want a mousy, overly curvaceous nurse from America. He needed a French supermodel. An English lady. An Italian heiress.

Just get the hell out, now. This time, both voices in her head were yelling the same thing. Maybe that cowardly streak was wider than she thought.

"Can I help you, miss?"

Resigned, she thought, Too late.

She turned and faced the speaker.

Connor threw his bag down and tossed his jacket over the newel post. The silence of the house washed over him and he dropped to sit on the lowest step and stare into nothingness.

When had his life become so meaningless?

Had it already been that way and it took leaving Ashlyn to realize it?

God, he missed her. Missed smelling the soft scent of vanilla and lavender on her skin. Missed the little touches, the friendly smiles.

Missed sinking into her tight, welcoming body. Feeling the press of her breasts against him, the tight wet glove of her sheath on his cock.

Two nights with her.

Very little, by the way, with just him and her.

But two simple nights and he had gotten addicted to her.

In the three weeks since he had left her, he had come to realize a few things.

He wasn't ever to going to be able to fuck another woman without seeing her face, without smelling her skin—and he wasn't sure he wanted to.

And . . . he had been an idiot to leave.

She had said good-bye to Kye, whom she had loved more than life. Had he expected her not to cry? Expected her not to mourn?

He had, hadn't he? He had expected her to cheerfully say good-bye to Kye and turn straight away to him. But because she cried herself to sleep after saying good-bye, he had taken it to heart and decided she was still too in love with a ghost and she'd never love him. Then he had walked away from her, left her sleeping with dried tears on her face, her thighs sticky with their combined climaxes.

"Stupid bastard," he muttered, grinding the heels of his hands against his eyes, then shoving his hands through his long hair he shot to his feet and started to pace.

Call her.

It wasn't the first time he had tried to talk himself into it. But he usually talked himself out of it. She needed time. He needed time. She would be too mad to talk to him after the way he'd walked away. She was at work. He had an irate artist waiting.

"Next thing you know you'll have to wash your hair, you stupid, brainless fuck," he mumbled, dashing the back of his hand against his suddenly dry mouth.

"Any other excuses now?"

The phone was in his hand before he realized it.

"Won't hurt a bit to call, now will it?" he muttered to himself, randomly punching buttons here and there.

A friendly voice kindly advised him to call the operator if he needed any assistance.

"Fuck off," Connor said easily as he tapped the button to disconnect.

He finally dialed her number, holding his breath. She wasn't going to be happy. He had walked away from her when she most likely had needed him the most. She would yell, or cry, or hang up. Or all three.

Or . . . she wouldn't be home.

As the phone rang on endlessly, he lowered it and stared at it.

Not home.

"Bloody figures," he said with a wry laugh.

On an oath, he hurled the phone across the foyer and watched as it fell to the floor in a number of pieces. Christ, he was falling into just as many pieces, going absolutely fucking insane without her.

He forced himself to his feet and climbed the stairs. And as he climbed he moved faster, until he was jogging up them. He was going to pack.

He was going to go to the airport and fly back to the States.

He was going to get her back.

If he had to wait, then bloody hell, this time he would wait until the moon fell out of the sky. He loved her—needed her—had to have her. He was going to get her back.

He was going . . .

. . . *to have a heart attack.*

Ashlyn stood in the middle of his room.

Wearing nothing but an unbuttoned shirt, her wild red hair falling halfway down her back in a riot of curls.

"Holy Christ," he whispered, falling back against the door. *Have I lost my mind completely?*

"Ash?"

"Surprise," she said, taking a step in his direction. The movement pulled the edges of the shirt further apart, revealing her pale body, the red curls between her thighs, her lush tits.

He reached out, grabbed and whirled her around, pinning her between his body and the door while he captured her face in his hands and took her mouth roughly, greedily, drinking down her sweet taste like a man dying of thirst.

Ashlyn's hands were at his waist, loosening his belt, unzipping his slacks, freeing his cock. He lifted her without ever taking his mouth from hers and shoved his length completely inside her.

She tore her mouth away, her head falling back as she gasped for air. He gripped her round butt in his hands and spread the cheeks of her ass, forcing her legs further apart while he pulled out.

She closed over his cock, a slick wet glove that clamped down around him as she started to shudder, climax building in her loins. Lowering his head, Connor caught one beaded pink nipple between his teeth and bit down as his hips pistoned against her, faster and faster.

He dropped to the floor, taking her with him, riding her to the down. He rose to his knees, draped her thighs over his and grasped her hips in his hands, flicking his thumb over her swollen clitoris from time to time as he fucked her hard and deep, holding tight to his control as she tightened around him in climax, sobbing out his name as she clamped down on him so tightly he had to work his cock back inside her each time.

Her back arched up, lifting her breasts high, her nipples tight and hard and red, a long lock of hair curling over her shoulder to lie between her breasts. A delicate flush pinkened her cheeks and her lips parted on a shuddering gasp as he pushed back inside her.

His gaze trailed down her body to her sex, to the neat thatch of red curls that shielded her, to the swollen red lips that spread tightly around him. Her clitoris rose stiff and swollen from her folds and he reached out, rubbing it with his thumb and groaning when it caused her to tighten around him.

"Again," he purred, lifting his hand to lick the cream from his thumb before he leaned back over her body, one hand burying in her hair, the other circling endlessly over her clit.

She cried out and gripped him closer, trying to lock her legs around his hips. "No, you don't," Connor muttered, catching her thighs in his hands, hooking his arms under her knees, using his weight to force her thighs wide while he shuttled his cock back inside her wet sheath.

"Connor . . ."

"I love you," he whispered in her ear as he shifted his weight and rode her slower, deeper. "I love you."

Her arms closed around his neck and she whimpered, straining to move faster on him.

"Say it back," he rasped, sinking his teeth into the exposed flesh of her neck. "Even if you lie, say it back, Ashlyn."

He pulled out and thrust his cock deep inside, and held there while she shuddered and bucked against him, screaming out as her climax grabbed and held her, cream pouring from her body and coating his balls, while she clamped rhythmically around his penis, pushing him closer and closer to the edge. "Say it," he pleaded desperately, his own heart shattering inside him, his own need for her driving any and all thought of sanity from his mind. "Damn it, Ashlyn, say you love me."

Bloody hell, he loved her. He had this insane need to stay right here inside her body for the rest of his life. And she was here. That had to mean she felt something. *Give me something, damn it,* he thought, starting to move inside her wet, slick passage.

Her clouded eyes drifted open a few moments later, when he started to rock against her again. His heavenly blue eyes were hot and full of need that she was just now recognizing. It had always been there, every time he had looked at her, that need had been there. He had just tried to hide it from her. A sweet, sexy smile curved her mouth while she reached up to cup his cheek. His golden hair spilled over his shoulders, his narrow handsome face naked with emotion. His whole body was tight and stiff with tension as he waited, his cock throbbing inside her, causing her muscles to contract around him.

She trembled under the exquisite pleasure that was racing through her, lifting her hips to take more of him as she said raggedly, "Connor, I can say it without lying. I love you. Why else would I be here?"

His hands tightened on her painfully and his control shattered as he drove into her mindlessly, filling her tight wet sheath repeatedly until he came inside her with hot flash-fire intensity, a dull sense of relief sliding through him as he felt her climax around him.

He wanted to fall asleep against her, to rest his weary body and take comfort just in her nearness.

But first . . .

He lifted himself off her slowly, settling down next to her before drawing her into his lap. "Did ya mean it, darlin' girl?" he asked roughly, cupping her cheek and lifting her gaze to his. "Did ya?"

She nodded slowly, staring up at him. "I meant it," she answered, leaning into his hand, rubbing against him like a cat seeking a caress. "I meant it. Do you think I'd fly thousands of miles to see you if I didn't love you?"

He only stared at her, his eyes nearly dumb with bewilderment.

And then—shock as she plowed her fist into his gut, her blow glancing off and causing no pain, thanks to her shitty leverage. But she got her point across, both with the blow and with how she shot off his lap and flounced away, grabbing the discarded shirt and pulling it on before glaring down at him with wounded eyes.

"You could have waited," she said, softly. "Given me a chance."

He watched as she lifted her chin, stiffened her body and prepared to argue. And he watched the fight drain out of her when he said, simply, "I know." Slowly, he rose and closed the distance between them. "I know. I was coming up here to pack, and then I was going back to America, to you."

A smile spread across her face as she asked, "Seriously?"

"Seriously," he echoed, reaching out and pulling her up against him. "Fuck me, but I love you. I have for all m'life. I pulled away from Kye, after that night, because of it. I didna want to hurt him, but it hurt me too much to be around him, knowing he had what I had always wanted."

He fell silent, as his eyes darkened with guilt and regret and his mouth tightened. Three years wasted. He had lost three years with his best friend and the man was gone forever. "I hate myself for that. If I had known . . ."

"Don't," she whispered. "He knew. Please don't be sad. Kye doesn't want that for us." Slowly, she drew him to the bed and urged him down, straddling him, stroking his shaft as he lengthened and hardened before she took his cock and slid down on it, impaling herself.

Her wet passage closed tightly around him and she rode him eagerly, hungrily. She was starving for him, trying to fill the ache he had left inside her when he had left.

His hands gripped her hips tightly, hard enough to bruise as he took control, slamming her weight down on him as he arched up, driving as deep inside her as he could go.

The climax hit them both suddenly, and Ashlyn screamed his name before she fell forward against him, nuzzling his neck as she murmured, "I love you."

When he exploded inside her, he rasped it back in his lyrical poet's voice, "I love you always, Ashlyn."

6

KYE WENT FROM hovering beside the stone while Connor and Ashlyn stood over it, straight into nothingness. Where he drifted for what felt like eons, in a fog that had no shape—no color—no scent. Where he was just an insubstantial thought with no body—just his memories.

And anger.

Impotent rage and immeasurable frustration.

Is this what he had hurried to? What he had told her she needed to let him go for?

Had he left watching her for this? To just hover in this nothingness?

And right when he was getting really pissed, he was thrown in a well of pain. Sharp biting teeth worked over his body and icy winds blew right through him. Bright lights burned his eyes and his naked flesh felt cold. Was he being born?

Again he was thrown back into the limbo, only it wasn't his world. And it wasn't Ashlyn he was watching.

A lithe, sultry brunette with a mouth made for sex, a tight, round little butt, full breasts, long legs . . . and a lover. And Kye didn't know either of them. Didn't know what in the fuck was going on.

Each time he muttered that out loud, there was an answer. Of sorts.

A deep aristocratic voice, almost familiar, that would sigh inside his head. *A mistake. So sorry lad, but this is your life. And that is your woman.*

"No. Ashlyn was my woman.

"And my life is over.

"Let me go on."

We can't. We can't change what is meant to be, or what is. This is where you were supposed to be all along. We brought you here, and here is where you must stay. With her.

With her? Granted, she was a sexy little bundle, with big almond-shaped eyes, full, golden breasts, a body that would have made a Playboy model jealous, but it wasn't Ashlyn.

Ashlyn isn't yours any longer. Let her go.

"*I have!*" he shouted into the nothingness. "Now let me go!"

Another rippling sigh sounded through his head and the voice whispered, *We cannot. She needs you.*

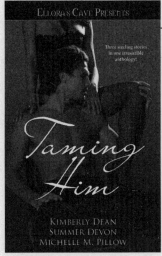
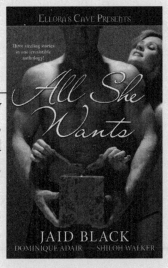